NO PERFECT MAGIC

UNEXPECTED MAGIC #6

Patricia Rice

No Perfect Magic

Published by Rice Enterprises, Dana Point, CA, an affiliate of Book
View Café Publishing Cooperative
Cover design by Kim Killion
Book View Café Publishing Cooperative
P.O. Box 1624, Cedar Crest, NM 87008-1624
http://bookviewcafe.com
ISBN 978-1-61138-683-7

NO PERFECT MAGIC

Patricia Rice

Author's Note

READER ENTHUSIASM keeps me writing, so you have only yourselves to blame for this series! I love my Malcolm and Ives, but they're a troublesome lot, and some days, I just wish for a simple maiden and her farmer hero.

As in most of my Magic books, the Malcolm gifts I describe have some physical basis, often in neurology. In this book, I give my heroine hyper-acute hearing, a topic discussed and argued today, not as magical but as a medical difficulty. The resulting behavior is often on the autism spectrum, which of course wasn't recognized in 1830. Neither was Will's dyslexia, although that's more of a nuisance than a gift. And if you believe in horse whisperers, I'm sure you already understand about dog whisperers! We really don't know the extent to which we can use our minds and senses because we're *all* different. May the *different* live long and prosper!

To my new readers: Don't worry. You needn't have read any of the other volumes to enjoy this one. The characters may be recurring, but each story and couple stands alone. The only problem you might encounter is if you're a stickler for title usage and don't realize Lady Aster is the daughter of an earl and thus entitled to be called Lady Aster instead of Lady Theophilus—not that the Malcolms care overmuch about titles anyway. So just enjoy!

One

DEAD MEAT, LEMME , lemme, oh no, must heel! Yummy bite, flower lady now, please. . .

Flower lady? William Ives-Madden cut off his mental connection with the mastiff's kaleidoscopic thoughts before he stumbled inadvertently into the path of one of the duke's daughters. The duke had felt safe hiring him because he knew Will wasn't a womanizer like his brothers.

Will wouldn't let the man down—he needed his grace's support to buy the kennel he had his eye on. Besides, the duke's daughters were too young, too dainty, and too toplofty for a big, uncouth bastard like himself.

When a man's voice carried through the arch in the hedge he'd been about to enter, Will fed Ajax another treat in approval for preventing his blundering in where he wasn't wanted. *Dead meat*? Will thought in amusement, recalling the scent Ajax had picked up on. Ajax was female, but the duke had chosen the name for reasons of his own. Maybe the duke was on to something. Ajax didn't like this gentleman and strained like any hero to get at him.

Deciding the tableau shouldn't be interrupted, if only for the entertainment value, Will waited where he could keep an eye on the scene. He'd lived in the shadow of Castle Yates the better part of his life. It wasn't as if he hadn't seen this play before, but one never knew how the farce would end.

On the other side of the arch, beneath the rose arbor, an elegantly attired gentleman rested on bended knee before a lady. "You are the dawn's golden light, the moon's silver glow, the light of my life, Lady Aurelia. Will you please do me the great honor of accepting my hand in marriage?"

Will admired the gentleman's way with words. In the eyes of every man over the age of six, Lady Aurelia was all he said and more. Her hair shimmered in the palest shades of corn silk. Her thick-lashed blue eyes matched the summer skies, and her dainty, feminine form made a man swell with protectiveness and desire.

Unfortunately, as the wealthy daughter of a duke, she had more suitors than dogs had fleas. She'd had so many proposals, she would probably disdain a prince if one offered. Proposing to her had become a sport wagered on in taverns in the same way hunters wagered on the number of quail they'd bring down.

Will pitied the foolish chap soaking his best trousers. As usual, the lady didn't even deign to look at him but tilted her head to admire a bird flitting from the trees.

The only real question was what the deuce she was doing out here without one of her family or servants with her. For good reason, the duke wisely shielded her from just this sort of inopportunity.

Familiar with the lady's eccentricities, and in lieu of a better guardian, Will lingered. His livelihood derived from training dogs to rescue lost animals and people, so watching over ladies was not his usual sort of task. But the duke wouldn't be pleased if Will let the lady come to harm.

"Lydia is playing the most beautiful waltz," she responded inexplicably to her passionate suitor. "Let us see if they have opened the ballroom."

She was always polite. She never made sense.

Without waiting for assistance, the duke's daughter rose in a graceful swish of sprigged muslin, revealing a waist so petite that Will knew his big clumsy hands could encompass it.

He went on alert as the scowling suitor groped his way upright by leaning on the bench she'd just departed.

"My lady, I have poured my heart at your feet. I think I have a right to expect an answer."

The mastiff stiffened at his tone. Will did the same, narrowing his eyes as the gentleman reached his feet and caught the lady's arm to detain her.

Dead meat.

Fearing the lady would not appreciate his intrusion, Will restrained himself and the dog.

Lady Aurelia donned her frostiest expression, her impossibly long lashes sweeping up and down in disdain as she regarded the hand on her person.

"Just say yes, my lady," the gentleman suggested. "We are well suited. I will see that you are never bothered by undesirable admirers."

"The waltz calls," she said, removing the hand crushing her sleeve by the simple expedient of bending a finger back until he had to jerk away.

Will breathed a sigh of relief as she swayed briskly in the direction of the duke's sprawling mansion. He really didn't wish to cause a commotion by pounding a rich lordling into the ground like a garden post.

Regrettably, the lordling didn't take the lady's form of dismissal as an answer. He caught up with her in a single stride, grabbed her arm, and swung her around rather forcefully.

The frightened look on Lady Aurelia's fair face was all it took to set off Will's protective instincts. Trying his best to remember he wasn't at home and couldn't do as he pleased, he snapped his fingers and set Ajax lose. The giant mastiff ran straight toward the couple.

Deciding the lordling didn't look as frightened of the dog as the lady did of his grip, Will silently ordered Ajax to jump. The dog enthusiastically obeyed as if the gentleman really were the smelly animal carcass she'd sniffed earlier.

Enormous paws landed square on the back of a tailored coat. The gentleman had to release the object of his desire if only to remain upright. Will noticed the nodcock did *not* attempt to block Lady Aurelia from the dog's paws, as a gentleman ought.

"Get off me, you beast!" the fool yelled, darting to one side while Ajax waved her tail and waited for a reward.

Will sauntered from his hiding place in the hedge. "Well met, my lady," he called, without explanation. He seldom gave explanations, and the lady knew who he was.

"Is this your bloody brute?" the angry suitor demanded. "Get him off me!"

"*Her.* Even females can be heroes. Ajax, down." Will snapped his fingers, then produced a treat from his pocket. The mastiff happily trotted over to where Will had placed himself—between the lady and the gentleman.

"Good afternoon, sir." The lady patted Ajax's massive head and accepted a drooling slurp. "Good doggie."

With legs down, the mastiff stood well over waist high. Her massive head and teeth turned toward the angry suitor, blocking his way. Without another word, Lady Aurelia swept down the gravel path, her petticoats swaying, head held high.

The lordling glared at Will and fisted his fingers. "Who the devil are you?"

"The one keeping the duke's dog from biting off your balls." That was one explanation he didn't mind giving. Feeding Ajax her treat, humming the waltz coming from the open window, Will aimed for his original goal, the kennel.

There. He had behaved like the gentleman he wasn't for a change. Did the soul good to occasionally refrain from pounding lordlings into fence posts.

Of course, he'd need a cold bath in the brook after encountering the lady's *flower* scent and seeing those huge blue eyes up close, wide with fear and anger and maybe a hint of admiration.

Even females can be heroes, Mr. Madden had said.

Aurelia wished she had the courage to be one. Given all the blessings she'd been given, her family expected her to accomplish marvelous things, not lurk in sequestered chambers.

Entering the cacophony of a house filled with over a hundred servants and guests, she rubbed her temple and tried to concentrate on the lovely notes emanating from the new piano.

Although she loved the music, she couldn't bear the penetrating, abrasive chatter of their guests in the music room. After the encounter with Lord Clayton, her head pounded from the assault of all the castle's noises, and she retreated to a quieter wing, shivering. She'd had enough company for a while—which was why she'd stupidly sought the privacy of the garden in the first place.

Recalling the ugly scene in the garden, she hurried to the parlor overlooking the path to the kennel.

A long line of yews sheltered the outbuildings from view, but Mr. Madden hadn't reached the hedge yet. At the sight of him, she took a deep breath of relief. The large. . . gentleman. . . strode along, unharmed, as if he hadn't just routed her suitor without lifting a hand. She didn't know what had come over the usually indolent Lord Clayton, but she despised altercations and was glad the dog trainer had behaved with more civility than the earl's son.

She had heard tales of Mr. Madden. His animals had pulled drowning people from ponds, found lost children in snowstorms, and more. She had thought them mostly local-boy-does-good stories, but his action in keeping Clayton away added corroboration.

Sheltered here as she was, she seldom had the opportunity to meet anyone outside the duke's elevated social circle. She'd seen Mr. Madden, of course, but only from a distance.

Mr. Madden had the build of an ox. Any attempt to hit his hard, very square jaw would have broken Lord Clayton's knuckles. Since Mr. Madden spent most of his time in physical exercise and had the taut bulging muscles to prove it, Clayton wouldn't have fared any better had he pummeled him elsewhere. She appreciated the trainer's long-legged stride and straight posture as he directed Ajax into happy circles to prevent the dog from chasing after a rabbit crossing their path.

She sighed in admiration over the overlong wealth of thick bronze hair brushing his loosely-tied neckcloth. Why couldn't the gentlemen who courted her look like that? She might even try to listen to them if they did.

Hearing an argument rising above the music, she decided maybe not. Even a dog handler would need to be a mute hermit for her to be comfortable. And her father and brother would shoot anyone less than an earl who came near her—which was why their current guests shouldn't be here at all. Her sisters had been mad to invite them.

Still, they were all gentlemen, as far as she was aware. Lord Clayton was heir to an earl. What on earth had caused him to overreact in such a manner? It did not seem in character, although she would be the first to admit that she was not a keen judge of behavior. Unfortunately, out of self-preservation, she preferred shirking society to observing it.

She peered around the corner to verify no one lurked in the corridor, then darted toward the library. If she was fortunate, she might find a book with pictures and sneak up the back stairs to her room before anyone found her.

She grimaced as she slipped into the library and Lord Baldwin rose from a wing chair with a rose in hand. As he spoke, she lost her concentration on the music, and the clamor of a large household invaded her head.

Don't you ever go in my pantry again or I'll take this knife. . .

Drip, drip, ping. Drip, drip, drip, ping.

A waltz please! We need to practice. . .

E, F#, G#, A, B, C#, D#, E, G
*You **bastard**, I thought you said there was no one out there. . .*
Is she really gone?

She nearly whimpered as the more emotional arguing dominated, intensifying the pain. Was that Lord Clayton shouting? At whom? Who was gone? Should she rescue the person threatened with a knife? How could she think with all these questions demanding an answer?

Vaguely, realizing Lord Baldwin had stopped speaking, not having registered half the words said, she dipped a curtsy. "How very lovely to see you again, my lord." Intent on no more than escape, Aurelia abandoned another bewildered suitor.

With her over-sensitive ears assaulted from all directions, she hurried up to her private wing, only to find her sisters waiting. Well, she had expected no less. She shut and bolted the extra-thick door, blessedly shutting out the worst of the aural storm. Stubbornly, she sat on a chaise longue near the window overlooking a quiet park filled only with birdsong, and waited for the lecture to begin.

"Did you accept Lord Clayton's suit?" Lydia asked, trying on Aurelia's diamond earrings and admiring them in the vanity mirror. Her round face and blond curls weren't classically pretty but pleasant enough. At nineteen, she'd already been presented and snared a suitor— because Aurelia had refused to go to London last season. The previous ones had been too horrifyingly painful and embarrassing.

She didn't know if she could put off her father's demands that she marry much longer.

"Or Lord Baldwin's?" Phoebe asked excitedly. "A spring wedding, just in time for my come-out would be wonderful!"

Phoebe was only seventeen. A shorter, plumper version of her older sisters, she was sweeter-natured but more impetuous.

"It won't happen," Lydia said in boredom. "You'd do better to anticipate my nuptials."

"Your betrothed will surely be home by spring," Aurelia said reassuringly, trying to follow her sisters' chatter with the din of a hundred voices buzzing and shouting from beyond her thick walls. In addition to extra thickness, she'd added heavy paneling and tapestries so she had some chance of sleeping at night. "Do you have your music prepared for the musicale this evening? Lady Bennet has such a lovely voice!"

"You won't even be there to listen!" Both her sisters glared at her. Accustomed to her behavior, though, they did not waste time bothering her again with questions she didn't hear or wouldn't answer.

"We waited until father and Rain were both in London to arrange this entertainment," Lydia continued, her anger superseding the buzz in the distance. "We brought in all the eligible young men you *haven't* rejected, the ones whom they would not invite. And you still cannot decide?"

"I don't *hear* them," Aurelia cried plaintively, hugging an embroidered pillow. "How can I marry someone I cannot hear?"

"As far as I'm concerned, that's a benefit, not a detriment. We made sure they were all handsome. All you need do is *look* at them," Phoebe said with a hint of desperation. "How will I ever compete with you next Season if you're not taken?"

"You won't," Lydia said. "None of us can. We'll have to put a sack over her head."

"Or beans in my ears," Aurelia said with a sigh. "Cook is threatening to knife someone again. Will one of you please calm troubled waters this time? I really don't want to push Lord Rush down the stairs. He's hovering on the landing."

Again, they didn't question her irrelevant response as everyone outside the family did. She hoped someday when she was a maiden aunt that they would come to accept her inability to deal with the world at large. Had she been a medieval lady, they could have bought her a place in a nunnery and gone on with their lives. As it was, her excruciatingly acute hearing rendered her perfectly useless and an obstacle to everyone's happiness.

"I'll go, if I can borrow your earrings for this evening." Lydia turned her head back and forth to admire the flash and sparkle.

"By all means." Remembering Lord Clayton's unusual behavior, Aurelia added, "Phoebe, go with her. Some of the guests have been a little unruly in Rain's absence. We'd best go everywhere in pairs."

That, of course, excited her sisters' lust for excitement. They left, chattering, completely confident that they were safe in their father's sheltered household surrounded by servants.

Aurelia wished she could be as blissfully ignorant. But she'd heard and suffered the result of neglect and violence and no longer pretended the world was a safe place.

As if her gloomy thoughts had taken on a life of their own, an anguished cry, almost a childish wail, pierced the normal cacophony in her head. Emotional cries always penetrated better than normal speech, but there were no children in the house. Even her younger brother Teddy was away at school. It wouldn't surprise her if the painful throbbing in her head started producing imaginary shrieks. Maybe it was her skull protesting.

Aurelia hummed, hoping to drown out the various noises so she might dress for dinner.

But by the time the musicale was ready to start, all she could hear was the child's terrified weeping. She could not think, could barely breathe with the anguish overwhelming all the more pleasant noises buzzing through the halls.

Aiieeeeeee, sob! Ahhhhhhh, sniff, sob, aiiieeeee!

They say. . . But really. . .

Tonight, we'll leave tonight.

Whimper, sob, waaaaaaaa!

She had done her best to learn to disregard adult arguments, but she could not ignore a terrified child. Neither could she go out into the world on her own. The daughters of a duke had the need for accompaniment drummed into their very souls from birth— especially in this tragic household.

Helplessly, she listened to the wordless wail. Everyone was anticipating a pleasant evening of music. Dragging footmen and her maid into the cold damp night on a fool's errand with no surety that she could find the child—or that she did not imagine it entirely— would only ruin her reputation even more than it was. Her father and Rain would be furious.

And then she remembered Mr. Madden coming to her rescue this afternoon.

HUMMING ONE of the tunes emanating from the duke's palace, Will scratched the heads of a few hounds, checked the kennel's water supply, and secured the gate. Moonlight peered from behind the clouds, enough to find his way back to the stable. He enjoyed the late hours when no one was about. He'd have to take Ajax on a nighttime patrol soon.

He favored Castle Yates over the grandiose home where his half-brothers resided. He'd been born and partially raised in Yatesdale. He was comfortable here, where people didn't expect him to be more than Maeve's bastard son. He had no inclination for science or politics as his brothers did. He didn't need the city. The land he meant to buy was in a peaceful valley of the Cotswolds, where he'd never have to wear a tailored coat or attempt to read a book again. He was built like a farmer, and a farmer's life suited him. No one accustomed to animals questioned his talking to them.

He could appreciate the beauty of the sprawling ducal castle from a distance, but he never wanted to live in one.

Lights flickered in the windows on the hill above him. Music poured from an upstairs gallery. He listened to the notes blending with the sleepy calls of birds and crickets. Perhaps, when he had his own place, he'd learn to make music. Or find a wife who could play.

Thoughts of a wife made him restless. Now that his brothers were almost all married, it was time he made an honest woman of Miranda. She was conveniently located not far from the farm he wished to buy. She wasn't a lady like his brothers' wives, but she was a good woman who didn't complain when his work took him far afield for long periods of time.

He was about to reconsider working off his excess energy by taking Ajax on a patrol of the grounds when he noticed a cloaked form racing toward him.

What the devil? There was no mistaking the lady's slight figure. Even should there be a maid of the same size, she wouldn't have been wearing a fur-trimmed cloak. For good reason, his grace's daughters never went out without escort, and this was twice in one day that the addlebrained female had risked her person.

Will hastened to put himself between her and any danger. He'd lived here half his life and never spoken a word to the duke's reclusive daughter. Twice in one day signified a change in the universe as he knew it, and he tried to maintain his usual composure. Difficult, he admitted, knowing the most-sought-after heiress in the kingdom roamed loose in his territory.

"Mr. Madden," Lady Aurelia cried when he stepped into her path. "Thank goodness. There is a child lost in the woods. I hear her cries, but I cannot understand what she is saying." She continued toward the stable, expecting him to follow.

Had she been anyone else, he would no doubt have balked without further enlightenment. But Lady Aurelia's daunting beauty concealed the fact that she wasn't entirely right in the head. She required all the security the duke could surround her with—and maybe some extra brains.

Following her, he listened to the night sounds, but if there was a child crying, he couldn't hear it. "Children cry," he said, searching for a thin thread of reason.

"Not like this." Impatiently, she tugged at the stable door that had been closed up for the night.

Ever aware of his size, Will knew he could fling the witless lady over his shoulder and haul her back to the house and to the people who ought to be guarding her. He feared she might break if he tried. Alternatively, he could let her tug at the bolted door for the rest of the night. Unfortunately, his mother had taught him better than that.

"Go back to the house. I'll fetch the dogs," he said, hoping she might have a rare episode of reason and agree.

"Excellent idea. I'll fetch Ajax, if you'll saddle the horses."

So, she heard only what she wanted to hear. Women were like that, especially women of this particular family.

Will saw no sense in arguing. In her eyes, he was a mere servant, and his duty was to obey her commands. He'd been thinking of walking out anyway. Might as well go for a ride with a madwoman. He grabbed the heavy bar, hauled it back, and heaved open one of the long doors.

Unwilling to disturb the grooms who had settled in for the evening, he threw saddles on a couple of the calmer mounts in the duke's extensive stable and led them out. The lady was waiting with Ajax already leashed.

"Shouldn't you have one of your sisters with you?" he asked, attempting a degree of sanity.

"They only make noise," she said, not exactly addressing the question. "It's quieter this way, and I can hear better."

Malcolm madness. He'd seen his brothers deal with their insane women. This one wasn't his and never would be, so he didn't have to listen. But if he wanted that kennel, he needed the duke's approval, and he'd lose it if his grace learned Will had let the witless Lady Aurelia go out alone.

"You'll explain this to your father if he objects?" he demanded, cupping his hands and lifting her into the sidesaddle. She was so light, he feared flipping her over the horse's back.

He liked his women heavy and substantial, he reminded himself. He was a big man and needed a big woman, like Miranda. Just because this fairy-like female fascinated him didn't mean he should see her as more than his employer's daughter—an employer who was likely to murder him should he discover he was out here alone with her.

She seemed momentarily startled at his assistance. Freezing, as if suddenly realizing the foolishness of this escapade, she glanced back at the lighted house spilling music.

And then she glanced down at him with what appeared to be a frown. "I can't hear the child if I'm surrounded by noise. You're so quiet, I can almost hear your heart beating."

Will snorted. Still not the answer he wanted, or even one that made sense. "*Annoyingly silent* is the usual epithet I hear." Deciding arguing with a madwoman was a waste of energy, he checked the girth and unleashed the dog. "Ajax has learned to heel. Let's see how she does."

"The child sounds so terrified," the lady murmured in despair, again not responding to his words. "How will we ever find her? I have no idea how close she might be."

Was the lady deaf to him while she listened to otherworldly voices? He was mad as she for not hauling her back to the house and letting them lock her up, where she belonged. Unfortunately, he had a little more experience than most at being outside the ordinary, and he couldn't deny her plea. Or that was his excuse anyway.

"Ajax has better hearing than I do. Let's see if he can pick up the sound." Linking his mind to the dog's, Will tried to hear what Ajax did.

Rustle, rabbits, badger! Hurry, tug, run. . . what's that scent? Human. Follow! Treats.

Will couldn't discern a child's cry in the dog's mind, but Ajax had been trained to track human scents. With no better guide, Will sent the bitch off to follow her instinct.

Tongue lolling, the mastiff took off in the direction of the untamed wilderness beyond the duke's manicured landscaping. The lady trotted in their wake as if riding out at night, alone, was the most natural event in the world. Having seen her ride these hills since childhood—in company with family and grooms—Will had no doubt she could handle the steed. His concern was returning her safely to her home before anyone came looking for them.

The lady rode silently, allowing him to stay connected loosely with the dog. He didn't need to know about every badger trail or dead vermin in the gorse, but he tried to hear with the dog's sharp hearing.

The sure-footed horses found paths around rocks and scree, carrying them downhill and into the gloom of the cliffs below. Will cursed himself for being so distracted by the lady's presence that he had not thought to carry a lantern. Even the moonlight vanished in the shadows beneath towering boulders. Ajax whimpered and dashed off down an animal trail. Will lost visual sight of her but kept the mental connection. Keeping his ears open, he tried to hear a child's cry but didn't.

The craggy moor appeared untouched since the beginnings of time. Tumbling rock, rough grasslands, and bogs were unsuited for human habitation. Miles from the village, cut off from other farms by the duke's vast estate, the steep hillsides were no easy hike from anywhere. He would dismiss Aurelia's fears as hallucination—except Ajax was definitely following a scent she identified as human.

"I *hear* her," Aurelia whispered anxiously, as if sensing his doubt. "How would a child ever find their way down here?"

"The same way you hear her perhaps," he said dryly.

"Inexplicably," she retorted, proving she could listen when she wished.

A rabbit darted from behind a rock. His horse shied, and Will heard Ajax's yip of excitement. If the damned dog was following a rabbit. . . He couldn't complain. He was rather enjoying this break in his dull routine.

He winced at that wayward thought. He'd chosen his simple path for good reasons—one of them being that he wanted freedom from society's unreasonable restrictions and lack of understanding.

He focused on the dog's mind—

Wet grass slapping her nose with the rich scent of earth. Push her nose into wet dog stench, tall plants tickling, yip, warning. . .

Will shook himself out of the bitch's unfocused senses. Ajax had evidently found a patch of thick ferns and the stench of wet fur.

Will still heard no child, but he gathered that Ajax had found an animal, possibly a dog, one that was alive but not moving. He held up his hand to halt the lady and swung down.

"She's not here," Lady Aurelia argued. "We're closer though."

"Let me see what Ajax has found." He couldn't abide to leave hurt animals suffering, and that was the sense he was receiving. He crept up to where the mastiff lay down, tail wagging, nose sniffing.

Among the frost-bitten ferns lay a bedraggled spot of dirty brown and white, wriggling pathetically. Will crouched down, removed his glove, and held out his hand for the creature to sniff. It did so eagerly, proving it was accustomed to human handling.

"What have you found?" Lady Aurelia asked, keeping her voice low.

Will scooped up the shivering terrier pup, stroking its bristly coat and searching for injury. He thought he found blood, and the rear leg appeared hurt. That was a discovery he would not relate to the worried lady, but it raised his hackles. This was a pampered puppy, not an animal accustomed to roaming wild. Damage like this usually happened from human brutality.

"A puppy. He may be injured." He held up the creature in the palm of his ungloved hand to show her.

"The child may be crying for her dog!" she exclaimed.

Will thought he might almost follow the path of that thought.

She reached for the bedraggled creature. "He's small enough to fit in my pocket. Will that keep him warm enough for now?"

He would rather take the dog back to the house to tend it than chase after unseen, unheard children at the insane demand of a woman who heard what others did not. But the presence of a pampered puppy asked questions he couldn't answer.

He fed the puppy from the treats in his pocket and let the terrier sniff the lady's much sweeter smelling hands. It scrambled eagerly to reach her. She cuddled him in her lap, stroking him into calmness. "A child's pet?"

"Possibly," he said gruffly, climbing back into the saddle. Quelling his resistance to tamper with a strange dog's mind, he probed until he saw the puppy's scrambled, page-flipping thoughts.

He might not read textbooks with fluency, but he could grab scenes from a dog's mind with enough accuracy to react in horror. *Blood, unbelievable amounts of blood. And screams. And pain.*

Unable, and unwilling, to explain those impressions, Will merely urged the horse into a trot, ordering Ajax to follow the puppy's scent. He appreciated that the lady didn't question his path.

His Malcolm sisters-in-law were nonstop chatterers, so he'd never thought of Lady Aurelia in the same manner as her cousins. Except he knew that her father was descended from one of the more mad of the Malcolm witches—one who heard spirit voices and saw ghosts. He didn't think the puppy was a ghost or that the scene of carnage in its mind was from beyond the veil, but it was possible that the lady might be hearing more than was evident in the real world.

Double damn and twice the trouble.

With an inexorable sense of foreboding, he led the way in silence, through darkness, until they reached the bottom of the steep hill. Ajax yipped and raced toward the south. The cold night air nipped at Will's nose, but this flat path was safer than the downhill one.

"I hear her!" the lady cried in a low voice. "We're close."

Will heard nothing human. He connected his mind to Ajax, sifting through the sounds and scents—until he heard a child's quiet weeping through the dog's ears. His stomach lurched, and he sent the lady a narrowed look. "Do you hear her in your head or with your ears?" he asked, cursing himself as he did. Ives curiosity often won over common sense.

"Both," she said curtly, straining to hear the impossible.

She seemed agitated but didn't do anything reckless like sending her horse galloping through the rocks to reach the invisible. He'd always known the lady as a cautious creature who seemed better suited to a fairy garden than the real world. Her reply proved him right.

"There, by those boulders," she whispered, distracting his wandering thoughts.

The terrain she indicated was too rough for their mounts. Keeping an eye on Ajax, Will found a grassy patch by the creek not far from the boulders. He dismounted and would have followed the dog alone, but the lady's impatient reaction forced him to reconsider.

"You'll terrify her. Help me down."

The night couldn't be any weirder. *Hold the duke's fragile daughter?* A few hours ago, he would have thought it more likely he'd encompass the moon.

Clamping down on his rioting senses, Will clasped the lady's tiny waist. He'd been right, his hands circled her. She smelled of cakes and biscuits, weighed almost nothing, and he had a need to cradle her against him. At the notion, he practically dropped her and backed away.

She didn't seem to notice. Removing the puppy from her pocket, she cuddled it in her arms, letting it sniff the air and whimper expectantly. Without hesitation, she lifted her skirt and cloak and picked her way across the stones toward Ajax, who had begun to yip quietly.

Feeling like an unnecessary appurtenance, Will tagged along. If the child had been crying, it wasn't now. That did not bode well.

Two

SNUFFLE, RUSTLE, hoot...

Startled by the loud cry and flapping of wings, Aurelia stumbled. Realizing the owl and the fox were actually some distance away, she swallowed and proceeded cautiously.

Heart pounding in fear that once more she may have arrived too late, she pushed aside tall ferns. Behind them, two boulders met, creating a crevasse at their base. The voice in her head had gone silent, but the dog watched her expectantly. She was useless without sound, but she *had* to be in the right place. She couldn't bear it if another precious life was lost because she was such an incompetent coward.

Behind her, she sensed Mr. Madden standing tall and strong, watching her back. His presence surrounded her with almost eerie humming vibrations. He might drive her mad were they elsewhere, but here she needed the reassurance he emanated.

If she had been able to fight past her hysteria earlier, she would never have considered this mad expedition. She would have hidden behind her usual weakness. But Mr. Madden's presence had oddly made the venture not only seem possible, but almost as normal as locating a lost kitten. Instead of arguing and forcing her to give up, he had accepted her need to find the crying child. And so, she had gone.

If her father or brother heard about this... It didn't matter. They already thought her worthless and had despaired of ever being rid of her. They'd vowed to return from London with a husband of their choosing, since she would not select one.

She reached through the forest of ferns for a scrap of color that seemed out of place, where she encountered what felt like a small foot. Crawling further into the narrow space, she reached deeper and felt a small chest rising and falling. Sending prayers of thanksgiving to the heavens, she buried her fingers in folds of cloth and gently pulled.

The child woke and cried again, a heartbreakingly odd cry with no words, only fear and grief. Will dropped to his knees beside her, helping her haul the weeping child from her hiding place. Aurelia held up the puppy, and the young girl cried out in joy, reaching for her pet.

The child made noises that weren't words as she crooned over the dog, which wiggled in ecstasy, despite its damaged leg.

"Can you tell if she's injured?" Will asked in a low voice, pushing the ferns aside to see better.

The child finally noticed him and scrambled backward in terror.

Oh, dear. Aurelia held up her arm, pretending to hold Will away. "He won't hurt you. Are you hurt?"

Wild-eyed, the girl just kept shaking her head and scooting backward, seeking her hiding place again.

"Don't." Aurelia caught her ankle. She couldn't guess the child's age. It was too dark. But she was small, all bone and tattered cloth. She'd lost one shoe and wore no cloak, and the temperature was dropping rapidly. "Let us take you home with us. We have a warm fire. Do you like soup? We can have a warm bowl of soup. And your puppy would like a bone, wouldn't he? Does he have a name?"

She spoke soothingly, stroking the child's leg and warming her cold toes in her glove. The girl quit inching away but continued glaring at Will with suspicion.

He stepped backward, out of the child's sight. "Can you lift her?"

"Maybe, if you'll take the pup." She grasped the wriggling bundle of fur and attempted to pry it from the child's hand, but she wouldn't let go. "That won't work."

"Wrap both of them in this, and maybe she won't be able to fight if I lift her." He dropped his very large coat over her shoulder.

Aurelia glanced up and saw him outlined in shirtsleeves and waistcoat in the weak light of the moon. "You'll freeze," she protested.

"Not any more than that child will. Wrap her up so she can't easily escape. I can carry her on my horse better than you can if she won't jump off."

Acknowledging the truth of that, Aurelia dropped the huge wool coat over the child's frail shoulders. Clinging to the puppy, the girl snuggled into the warmth. Aurelia wrapped the heavy fabric around her nearly twice, bundling child and dog into a cocoon. "All snug and tight?" she crooned as if to an infant. "Let's go for a ride and find some warm food."

When the girl still only made *ummm ummm* noises, Aurelia lifted the bundle from the fern bed and nearly staggered with the awkward weight until Will slid his big arms beneath her burden. The girl wriggled and cried out in protest, but she didn't have a chance of fighting off his embrace. Aurelia continued speaking reassuringly as they walked back to the horses.

While she found a boulder she could stand on to mount her sidesaddle, Will tucked his protesting bundle into the curve of one arm, and pulled himself up with ease.

"Men have it too easy," Aurelia complained as she wrapped her hindering skirt and leg around the pommel. "You're bigger, stronger, and you don't have to wear petticoats."

"Women are smaller and softer so they don't frighten little children," he countered, hanging on to his writhing bundle of yipping, protesting dog and child while setting his horse in motion.

"Small children wouldn't be afraid of big men if men didn't hurt them." She had to air that fear if only to take it off her chest.

"There are equally wicked women," he said, "but admittedly, men have the strength to do more damage. But this one seems to have all her bones in place. They're pummeling me viciously."

Apparently they were far enough from human occupation that the only sounds her acute hearing picked up were the silent animals going about their nocturnal business. Amazed that she could have an actual conversation, Aurelia laughed at the notion of those tiny hands causing his muscular chest any harm. "I wonder why she does not talk? Surely she's old enough to know how."

"Unless we wish to believe she's lived out here alone, raised by rabbits, she may just be too frightened."

Aurelia didn't think she'd ever heard Mr. Madden string so many words together at one time. His voice was a low rumble, calming in the same odd way his vibrations soothed instead of irritated. She thought even the child sensed it and settled down to simple sobs. Out here, with only the dog trainer for company, she experienced a tranquility she'd never known.

It didn't last long. The closer they came to home, the more the din of her company invaded her head. Although Mr. Madden's noiseless hum soothed, she could still hear the castle occupants shrieking with repressed excitement, fear, and worry. Apparently the guests had decided on a late night—or her suitors were waiting for her to reappear.

"We should take her in through the kitchen," she murmured as they entered the stable yard.

"Cook will not appreciate the dog," Mr. Madden countered.

"And the child won't be parted from it, I know. But she needs a hot bath and hot food. If I am very fortunate, Cook will have retired, and I can call a maid."

"I'll go with you. The horses can wait in the paddock." He led the way back to the gate.

He swung down with ease despite his burden, then held her horse as she used a stepping block. Aurelia wanted to take the child and do this herself, but she knew she needed assistance. She was comfortable accepting the aid of servants, but Mr. Madden wasn't family or servant. He existed in a limbo with no societal definition, and his shirt-sleeved proximity unnerved her.

Descending the back stairs, she wished herself back outside in the relative silence of the fields.

Bang, clang, look what you've done! **Where the devil is she?** *We must leave. Why stay here? The lady is quite mad. Splash, scrub, grumble. . .*

Two kitchen maids and a pot boy were washing up as they entered the kitchen cellar. The servants stared in mute amazement at her presence.

With the clamor of the guests building above, Aurelia wasn't in the best of humors. She snapped orders for hot water, hot broth, and sent for her maid. The servants scurried, unwittingly leaving her alone with Mr. Madden.

"And people claim you're addlepated," he said in amusement, releasing his terrified captive from his coat and setting her on the floor.

The child clung to her pet and studied the enormous kitchen with alarm.

"I *am* addlepated," Aurelia retorted. "I am holding on by a thin thread and not certain how I'm doing even that much. I suggest you leave to take care of the horses before I snap."

She wasn't generally so blunt with gentlemen, but Mr. Madden wasn't a stranger or a gentleman. He'd been rude, and now he was standing there with his massive arms clad only in shirtsleeves, exuding masculinity with every breath. She was too nervous to dissemble.

Instead of donning his coat, he removed a round laundry tub from the wall and set it before the fire. One of the maids returned to fill it with pails of hot and cold water at his silent direction.

Only when Aurelia's maid hurried into the room did he bother shrugging his battered coat back on.

"Should I take the dog or will you handle it?" he asked, making no comment on her claim to addlepation.

Aurelia looked at the terrified pair on the hearth and hadn't the heart to separate them. "We'll have to dunk both of them in the bath together."

He nodded agreement. "As best as I've been able to tell, his leg seems bruised but not broken. He'll bite if you're not careful."

How could he determine that when the child wouldn't even let him near her pet? Aurelia was too exhausted to question. "I'll be careful."

"Send for me if there is aught I can do." He edged for the door.

Despite his lack of finery, unshaven jaw, and overlong hair, he looked as out of place in the servants' gloomy cellar as she did. Awkwardly, she gestured at the child on the hearth. "I thank you for understanding."

"I am always at your service," he said, making a polite bow and doffing an invisible hat.

Her maid watched him, open-mouthed, as he departed. "Lordy, is he man or mountain?"

Remembering his concern for a lost urchin and his unquestioning aid, Aurelia sighed in confusion. "Not a mountain," was the best she could do. There was nothing cold or rocky about Mr. Madden.

A#, C, C#, D#, F, F#, G#, A# plink plank plunk
 She's not in her room. . .
 She's not worth your time. . .
 You promised. . . !
 *And **Rose?***

You needn't worry. . .

Creaaakkkkk. . .

Fighting exhaustion and the odd confusion of guilt and fear exhibited by the voices in her head, Aurelia watched the maids tuck in the sleepy child before striking out for her chamber. She'd almost reached the end of her strength and really didn't need another encounter with her insistent suitors, so she used the servants' dark stairs.

The masculine argument grew more heated. Even normal hearing might detect the shouting, but with her acute ability, the words graduated from background noise to clarity. She tried desperately not to sort out the various sounds she heard when she was this close to their source. If she concentrated hard enough, she could force the clamor into a monotonous rhythm rather like a waterfall or rain storm. But other times, especially when she was weary, the sounds would penetrate and she could separate the impassioned lovemaking from the drunken laughter or malicious gossip and hear every word.

The silly cow won't give me an answer! That shout leapt plainly from the other cacophony. *She's avoiding me. I haven't seen her all evening.*

Aurelia winced, recognizing Lord Clayton.

She's your last damned chance another male voice roared. He sounded almost close enough to hear normally, which meant they were probably in the library, one of the rooms nearest to the servants stairs. *I need my blunt or I'll lose my mother's house!*

Charming. Leaving the ground floor to the quarrelling men, Aurelia climbed to the next floor and peered down the corridor to make certain it was empty. A light under her door welcomed her.

I'll bring her around the Clayton voice argued inside her pounding skull, despite the distance she was trying to put between them. *You don't think I want to cool my heels in debtor's prison do you? All you have to do is go along with anything I say, and the deed will be done before her father returns.*

Aurelia thought she really ought to find a big stick and part his hair to the crown, but what was the point of proving she wasn't a stupid cow if she behaved like one?

You touch a hair on her head and Rain will part yours from your neck. The voice of reason spoke. She wished she could appreciate it.

Don't be foolish. One doesn't need force with a simpleton, just wit.

Aurelia took exception to the direction of this conversation. She assumed both men were in their cups, but any reference to her brother warned they'd worn out their welcome. Rain had enough problems without adding obstreperous suitors to them.

Fortunately, the men had vented the worst of their anger, or she had moved far enough away that even her sensitivities could no longer discern all their words. They blended into the background hum. She probably should seek them out and attempt to learn their nefarious plans, but it all seemed too foolish at this hour. She would simply put an end to their fun.

Her sisters waited in her bedchamber, helping themselves to her jewelry and paint, amusing themselves while they waited to pounce.

"Where have you been?" Lydia demanded. "We've had to lie for you all evening."

Lord Clayton and his friend might no longer be shouting, but someone in the next wing was delivering a sharp scold and another couple was turning amorous. Aurelia simply wanted to bury her head in her pillows and sleep.

In the morning, she would worry about why a child wandered the dale alone.

"This house party was a mistake," she informed her sisters, flinging her cloak over a chair. She could concentrate when the topic was of this importance. "Everyone needs to leave in the morning."

"You're simply having one of your episodes," Phoebe said. "You'll feel better after a good night's sleep. Shall I send for tea?"

"No, I do not want tea. Lord Clayton and one of his pockets-to-let friends are plotting. I will not marry him no matter what scandal he means to provoke. If you wish to avert disaster, you will send them packing." Aurelia sat down to remove her muddy boots and glare at her bewildered sisters. "Without Rain or Father here, we have no defense. Aunt Tessie is not enough."

"They're gentlemen," Lydia protested. "They wouldn't do anything to harm us."

"They are plotting as we speak. Lord Clayton thinks I am a stupid cow, and he's probably convinced himself that I am better off behind closed doors, in his bed, bearing his children, than running loose. Cows, after all, need tending." Scowling, she presented the back of her gown to Phoebe to unfasten. "He may be an earl's son, but he hasn't a feather of his own to fly with, and he's seeking an heiress. If he can't have me, he'll take one of you."

"Not me," Phoebe piped up in alarm. "He's too old. And I want a glorious come-out where I may bedazzle all of London."

"And I'm already betrothed. You worry for naught. Take your headache powder, and you'll feel better in the morning." Lydia removed the diamond earrings and returned them to Aurelia's jewelry box.

"Desperate men do desperate things. You will stay in your rooms in the morning. I will send word that you are ill, possibly with something contagious, like the mumps, and everyone has to leave." The cries in her head were lessening somewhat as their guests settled in for the night, but the pain did not recede. At least the frightened child had fallen asleep.

"Lela, you cannot mean it!" Lydia cried. "Where will they all go? We promised entertainment. You will make us laughingstocks in all society."

Bodice unfastened, Aurelia circled to face her sister. "I am already a laughingstock, you'll remember. There is nothing more pathetic than a *compromised* laughingstock. If I absolutely must marry, then it needs to be someone of rank, who can accomplish great things with my wealth, as father says. This party was a mistake, I am sorry. Either they go, or I call Rain and Father back from London."

She'd done it before. They knew she did not make idle threats. They might be too young to remember the earlier disaster, but Aurelia had the tragedy imprinted on her mind forever. So did Rain.

"Papa says the future of the kingdom rides on the Reform Bill," Phoebe whispered in concern. "He will hate to leave."

Because of the family peculiarities, their father and brother almost never went to London. That they had done so to aid the cause of reform spoke of the importance of the current parliamentary session. Aurelia felt guilty about making the threat, but the clearness of Clayton's anger in her head spoke of his desperation. She might risk herself, but not her sisters.

"Would Lord Clayton really hurt us?" Phoebe asked with the uncertainty of the child she still was.

"Men who think of women as cattle can justify their behavior with impunity. They do not believe they are hurting us. We are just pawns to be traded in their quest for riches." Removing her gown and corset, Aurelia slipped into a robe in relief. "I am sorry. This is the reason we should never entertain without Father or Rain in attendance."

She was painfully aware of the hypocrisy of her orders. She'd ridden out with a man she scarcely knew this evening. Perhaps she'd frightened herself more than she'd realized. But she would not change her mind about the party. It had been drummed into her head from an early age that the children of dukes were expected to accomplish great things, and for that reason, they must take as much care with their persons as royalty. She understood better than they why this had to be so, but she'd been as bored as her sisters and had relaxed her guard.

Looking worried but not chastened, her sisters finally departed. Aurelia sank into a chair and rubbed her temples. Her gift was mostly a curse, but if she could occasionally save her family from harm, she would endure.

Thinking of the quiet giant no doubt sleeping in the stable, and the mute child in the cellar, she wondered what it would be like surrounded by people who seldom spoke. They could live in a cottage on the moor, away from all civilization.

But she was the wealthy daughter of a duke, destined to make the world a better place. A hermit's wife she could never be.

Which meant—she had to venture out into the world on her own. Again. Sometime.

Three

LEANING AGAINST a fence post the next morning, testing Ajax's ability to follow any scent he gave her, Will watched a steady trickle of guests departing down the drive.

He'd been waiting until he was certain the household was awake before inquiring about the mystery child. Consumed with curiosity about the unhappy, anxious parties deserting the castle, he debated the wisdom of heading that way. His business was with the duke, after all, not the duke's afflicted daughter. He had no right to approach her.

Deciding he had a right to inquire after the child, he returned Ajax to her pen and descended the kitchen stairs. He might possess the blood of an aristocrat and the privilege to enter the front door, but the staff accepted him as one of their own. He preferred the back stairs.

Lady Aurelia and her maid were already there, bundling the girl into what he assumed were outgrown attic discards. Clean, fed, and dressed in a well-made child's frock, the girl appeared much sturdier than she had the prior night. She still warily backed away from him, but she did not cry.

"Oh good," the lady said in relief. "I need to go into the village and make inquiries. I cannot persuade her to even give me her name."

Horrified at the thought of the delicate lady descending to the rough-and-tumble cottages that constituted Yatesdale, Will put a halt to that dangerous thought. "I can go," he said. "You have guests." That was easier than putting together the retinue required to surround her.

The lady stubbornly set her small chin. "The guests are leaving. And the child won't go with you. I need to see if anyone recognizes her."

"Then send your maid with me," Will argued, horrified down to his toes at the notion of allowing the princess out of her castle.

An older woman with threads of gray in her brown hair, the

maid sent him an approving look but said nothing. Will felt as if he
were leaping ice floes over a raging river. What was she proposing?
They couldn't question a soul if she was surrounded by servants.

"I want to go," the lady insisted. "The child can't talk, but I. . ."
She sent him a piercing look. Apparently deciding he'd already
called her addlepated, she continued. "When people speak, I can
sometimes. . . sense. . . if they're hiding anything."

"Why would anyone hide their knowledge of a lost child?" he
asked in genuine puzzlement.

The lady exchanged looks with her maid, who nodded approval
of some unspoken question.

"She is badly bruised. Not all of them are fresh." She waited for
him to understand.

Appalled, Will studied the silent little girl playing with her
puppy. The bloody scene he'd caught in the dog's mind had played
through his sleep, but the scene hadn't included the child. Of course,
dogs reacted stronger to smell than other sensations, and blood was
a particular trigger. That brief glimpse reflected the dog's reaction
more than the actual sight.

He frowned as he followed the path of her thoughts. "You
cannot go about confronting violent men. Or women," he added out
of fairness.

For a moment, the lady looked relieved. Then she rubbed her
temple and studied the child. "No confrontation," she agreed. "I am
very bad at it. If I hear or sense anything untoward, I will wait until
we're away before telling you."

Will wanted to shout that fairy princesses should stay in their
damned fairy hills where they were safe, but the lady was of age and
knew her own mind. Well, her own addlepated mind anyway.
Reluctantly, he admitted it was not his duty to tell her what to do,
although he was beginning to understand why the duke kept such a
close guard on her. Her beauty attracted too much notice, but her
eccentricity no doubt led to dangerous behavior—like this.

"I'll agree only if you take a closed carriage, a groom, and a
footman. A maid isn't sufficient," he said, brooking no argument.
Although by all rights—he had no means to stop her.

She scowled. "I sent some of our guests home in the barouche.
I'll have to take the curricle."

Which she no doubt meant to drive herself. Will had an inkling of why his half-brother, a powerful marquess, spent half his life growling and shouting at the reckless behavior of people for whom he was responsible. Which was why Will didn't want responsibility for anyone but himself and certainly not the sheltered daughter of a damned duke.

Miranda had her own small acreage and had been taking care of herself for years. The widow was definitely his best choice if he meant to marry and continue his guilt-free travels.

"Take the safest carriage you possess," he ordered unhappily, "and the largest footman or stable hand you can summon to ride on back. I'll ride beside the carriage." With anyone else, this would be a ridiculous request. For this sheltered, retiring—addlepated—princess, a full retinue was a necessary safeguard.

She considered his command. "An entourage like that will not terrify everyone in the village into hiding?"

"Of the two of us, which do you fear will cause terror and consternation?" he asked dryly. "I don't think the people whose business depends on your family will cower at sight of you."

"And they know you," she said in relief. "That will be all right. If you'll call for the curricle, I'll verify that our guests have departed. I don't wish to bump into them on the road after I've heaved them out."

Will would have liked to have heard the story behind that statement, but he'd already tested his limits. He'd hear the tale from the servants later.

"I SHOULD HAVE left Mr. Madding to protect my sisters," Aurelia murmured to Addison, her maid and companion. Now that she was away from the Hall and not yet at the village, she could think more clearly. The trotting click of the horses almost nullified distant sounds. "I am not convinced some of the guests won't turn around and come back."

"Your man-mountain goes where he wishes, and he wishes to know about the child as much as you do," Addy said. "Besides, you are as valuable as your sisters."

Addy was twice Aurelia's age and had been her nurse when she'd been an infant. Bossy and efficient, her maid hadn't given up teaching lessons once she'd taken over Aurelia's wardrobe. Aurelia would resent that, except Addy was as close to a mother as she'd had since the duchess had died giving birth to her youngest son almost a dozen years ago.

"My sisters are sensible. They will become the women behind powerful men that they've been raised to be, if we protect them from their adolescent foolishness."

"You do not need a man to make you valuable. But they are very convenient beasts of burden when we want them." Addy stole a glance around the hood at the large man trailing behind them. "Maeve's son grew up nicely, didn't he?"

Aurelia wasn't supposed to know about innkeepers and their bastards, but everyone in the village had known Maeve and her son. Mr. Ives-Madden had gone off to school at some point, then left home entirely to live with his father's family after Maeve died of a painful wasting disease, but he'd not forgotten his old friends.

And yes, he'd grown up nicely, although he dressed like a farmer in baggy clothing and slouchy caps, with his overlong hair rubbing his neckcloth. But she'd noticed his boots were well made and well kept, and she really shouldn't be noticing his form in the saddle. But she did. He was an expert horseman.

"The Ives men tend to be large," Aurelia said dismissively. "They are also said to be stubborn, autocratic, and eccentric. I understand Maeve was no better, so he is probably twice as bad as the others."

"You, above all else, ought to know better than to judge by appearance."

Which nicely put her in her place. How else was one to judge when appearance was all one saw—until it was too late. Her looks belied her disability so gentlemen trusted her form and not her behavior. She should wear sacks.

The child wriggled between them, trying to hold onto her pet and stare at the countryside at the same time. Now that she was cleaned up, she didn't appear to be a forlorn waif any longer. She had brownish curls and brown eyes in a heart-shaped face on a small but sturdy body. Judging from her missing front teeth, Aurelia guessed her to be about six, so she should be talking. Occasionally, she made sounds that sounded as if she meant to speak, but no one could understand her.

"Mmmnnn?" she asked now, watching Mr. Madden ride ahead to chase sheep from the road.

"Man," Aurelia responded, looking for words with a similar sound. "Gentleman."

The child sat back, unsatisfied, to judge by her frown. "Bbbbdmmmnn."

"Bad men?" Addy guessed, speaking louder to catch the child's attention.

The girl swung around, pressed her fingers against Addy's lips, and repeated, "Bbbdmmnn."

With her sensitivity to emotional sound, Aurelia heard the child's fear, and her heart fell to her stomach. "Bad men?" she said loudly, loud enough to cause Mr. Madden to startle and turn around.

Frowning worriedly, the child pursed her lips and repeated, "Bbbddmmn."

"My word, she's almost deaf," Aurelia said.

Her expression must have alerted their escort. He trotted back, Ajax at his gelding's heels. "What is it?"

"You wouldn't happen to carry pencil or paper on you, would you?" she asked.

"We can find some in the village. Are you preparing a ransom note?"

She could see curiosity and amusement in the way his dark eyes danced and his lips curled. Really, the gentleman, if he could be called that, was too annoying and too forward. And she had no idea how to treat him. "I think she's almost deaf and wondered if she might be able to read and write. It would help to know her name."

Amusement turned into a frown. "That would explain her inability to speak. How the deuce will we find her parents if we don't know her name?"

"I had hoped you would take Ajax out to follow her trail today. She didn't fall from the sky."

"We went as soon as the sun was up. But the rain last night has washed away the scent. Ajax followed for a little while, in the opposite direction of the Castle. But she lost the trail before we were half way up the hill."

That took her down a notch. He'd been out at dawn, after she'd kept him up half the night. "I'm sorry. I'm not accustomed to gentlemen who rise with the birds. I don't think there is much in that direction but sheep crofts, is there?"

"Not that I'm aware. I'll take Ajax around to that side of the valley if we find no answers in the village. It would be useful to take her terrier, but I'm assuming that's not possible." He studied their small passenger's defiant frown and determined grip on her dog.

Aurelia shook the reins to speed up her team. "All we can do is ask around for now. Let's start there."

He made her impossibly nervous for no good reason. Perversely, she trusted him, perhaps because she sensed his reserve hid secrets like her own. He had Malcolm ancestors, just as she did. He'd not questioned her ability to hear things he couldn't. All in all, Mr. Madden was rather restful to be around. At least he wasn't calling her a stupid cow and thinking of her as a pot of gold waiting to be claimed.

He was, of course, bossy and autocratic. When they reached town, he directed her to the inn he preferred, not the larger one she had intended to visit. He ordered the stable hands around as if he owned the place, which made her give herself a mental slap.

"Is this his mother's inn?" she whispered to Addy.

"His now, I reckon," Addy said. "Old Butler's been running it forever, though."

This was what happened when she never left the house—she knew nothing of the people around her. Mr. Madden offered his gloved hand to help her down before her footman could clamber off his high perch on back. Usually distracted by the din in her head, she seldom noticed when other men did this, but Mr. Madden's hand was large, and powerful enough to muffle the noise for the brief moment he held her.

But the cacophony of an entire village shouting, singing, and laughing intruded, and she hastened to hide behind the thick stone walls of the inn.

WILL HAD KNOWN Butler would hear about the lady's arrival well before the curricle pulled into the yard. It would have been worth his life to bypass the inn without stopping. He not only wouldn't insult the older man by doing so, he relied on his trusty innkeeper to provide a secure and private room for the duke's daughter.

By the time Will had directed a stable hand to look after the team and followed the ladies inside, Butler had donned a crisp white apron over his portly belly and combed his thinning gray hair out of his face. He had the maids lined up to curtsy a greeting, and a tea tray waiting in the private salon Will used when he was here. The maids were so awed by the presence of aristocracy that they did not even bother to flirt with him for a relaxing change.

The fairy princess had no inkling that this was not normal behavior. Winking at the staff, Will let the lady's servants surround her while he held back to order refreshments and pencil and paper. The maids giggled and fell all over themselves in their effort to please him and see a duke's daughter. The modest inn seldom attracted aristocrats.

"I heard there was mumps up at the Hall," Butler whispered as the salon door closed. "They not be bringing 'em down here, be they?"

"Mumps?" Will chuckled after working that through the other gossip circling the servants hall. "More like the lady was tired of her guests and had better things to do."

Butler nodded in relief. "The duke ain't home to make the young louts behave. What brings her here then?"

Will turned serious. "The girl. Did you see her? Do you recognize her? She may be deaf and mute."

Butler wrinkled up his already wrinkled brow in thought. "Can't say that I've heard of such. Want me to ask around?"

Will hesitated. That was the method he would prefer, but if the lady had some Malcolm means of determining if a man was lying. . . "Ask if anyone has heard about a missing child. Don't be specific. Bring anyone here who might know something. And send for the vicar, if you will."

Butler snorted. "He'll be on his way soon enough. The church needs a new roof."

There were many reasons a duke's daughter might not visit the village, Will realized. But he was reasonably certain that money wasn't one of them.

When he entered the salon, the lady, her maid, and the girl were already sipping hot drinks and working with a pencil and paper. The girl shot him a suspicious look but bent determinedly over the paper, nearly crushing the pencil with her small hand.

"She can write," Lady Aurelia said aloud. Since the child apparently did not hear well, they had no need to whisper.

"I'll send for a slate and chalk if she can write more than her name. She's a bit young for writing more than her alphabet, isn't she?" Will nodded gratefully as one of the inn maids handed him his preferred mug of coffee. Tiny teacups didn't fit his fingers well.

The child smiled triumphantly and pushed the pad at the lady. In the big awkward letters of a beginning writer, she'd printed ROSE.

"Rose!" the lady shouted in delight. The child apparently heard, because she looked pleased.

The lady printed LELA in large letters and pointed at herself. *Lela?* That must be her pet name Will realized in amusement.

Rose attempted to sound out the letters by watching the women's lips as they repeated the name. Clever, Will concluded. "What is the dog's name?" He pointed at the skinny creature.

Rose followed his gesture, held up her terrier questioningly, and at Will's nod, eagerly picked up the pencil again. She printed TINY with a backward N.

"Tiny!" the lady shouted, and the child beamed.

Behind her back, the lady gestured at Will, then turned to cast him a warning glance. Not entirely certain how he should interpret her request, he angled his head at the door, and she nodded. All right, then, silent communication it was. Weird, but not dangerous.

She'd already proved she could hear what he couldn't. He slipped away to find out what she might have perceived. He recognized nothing untoward in the inn, so he stepped outside. He had to leave the yard and walk into the street before he caught more than the whickering of horses.

"My daughter's been missing this year or more!" a big blustering fellow roared from well down the street.

How the devil could the lady hear that from deep inside the stone walls of the inn? Will studied the burly, disheveled man approaching with a rolling gait, shouting at no one in particular. He looked too old to have fathered a young child. No wife walked beside him, but she could be young, he supposed. He also appeared to be a sailor if his bearing was any indication. A sailor this far from the water wouldn't find much work.

One of Butler's young messenger boys ran to keep up with the man's hurried stride. Will was reluctant to let such a dubious specimen in the lady's presence. He stepped back inside and signaled to the innkeeper. "Do you know the fellow? I don't recognize him."

Butler peered out the mullioned window as the loud sailor approached. "The blacksmith's brother, cashiered out of the Navy, I heard."

"Married?" Perhaps it wasn't a good idea to find the child's family, given the bruises on her.

"He has a woman," Baker said. "Don't recollect a child."

"Hold him out here until I speak with the lady." Will strode back to the parlor where the women were merrily feasting on teacakes and shouting at each other, presumably so the girl could hear.

The lady actually smiled when he entered the room. He wasn't certain he'd ever seen her smile. Perfect, petite features, big blue eyes, rose lips, and stacks of golden silk were enough to make a man twist his head backward to watch her. But that smile altered pleasant into radiant. No wonder she had men groveling at her feet! He waited warily for explanation.

"Shouting is very useful," she told him with amusement. "I cannot hear others over my own voice."

"And it took a child to teach you this?" Not that he totally understood, but he was learning more about her idiosyncrasy with each passing insane minute. "You heard the bluff fellow heading this way?"

"Only that he is loud and coarse, and he's hiding something. Is he out there now?"

William processed this amazing statement. "Will you be able to tell what he's hiding if I bring him in here for questioning?"

"I cannot read minds," she said. "I only hear what they're feeling, and even that is uncertain because people generally do not feel just one thing. Unless they're in a rage, maybe," she added, wrinkling her perfectly proportioned nose.

"Will you let me interview him, then?" Will asked. "Perhaps Addy and Rose can go out where he can see them, and we'll see how he reacts. I'd rather not have him near you. He looks the sort to take advantage any way he might."

Her eyes widened in understanding. "Yes, I know the sort. And it would figure that sort would be the first to arrive."

By this time, the girl and maid were watching them, and the new arrival could be heard blustering from the front of the inn. Rose, of course, could not hear him. She simply hugged Tiny and studied the adults for answers.

"I'll let you know if he seems a possibility." He forestalled any attempt for the duke's daughter to solve this on her own. Malcolm women had a tendency to take things too far, he'd learned from watching his brothers' wives. He'd been mad to agree to this expedition.

Will let himself out. Snapping his fingers, he brought Ajax running from the kitchen.

Butler had handed the fellow an ale and listened to his tale of woe. Will took a seat nearby, and let Ajax sniff the air. Connecting to the dog's senses merely told him that the oaf stank of horse shit and ale. He could tell that on his own.

"You're missing a daughter?" Will asked as the man roared his tale.

"George Acres," Butler said in introduction. "Harry's brother."

Will didn't offer his hand or his name. He let the sailor speak for himself.

"My wee daughter was no more than a babe when I saw her last," George cried, drowning his sorrow in a swig of ale. "M'wife stole her, she did. Came home from sea to find strangers in my home and no sign of her a'tall."

"How long ago was that?" Will asked, sipping from his mug.

"Ten years, ten years I been without the comfort of me own family! How's a man to live like that, I ask ya? It's a right sin, it is. You the gent what found the lost girl?"

"Did you tell him we'd found a girl?" Will asked the innkeeper.

"Not nothing of the sort," Butler said, polishing a glass. "Just asked if any children had gone missing of late. Ten years is a little more than lately."

Will wouldn't have been particularly suspicious of the error if the lady hadn't said the blustering fellow was hiding something. He probably shouldn't be suspicious now. The man had in all probability lost his family when his wife ran off with someone more useful than a belligerent drunk who was never around. It would be perfectly natural to assume the missing child was his own missing daughter. But if the fellow hadn't looked for her in ten years, then chances were good that he was up to something.

"Sorry, old fellow." Will dismissed him by returning to his coffee. "No one has found any ten-year-old girls around here."

"She be older than that now," George said eagerly. "And comely, like her ma. Bring her along and let me tell for myself."

The terrier yipped in the lobby. George didn't even turn to look. Will assumed that ruled him out as knowing anything about Rose since she and the pet were inseparable.

"Did you ever ask your wife's family where she might be?" Butler asked as William stood up.

"The snobbites live up Edinburgh way. I'll not be going after a woman what don't know her place," George said bitterly into his ale. "A man's got a right to expect his dorter to look after him."

Will snorted at that self-centered twaddle. The only thing the drunk was hiding was an eagerness to grab a lost female to do his bidding. He walked out and herded Addy and Rose back to the safety of the salon.

At Lady Aurelia's questioning look, he shrugged. "He's a drunken lout looking for a child he hasn't seen in ten years. I doubt his interest is a moral one." He glanced at Rose, who climbed up in her chair and returned to her hot chocolate and cakes, unfazed by the encounter.

If the girl didn't recognize George Acres, then he wasn't of any interest.

"I should speak with the vicar," Lady Aurelia decided. "He will preach at me for not attending regularly, but he knows more about the village than anyone."

"He should be coming. Are you comfortable here? Shall I ask for anything else?" Will had spent time as an innkeeper's son. He knew the basics of offering hospitality. He simply had never needed to use his knowledge since he had no home of his own. He'd grown up in an all-male household after Maeve's death, one with servants to attend guests. But even he knew a lady of Aurelia's status ought to be treated with kid gloves.

"Unless you know someone who plays loud music, we will simply keep shouting at each other. You might look into your weeping kitchen girl and tell your cook that raging at her won't help." Aurelia beamed at him expectantly.

Addlepated, but quite possibly right. Will gave a finger salute, checked to see that everyone was settled in, and jogged off to the kitchen.

AURELIA ALMOST broke out laughing when a fiddler began playing loudly in the tavern. It was mid-day and even she knew fiddlers did not play until evening, when the tavern was full.

The kitchen girl had stopped weeping shortly after Will had left the room. Since the cook had also gone silent, Aurelia assumed she was no longer in a rage. There were other, more subtle noises, as expected in an inn full of people. But on the whole, the level of cacophony was less than a house party full of aristocrats. Everyone here was working and minding their own business.

Mr. Madden had performed the equivalent of miracles—without being told. She knew better than to become used to his brand of magic. He was a traveling dog trainer who never stayed in one place long, but it was nice to have acceptance of her eccentricity for a while.

She heard the vicar's excitement in his greeting when he finally arrived in the lobby. Even the fiddler stopped—to doff his cap, she expected. She braced herself for the church man's effusiveness. She hated being like this. She would run and hide if it were not for Rose. But she couldn't abandon the child to an orphanage if it could be prevented.

Will accompanied the vicar when they entered the salon. Mr. Richards was a round, affable gentleman of middle age. He bowed and beamed at Aurelia, then everyone else in the room.

"What a charming gathering! Thank you for inviting me to join you." He took the seat Aurelia indicated, and a maid returned with a full teapot.

Rose looked at him with curiosity but returned to her paper and hot chocolate.

The vicar did not appear to recognize her. Disappointed, Aurelia glanced at Mr. Madden, hoping he would stay this time. He hesitated, then took a chair beside the fire, out of the way. It was as if his large size blocked the worst noise the way her tapestries did, and she relaxed.

"We are hoping you will solve a mystery." Aurelia poured the vicar's tea and nodded in the direction of Rose. "We have found a misplaced child, and so far, no one has come forward to claim her."

The vicar studied Rose's bent head with a frown. "She has not been taught her manners, but she's a pretty child. I would remember seeing her at services."

"She cannot hear us unless we shout," Aurelia told him. "It must be hard to teach a child who cannot hear or speak."

The vicar's eyes widened, and he stopped reaching for a teacake. "I have heard. . ." He puckered up his brow. "I know I should not listen to gossip, but it's difficult to scold my parishioners when they have no other topic of conversation."

"Gossip is how a village survives," Aurelia suggested. "It warns us of dangers and celebrates triumphs."

"It can be very wrong, as well. People see with blinders sometimes. But I have heard of a couple newly arrived this past week or so. Titus Brown has several sheepherder crofts he lets out. He's said the young couple appear to have some troubles, but my horse has an injured hock, so I haven't been out that way lately."

"What makes you think this couple has a child?" Will asked from his place by the fire.

"The gossips," the vicar said with a sigh. "They talk of a devil child and a witch who walks the night. I had hoped they might take Brown's cart into town of a Sunday, but they did not."

A devil child and a witch. Aurelia could almost feel Mr. Madden twitch in exasperation. Her reaction was a little more concerned.

Four

WILL HAD NEVER done a reverse rescue before, but if Rose had been living out with the sheep, he knew how to find out where. He rummaged through his pockets filled with various scent identifiers that he squirreled away for training. Finding one of Rose's torn stockings, he gave it to Ajax to smell. Then he set the bitch off over the hills in the direction of Titus Brown's crofts. Singing quietly to let Ajax know he was there, he rode behind her, keeping an eye out for the unusual.

The duke's daughter had been easily persuaded to retreat to her sheltered castle with the child and servants—after promising the vicar a contribution for his church roof. Will was relieved that she had the sense to stay behind secure walls where she belonged. He had a bad feeling about what he might find.

Children and dogs occasionally hurt themselves. They did not *continually* hurt themselves so as to leave multiple days of bruises. The ugly scent of blood in the puppy's mind and the fact that no one had come looking for a child added up to disaster in Will's head. This was his true calling—finding and helping the lost and endangered.

Normally, he'd be told of a missing child or woman—or upon one memorable occasion, an escaped murderer. His business was to train dogs to follow the lost, swim after drowning victims, and track through snowstorms as well as to guard people. He justified his lack of book learning by believing he made a difference in other ways—not that he could explain that anymore than the lady could explain her peculiarity. Unlike the lady, his occupation allowed him to keep his wits about him, most of the time.

Fragile fairy ladies belonged sheltered by their fairy hills. Big louts like him, with more brothers and male cousins than he could count, got shoved roughly into the real world at an early age. He'd learned to survive. He doubted Lady Aurelia could endure his rough world for long. Whatever caused her sometimes witless behavior had cut her off even from the privileged confines of her own society.

He was relieved he hadn't needed to argue the point.

Titus Brown had given him a rough map of his various crofts. Dusk was closing in by the time Will rode toward the last one far back into the hillside. Picking up a familiar scent, Ajax stepped up her pace, even though the mastiff ought to be weary by now. Will prepared himself. He kept his inventive brother Erran's multi-barreled pistol in his coat pocket and a musket on his saddle. Usually his size was sufficient to deter any threat, but he had a suspicion Rose feared men for good reason.

Ajax uttered a mournful howl that sent cold shivers down Will's spine. The dog had found a stronger scent. As he rode over the ridge, Will easily located the one-room stone hut on the far side. There was no cover out here to hide behind and no way he could approach silently. He felt like a moving target for anyone watching from the one window.

The mastiff followed a trail past the cottage and down the cliff in the direction of where they'd found the child. Since he'd ordered her to follow Rose's scent, that was telling in itself. Will whistled her back.

Even in gentleman's garb, he didn't have the ability to look unthreatening. Stoically, he rode up to the hut, waiting for a musket blast or a mad farmer rushing at him with a shepherd's hook. He could manage that last but musket balls were damned painful and often deadly.

He saw no movement in the unglazed window as he approached. That didn't ease the tension in his shoulders as he dismounted. Given the scene in the puppy's head, no movement probably meant no life.

He rapped on the crude timber door and received no response. Ajax pushed worriedly at the gap beneath the wood and whined. With night closing in and the drizzle turning to rain, it was damned cold out here. Will smelled no smoke, although there appeared to be a supply of peat and coal in the bin by the door.

The door latch wasn't fastened. Will lifted the warped planks and swung them wide so what little light remained outside could pour into the hut. No one shot at him or shouted. Ajax pushed past, but her tail wasn't wagging. She whimpered and sniffed at a bundle of clothes near the hearth—a bundle that moved.

Will had pulled dead bodies from ponds and half-alive ones

from snow drifts. Neither involved buckets of gore and seldom involved women. He could smell the stench of blood and evacuation and steeled himself as he approached the huddled form in front of the dead fire.

The blood had dried. The form was female. Heart in throat, Will crouched to find her pulse in search of some sign of life. He had to stop breathing to feel it, but she was not dead. Yet.

And then the shawl wrapped around her arms wiggled and uttered an almost infinitesimal gasp.

Will wasn't a praying man, but he sent pleas to the heavens now as he pushed the shawl back.

A small thatch of matted hair and a wizened baby face appeared.

Ajax bayed mournfully. Will wished he could do the same. He despised helplessness, but what could he do? Crippled with anguish, unable to think, he responded like a dog, only with the sense to go outside, where he released his torment in a howl. He had no mate, no pack to call, so he threw his turmoil at the fairy hill on the other side of the valley. "Lela, please, for the love of God, if you can hear me, *I can't do this*! I need help!"

He was a strong man. He could move mountains. He could not save dying women and babes. Realistically, he knew howling didn't help, but it cleared his head and let him do what he must.

He was not a man who put words to paper, but he'd picked up pencil and paper at the inn earlier in case he needed to communicate with the child. Not trusting his abilities, he returned to the cottage and kept the message short. Rolling it up, he tied the paper to Ajax's collar with thread from one of his buttons.

"Find the lady." Easily calling up Aurelia's lovely form and features in his head, he shut his eyes and showed the image inside the dog's open mind. Dogs didn't think as men did. He couldn't pass on scent with the picture. So he fumbled in his pocket for a handkerchief the duke's daughter had left at the inn and let Ajax sniff it at the same time.

His bad habit of squirreling away scent identifiers sometimes came in handy. The linen the vicar had rubbed his hands on at tea was in his other pocket. Inns were a good place for locating human musk, he'd learned growing up. The scent didn't last forever, but dogs had better noses than he did.

The mastiff had to be tired, but she yipped loyally and trotted off—in the same direction Rose must have taken when she'd run after her pet. Will was glad he couldn't read human minds. He didn't want to know what horror had sent the puppy and child fleeing into the night. The brief scene in the puppy's memory and the blood staining the croft floor was more than enough.

For good measure, he shouted "Watch for Ajax" at the hills, hoping for a little Malcolm magic. The cry let off steam and made him feel as if he was doing something. It didn't give him hope.

He gathered peat and coal and returned inside to heat the chilly hut so the last moments of woman and child would be warm.

AURELIA RAN her fingers over the piano's keys but she lacked Lydia's talent. She simply needed to counterbalance her sisters' whining, the hissing fit of two servants below, and her own tension. With the guests gone, the castle settled into a familiar hum, but she could not relax. Rose wasn't at fault. The child remained silent in her own little world, entertained by old dolls and books from the nursery.

"You are mangling that tune," Lydia complained from her seat by the fire. "If even you're bored with no company, why can't we go to London with Father?"

"Because Father and Rain aren't entertaining, and Aunt Tessie won't go with us. Because the weather is bad this time of year, and we could be stranded at an inn in a rainstorm. Write to our cousins and see if any wish to visit. Make plans for Father's return. Be useful."

An anguished cry played through the back of her mind as she spoke, but she resigned herself to ignoring it. Mr. Madden had not returned, and she could not plunge into the night alone again, not in this rain. It would be madness. She knew people thought she was nicked in the nob at best, demented at worst, but she knew she was rational, most times. It would do no one good if she harmed herself following all the insane voices in her head.

She had given up on the piano and decided to settle in her room with a book when the cry in her head made her almost double up in pain. She could swear the voice wailed *Lela*. Mr. Madden? Would he use her childhood name?

Giving in to folly, she lifted her skirt and ran down the stairs, aiming for the side door and the kennel. She would make certain Mr. Madden had not yet returned.

A footman entered, waving a paper at her before she could reach for a cloak.

"Ajax came back alone, m'lady," he said. "She was carrying this."

Swallowing hard, trying not to shake, she took the paper to the nearest lamp and read the penciled scrawl. *Bruns crotf. Baby. Bring crat.*

Bring crat? She had no way of knowing if this was Mr. Madden's writing. It certainly wasn't the penmanship of an educated gentleman. But Ajax had been with him the last she'd seen.

And there was that cry. . .

She's dying wailed through her head, a very male, very desperate wail.

Baby. He could carry a baby as he had a dog, but where there was a baby, there had to be a mother, didn't there?

Knowing she would sound ridiculous, but accustomed to overriding protests, she gave the waiting footman his orders. "Have a team saddled to a wagon. I need a driver and whichever grooms are willing to go with me. Have someone ride ahead to Tobias Brown and ask where Mr. Madden went."

"His grace. . ." The footman tried to object.

"My father and Rain aren't here," she said with the sternness she had learned to muster in emergencies—a lesson she'd learned the last time no one had listened to her. "Someone is in trouble, and a woman is needed. I'll have Addy with me. Go, and hurry." Rather than listen to more objections, she raced back up to her room. Addy would probably kill her.

But who else could she send if a woman was needed? Certainly not Aunt Tessie and her bad hip. Not her younger sisters. If she wasn't willing to go out, then she really had no right to send anyone else. She either answered the plea or didn't.

She could not ignore it. It simply wasn't in her.

Her father was a physician and usually answered calls for aid, or he sent Rain, who was also educated as a physician. They had grooms and gardeners and footmen to deal with mechanical matters or field disasters. Rain acted as steward and had men under him to go out when he wasn't available, but this was a *baby*. If the wretched men of the household wouldn't marry, someone had to step up and do the work of a duchess.

It had never been Aurelia. Even Lydia had gone out upon occasion, during the day, to help the vicar visit the ill. Aurelia's disability confined her to the safety of thick walls. Or her family confined her by not coming to her in the first place, she realized—for good reason, admittedly.

She doubted her decision to go out on her own every second that she pulled on warm clothes and Addy scolded. Her youngest sister offered to go with her, but Phoebe was far too naive to be exposed to whatever happened this night. Lydia was affianced to a gentleman who would one day be a powerful reformer with the duke's aid. She couldn't be risked.

Aurelia was the worthless one.

"Bridey should have married Rain," she muttered as she and Addy ran out into the drizzle to the waiting cart. "She would know what to do. She would have been riding the hills to look for trouble before it happened."

"Your cousin would eat your brother alive," Addy grumbled. "Or your brother would strangle her. He needs a gentle lady, not a termagant."

"A gentle lady who will ride in the middle of the night when a tenant needs them? Such a creature doesn't exist," Aurelia said in scorn. "That renders Rain as useless. We'll have to place all our hopes on Teddy marrying early to someone worthwhile. I shall be an aging spinster by then. I might as well learn to be helpful before I take up knitting."

Since her youngest brother was twelve and not likely to marry for another decade or more, that was a lot of cries for help not answered.

Aurelia didn't hear the voice in her head anymore, just the despair echoing in her memory. The night creatures were quieter than they had been the last time she'd ventured out. Perhaps they stayed in their holes in the rain. No other anguished cries reached her. Even the tavern was reasonably quiet as they rode through the village. There was music and laughter, of course, and loud male voices, but no anguished cries to make her wince.

The groom who had ridden ahead galloped down to direct them.

"Brown says as Mr. Madden was hunting the crofts. He'll meet us at the ridge, but there's half a dozen of them huts."

Aurelia had ordered the exhausted mastiff to ride in the cart. The kennel keeper had fed and rubbed her warm and given her a blanket and complained the whole time about sending her out again. But Ajax could find Mr. Madden faster than Mr. Brown could. She offered the dog the glove she'd had one of the men fetch from wherever it was he stayed.

Well-trained, the dog sniffed, yipped, and stood up, eager to be on her way.

As soon as the cart reached Mr. Brown, she had the grooms let the dog down. Ajax took off in the direction of the cliffs where they'd found Rose.

"Looks like she's aiming for Crockett's place," Brown said, tipping his hat to Aurelia. "It ain't no place for a lady out there in the hills. You could stay with my wife," he said stiffly. "She'd be pleased to have you."

Aurelia doubted that. She didn't really know Brown's wife except to see her on an occasional visit to church, where she could hear her spiteful whispers.

She wanted to believe the voice in her head was Mr. Madden calling for her. *Calling*, as if he understood she might hear. The possibility that he didn't scorn her but might actually find her useful forced her to stay focused. He hadn't necessarily meant for her to come personally, but the message had said *baby*.

"I have a notion a woman is needed, Mr. Brown," she said coolly. She'd heard the disdain he tried to disguise behind politeness. She knew the villagers perceived her as arrogant. She had no help for that. She could either go to town and listen to the private conversations of every person there, or keep her distance. For the sake of sanity, she chose the latter. "Let us go on."

Mr. Brown and several of the grooms rode ahead since horses were faster than the cart over these rutted lanes. Addy complained bitterly. Aurelia had half a mind to leave her with Brown's wife, except it would take them out of their way.

Why couldn't she hear the baby or the woman who presumably needed her?

It was almost restful out here in the hills with the gentle rain pattering. The men accompanying her were silent. If anyone was awake in the crofts, they weren't talking. She could almost fall asleep to the sway of the cart—except she was too tense worrying if she was making an utter fool of herself. Oh well, then even Mr. Madden would think her crazed instead of just mildly addled.

She could smell the peat fire before she saw the hut. They rode over the ridge to find a small stone building with light gleaming through a narrow window and a lantern hung to guide them down the nearly invisible path.

At their noisy approach, Mr. Madden ducked his head to pass through the doorway. He waited outside the door, fists bunched at his side, as if to restrain a volcano of rage. Despite his casual clothes, she'd recognize his wide shoulders, barrel chest, and aristocratic posture anywhere. Not too many gentlemen were built as he was.

Once the cart halted, he covered the distance in one long stride to lift her down. The sensation of his gloved hands around her waist jolted her with the force of lightning. She could barely hear him through her startling consciousness of his physicality.

"They're still alive. I have no notion if it's safe for them to be out in this mist or if the cart will kill them. Thank you for coming, but it was mad of us both."

Alarmed by this many words rushing from the usually taciturn gentleman, Aurelia daringly squeezed his massive arm and hurried into the hut.

A fire warmed the small space. A crude bed dominated the room. A frail face surrounded by a cloud of dark hair rested against what appeared to be a saddle padded with a blanket. Eyes closed, the woman didn't appear conscious. Addy hissed in dismay. The grooms had stayed outside with the horses, but Mr. Brown and Mr. Madden hovered nervously on the edges of the chamber, out of the lantern light.

Aurelia was not a physician. She had lived with two all her life though. They'd done their best to protect her, but those things they most wished to hide were the ones they transmitted clearest. Biting her lip, she approached the opposite side of the bed from her maid. The patient was dressed in a worn white nightshift, but the fabric seemed of decent quality and looked clean. If a baby had been involved... Deliveries were messy. She noticed a bucket in the corner and for the first time, recognized the odor of strong soap.

She shot Will a look. He merely looked tense, waiting for a

command from her—as a woman who should know these things.

Was he responsible for the normalcy of the scene? If so, he'd gone far beyond the call of duty. She must do the same. Where was the baby?

Old linen covered the mattress, the kind that her housekeeper would have turned to rags long before it reached this stage. Addy lifted the blanket over the woman's still body. An infant wrapped in a rather expensive shawl suckled weakly at a bare breast.

Bruises covered the woman's face and shoulders. Stifling her horror, Aurelia brushed the mane of hair out of the woman's face. A recent gash on her brow had scabbed over. An older, deeper one on her shoulder had re-opened and left blood on her nightshift. But she still breathed.

Judging by the newborn, someone had beaten this woman within an inch of her life—while she carried a child!

Ice formed around Aurelia's heart. Glancing at Addy, she could tell her maid was about to be ill. Balling her fingers against her own fury and nausea, she gestured for Addy to step back. "If anyone finds this woman's husband, beat him into mash before you bring him to my father. It will save him the trouble," she announced to the room at large, needing to release her anguish and anger before she cried in front of all.

Mr. Madden had distanced himself to a far corner where only shadows from the firelight crossed his face. But he emanated such tension that she knew. . . she did not doubt in the least. . . that if he'd been able to find the monster who had done this, he would have murdered him with his bare fists. A man like Mr. Madden did not let down his pride to howl as he must have done earlier. That he'd also set himself to the humbling woman's task of presenting the new mother as decently as possible spoke much of his character, and for the first time in forever, she admired a man not of her family.

"We have no choice," she said unhappily to the waiting men. "We must at least take the babe to where he can be fed. The mother needs warmth and rest, someone to pry broth into her, and her wounds tended and watched for infection. Can we find enough cover to put over her to take her down in the cart? I can wrap the babe in my cloak." Hating to part mother from child, Aurelia lifted the naked babe and looked about for swaddling beyond the expensive shawl.

As if they'd only been waiting for a woman's approval, the men surged into action. Mr. Brown called for the grooms. Will raised the unconscious woman from the old mattress, wrapping her in the discarded shawl and blanket as he did so. The others carried the mattress outside, while a groom gathered up what must have been Will's saddle and horse blanket.

Clucking angrily, Addy tore up a man's ragged shirt to wrap around the infant. "You should not have to see this," the maid scolded. "You should have sent me."

"I didn't even want you to come with me," Aurelia said. "It's not what you're paid to do, and you lack the authority to tell others what to do. I'm the useless one showered in riches who ought to have some purpose."

"Your father, your brother, the damned vicar—any of them could have married so there'd be other women to do this," Will said angrily, still holding the lifeless mother. "Any woman in the village could have helped here, if any had cared."

"Your mother used to be the one to travel back to these places when she heard a woman needed help," Aurelia said, understanding his anger. "Now, everyone must rely on my father and brother, who simply lack the time to do everything, as does the vicar. We all have limits."

The babe was too silent as they swaddled him. Aurelia held him under her fur-lined cloak. It was damp outside, but she was still dry. If it did not rain harder, the babe should be warm.

The men shouted that the cart was ready, and Will effortlessly carried the patient outside, even though she appeared to be far larger than Aurelia.

"Do you think this is Rose's mother?" she asked, following Will out and watching as he lifted the patient up to the cart. Addy settled her in with all the blankets the men could find.

"I fear so," he said grimly. "Should we take them to Lady Pascoe?"

Unaccustomed to thinking of her cousin by her new name, Aurelia took a second to follow his thoughts. He'd said *we*. Did he mean for her to go too? Bridey was only a few hours away. . .

"In the morning," she decided. "Let's take them to the inn tonight, try to get some food into them, and see if they rally at all in the morning."

A little piece of pride lodged in her heart when he nodded acquiescence, as if she had said something worth listening to. As if she weren't an addlepated worthless piece of pretty glass.

"I'll have one of girls at the inn help," he said, crashing her back to reality. "If you don't mind my borrowing the cart and one of your men, you can ride back on his horse."

"Addy doesn't ride," Aurelia said in a tone of dryness to hide her hurt at being thus dismissed, *again*. "She can stay and help, if the inn has room for her."

Of course she couldn't stay at the inn. What had she been thinking?

Cursing, she climbed up in the wagon with the babe in her arms and waited for everyone else to do what must be done, as always.

Five

THE NEXT MORNING, Will wearily sipped from his coffee mug and paced the inn's hall.

He had sent Ajax home with the duke's daughter and her retinue last night. It had been inexcusable of him to call on the duke's household to aid a woman they didn't know, but at the time, it had seemed his only hope. And miraculously, Lady Aurelia had responded—whether to his howl or his message, he couldn't say. He had understood that she wasn't as addled as she seemed, but now, in the clear light of morning, he knew that both of them had been out of line.

He'd refrain from howling from here on.

He wasn't certain how he'd become the one in charge of transporting the patient to his uncle's medically-trained wife, either, but it was evident there was no one else to take charge. He couldn't expect Lady Aurelia to come down out of her castle to do so.

He bred and trained dogs. He delivered *puppies*. He knew damn all about women and human babies. He waited as the maids prepared the patients for travel, wondering how he'd been roped into this. His rescues normally ended with the happy family taking the victim home and leaving him to travel to his next task.

Lady Aurelia's maid, thank all that was holy, had remained at the inn. While Will paced, Mrs. Addison emerged from the sick room holding the wailing infant. "He's starving, poor thing. He's all but eaten the pap we've given him. You'll need someone to ride with you to keep him fed since his mother can't."

"He'll survive?" Will asked gruffly, hesitant to even look at the squalling bundle. His half-brothers had been producing infants at a prodigious rate lately, but he preferred avoiding the creatures.

"I don't know how Mrs. Crockett did it, but she must have delivered him alone and kept him warm for as long as she was able." Mrs. Addison bounced the crying bundle almost angrily. "Is anyone looking for her husband?"

"I could. It's what I do." Will tossed back the rest of his coffee.

"But he'll be long gone. Unless the duke orders him found, we're better off trying to save the woman. I'll see who I can find to go with me to Alder."

He could practically feel the lady's maid vibrate with some unspoken suggestion. Normally, he went his own way without aid of others, but the duke's daughter had inexplicably come last night and brought this woman with her. He owed them respect and more. He lifted an eyebrow and waited.

"The child, Rose, should go with her. It might help bring Mrs. Crockett around if she knows Rose is safe." Mrs. Addison looked worried.

"The girl is afraid of me," Will reminded her. "She's likely to flee again."

"I hate to suggest this. . ." She frowned and sought words.

Impatiently, Will tapped his mug against the wall. "Just spit it out. I need to look for a woman willing to spend hours in this weather holding a screaming infant. If you know someone who can manage the child, I'll listen."

"Lady Aurelia," the maid said hurriedly.

"Absolutely not," Will responded. He removed his shoulders from the wall and started for the stairs. Maybe Butler would know of an old woman willing to go with him in return for coin.

"Wait! Listen," the maid called after him.

And because he'd just decided the maid was deserving of respect, Will glowered and waited.

"It's painful for my lady to go where there are too many people," Mrs. Addison said hurriedly. "But she's fine on her own. She's good with Rose. The duke has kept my lady wrapped up like a porcelain figurine so that even she believes she's no more than a pretty ornament. But she is so much more. . ."

"There we agree," he said. "She's a duke's damned daughter. She doesn't go visiting in farm carts, caring for bairns not her own. Or even her own, for all that matters."

"The duke has a landau. It will keep Mrs. Crockett and the children covered better than a cart. It's large enough for me and Lady Aurelia to travel inside. It will be more comfortable for the patients."

A landau and four horses—for a woman no one knew. Will narrowed his eyes. "Why?"

The babe cried hungrily. The maid looked uneasy. "My lady will waste away if she never learns to set out on her own. The duke trusts you. She'll be safe in our company. She simply needs to go into the world and discover it's not all frightening."

"She's been to London," he scoffed. "There is nothing more frightening than that place."

"Twice. It was not successful. She refuses to return. The duke has threatened to return with a man of his choosing for her husband, if she will not choose one. That will make my lady miserable." Her expression turned stubborn. "You said yourself Alder is only a few hours away, and Lady Pascoe is her cousin. They'll be happy to visit."

"Last time I was at Alder Abbey, the place was Bedlam. Pascoe has his twins there." And Bridey was setting up a midwife's school and stirring trouble with the locals, along with another of the Malcolm cousins. It had been all female madness and mayhem. But if the lady was also some sort of Malcolm. . .

Warning bells clamored in his head.

"A landau," Mrs. Addison repeated. "Someone to help with the children. What happens at the abbey is not your problem."

True. And Bridey had said the deerhounds had pups ready to train and sell. He could leave the women to their own devices. In the interest of looking after his own business, he stifled the warning of his instincts. "If you can convince the lady," Will agreed grudgingly.

He didn't have to ride in the carriage with the lady, he told himself as messages flew back and forth between the inn and the castle. She would have footmen to help her in and out so he needn't experience any more bolts of unseemly lust like last night, when he'd helped her off the cart and felt as if a choir of angels sang. That had probably just been the result of pure gratitude for the arrival of help.

If he hadn't made a rule about swiving the wenches in his mother's inn, he'd occupy himself more usefully while he waited for a duke's carriage to arrive. But his mother had suffered the village's contempt for bearing his father's bastard, and he wouldn't submit another woman to the same. Besides, he could ill afford to support one. His savings were destined for a better purpose than a child he didn't want. Miranda understood that, he thought.

So Will spent his time badgering Butler by going over the inn's books, suggesting changes, then criticizing the maids on their lazy housekeeping skills. He'd toted buckets and mops and polished every damned piece of furniture in the place in his youth. Maeve had beat cleanliness into his soul, and he'd discovered a penchant for it. It had kept his hands and mind busy last night, when he'd been helpless to do anything for the babe and its mother.

By the time the lady and the landau arrived, he'd bathed and put on fresh clothes from the trunk he kept here. They weren't fancy clothes like his half-brothers wore, but they were sturdy enough for riding in the steady rain and good enough for visiting Pascoe.

He barely glimpsed Lady Aurelia while the grooms carried Mrs. Crockett down and the women settled her inside the carriage. He could hear Rose making her strange cries and suffered the sick realization that the child's deafness could have been caused by a beating. It was a good thing to remove the family before Crockett returned from wherever he'd gone. If the world was lucky, the scoundrel had fallen off a cliff in a drunken rage.

"The stagecoach said the London Road was clear and still solid," he told the carriage driver. "We should make decent time."

"As long as we arrive before nightfall and there's a stable for the team," the driver said prosaically. "The lady don't go out often. It's good to take the cattle out every oncet in a while."

A fortune in carriages and horses and no one ever used them, Will mused, swinging onto his gelding. At least such waste kept carriage makers in business and the grooms employed.

He caught a glimpse of Lady Aurelia inside the landau as he ordered the team into motion. She was a vision in blue velvet and lace, so far removed from his rough countryman's world that he could only admire her like a painting on a wall. While he watched, she placed a hand on the window, and he could swear she mouthed a *thank you.*

What the devil did she have to thank him for? Irritated that the gesture had buoyed him as if she'd given him his heart's desire, he dug in his spurs and rode ahead to scout the road.

AS THE DAILY noises of the village faded in the distance, Aurelia could let down her guard and pay more attention to her companions. Mrs. Crockett was too tall to comfortably occupy the rear-facing seat lying down, but they'd folded her up and covered her with blankets. That she was still fevered and unconscious was not a promising sign. Aurelia suspected childbed fever for which there was no real cure.

Addy held the mewling babe. Rose sat between them, anxiously watching her mother, paying no attention to her new brother. A child that age had little understanding of childbirth, and it was almost impossible to communicate to explain. Rose clung to a doll that Phoebe had given her. Her puppy slept in a basket at their feet.

"Are you certain that Mr. Madden wanted us to come?" Aurelia asked. "He seems to be avoiding us."

"He's scouting the road ahead as a gentleman does," Addy said reassuringly. "You know Lord Rainsford does the same when we go to London."

"Rain rides ahead to avoid our chatter," Aurelia said in scorn. "He's too toplofty to speak to mere females."

"And Mr. Madden isn't?"

Aurelia thought about it, remembering the clean cottage last night. Toplofty gentlemen did not bathe poor women, babes, and scrub floors. "Mr. Madden prefers the company of dogs, perhaps, but I don't believe he's toplofty."

"There you are, then. Hang Tiny out the window and see if that brings him," Addy said with a chuckle.

The woman on the far seat moaned and stirred feverishly. Aurelia dug into another basket for the sweetened water they'd brought to put between her lips in those brief moments she woke. Addy handed her the babe, transferred to the other seat, and held Mrs. Crockett's head to persuade the liquid between her lips.

"Mmmmaaaa?" Rose asked in concern, glancing from her mother to Aurelia.

"Sleeping." Bouncing the babe in one arm, Aurelia hugged the little girl, then imitated rocking the babe to sleep. She tilted her head, closed her eyes, and opened her lips in a mock snore. Straightening, she placed Rose's fingers against her mouth as she'd seen her do the other day. "Sssssllllleeeeping."

Rose offered a tentative smile. "Ssssseepng."

"Good girl." She pressed a kiss to the child's curls and wondered if anyone knew how to teach the deaf to communicate. Rose was so smart, she deserved a chance in life.

Reassured, the child snuggled down in the fur blanket covering the seat and slept. Whatever she'd suffered these past days had undoubtedly not allowed her to rest peacefully.

Aurelia heard Will riding back at a gallop a while later. Anxiously, she watched out the window for a sign of him. When he appeared, he was mud spattered and looked impatient and unhappy. The coach driver slowed. Will cast a glance toward her, apparently worried that she would hear him. She could have told him that if he was upset, she'd hear him had he been miles down the road. Unfortunately.

"Water has risen over the road about two miles out. A coach hit it taking a curve too fast and overturned. There's baggage and people all over the place. We won't drive through for another hour. There's a decent inn at the next crossroads. We might as well stop and rest the team there."

An inn, oh dear. Aurelia grimaced. She'd certainly tolerated busy inns before, but it had been so peaceful rolling along open road with no people about. She'd hoped to have a long, quiet journey to prepare herself for the chaotic evening. She'd not met Bridey's new husband. It would have been nice to be introduced while she was calm and not reacting like a halfwit.

The landau pulled into a small inn that was probably more tavern than resting place. At this hour, there were no other carriages and only a trio of horses in the paddock. Aurelia breathed a sigh of relief. Her acute hearing picked up little more than men grumbling.

Mr. Madden was waiting when the footman opened the carriage door. "I've had a word with the innkeeper. There's a private salon available. Should I carry in Mrs. Crockett? There will be no bed."

"I'll stay out here with her," Addy offered. "The children need a fire and something warm in them."

"You're the governess," Aurelia protested. "You're the one who should be with the children." Then she could avoid the inn and its inhabitants.

Mr. Madden impatiently offered his hand. "I'll carry her inside. We'll see what we can do about a pallet. The footmen deserve relief from this mizzle."

The servants would have had to huddle on the back of the carriage looking after her otherwise. Aurelia grimaced at her lack of understanding, took his hand, and stepped onto the planks over the sea of mud in the coach yard. Even though they both wore gloves, she could feel the heat and strength of him—and nickering horses and talking people faded into the distance. Strange, but restful.

He released her to help Addy and Rose down, and she had to follow her footmen inside.

The innkeeper hovered anxiously at the entrance. His eyes grew wide as Aurelia stepped out. She couldn't pull her bonnet over her face and hold the babe at the same time. He wiped his hands on his apron and nearly fell over his feet to assist her over the planks and into the dreary tavern.

Trying very hard to focus on the babe she carried and not the chaos in her head, Aurelia paid no attention to the men at the bar until one shouted, shattering her concentration.

"Lady Aurelia! We thought you were ill!"

She winced. She could stalk by and cut them cold, but she didn't like being intentionally cruel when she was often inadvertently so. She glanced nervously for Addy, but her maid was following a serving girl down a dark corridor to the promised parlor.

Aurelia hesitated near her footman, as far from the tavern seats as she could arrange. "Lord Clayton, Lord Baldwin, Lord Rush," she acknowledged. "My sisters are ill. I've had the mumps before. Now, if you don't mind. . ." She started after Addy again.

"What are you doing here with him?" Lord Clayton demanded, throwing an angry look at the entrance.

Oh dear. She hadn't heard Mr. Madden enter. The man was a blessed wall of silence—except when he was not. His boots echoed loudly on the wooden floor as he caught up with her.

"Excuse us." She hurried down the corridor. She disliked argument even more than she disliked being cruel. She prayed Mr. Madden wasn't a combative sort of man. Since he carried their patient, he could not get into too much trouble, she hoped.

Even after escaping into the dark parlor and shutting the door, she could hear her suitors grumbling complaints. The babe cried. Rose made anxious sounds. The puppy yipped to be let out. Addy ushered orders to the inn maids for a pallet for their patient. And Aurelia could still hear her suitors' low growls and epithets from the front of the tavern. Their anger, curiosity, and *fear*? carried their voices, but not as clearly as expected. Interesting. Did the castle carry sounds better than a tavern? She rubbed her temple and wished for ear muffs.

A footman took out Tiny. Mr. Madden settled his burden on a pallet the maids carried in. Addy led Rose behind a screen to a chamber pot. The innkeeper arrived with a tray of tea and hot chocolate. How had Mr. Madden ordered all this so quickly? Shouldn't she have been the one to order the servants about?

But she didn't have the experience, and Mr. Madden was a traveling gentleman who did. She offered him a tentative smile. "Thank you for seeing to our comfort."

He removed his wet cap to reveal his unruly tangle of bronze hair and bowed. "I'm the one who caused the discomfort in the first place. It's the least I can do. I'll wait in the tavern until we hear word that the road is open."

"Is that a good idea?" she asked worriedly. "They are saying very unpleasant things out there. I had no idea gentlemen could be so crude."

He quirked a wicked eyebrow. "You *hear* them? Then I should remind them that there is a lady present." He bowed and walked out before she could stop him.

Oh dear, she didn't like the sound of that.

"I think we need to start shouting again," she said when Addy and Rose emerged from behind the screen.

She winced as male voices carried more loudly through the walls.

Six

"WHO THE DEVIL are you?" the drunker of the three lords shouted as Will entered the tavern. That would be the cad who had grabbed the lady after she'd ignored his proposal.

Will signaled the innkeeper to serve the footmen and driver, placing a sovereign on the counter to quell any protest over what he was about to do.

He'd learned early on that his aristocratic half-brothers might demand respect with their titles, names, and family crest, but a bit of gold commanded equal deference.

Will picked up his ale, saluted the wary innkeeper, and took a warming sip.

"I demand an answer, sir," the lout insisted. "You are in the company of a peer of the realm and your obedience is expected."

Will snorted and took another drink. Did that lordlier-than-thou trick really work with other men? Maybe with those whose livelihood depended on the prick. That wouldn't be him.

Setting down his mug, Will straightened and grabbed the front of the drunk's waistcoat. While the man with the book and the other with a lavender pocket handkerchief watched in shock, Will hauled the drunken lout's muddy boots off the floor, and carried him out the front door. The *peer of the realm* squealed like a stuck pig, kicked, and threw futile punches, since Will's arm extended well beyond the lord's puny reach.

He could explain that he was the son of a marquess, but he seldom saw good reason to bother when his name, character, and the company he kept should have the same effect. He flung the sot into the yard muck and placed his big boot on his chest to hold him down. "One does *not* accost the daughter of a duke in a public tavern. Sober up and call on her at her home with the duke's permission."

While his holy lordship screamed and flailed, Will rummaged in the man's coat and found his last coin wrapped in a handkerchief. "Your host deserves to be paid for his ale and trouble."

Out of habit, Will stuffed the linen in his pocket. Flipping the coin in his palm, he returned inside to lift his eyebrow at the other two lords, who didn't appear inclined to help their friend. One of them, the older and more foppish of the pair, merely pulled on his mug and ignored the shouting in the yard.

The other removed a pair of spectacles to peer at Will. "I say, you have the look of an Ives, except for the goldish hair. Are you a relation?"

Will slapped the coin on the counter and returned to his ale. "One of the bastards," he said, just because he felt like it. Anger simmered below his surface, but he had learned to deal with it.

"Ah, that is why the duke trusts you with his daughter. You had only to explain."

"No, I had not. You and yon sot had no right to question the lady." Ah, there was the reason he was simmering. He'd lived with insults to himself often enough not to care, but they had shouted at Lady Aurelia and thought her incapable of choosing her own companions. For some reason, that angered him, even though he considered her half-witted most times.

The bespectacled lord had sense enough not to argue the point. He set down his mug and fumbled for his coin.

"If you take away your friend out there, your drink is covered," Will said, downing his ale. He knew he had the duke's men at his back, but he didn't see any reason for them to dirty their livery.

"That's generous of you," the talkative lord said with a hint of wryness. Obviously, he wasn't as drunk as the other. "Give the lady my respect, if you please, and tell her I will call again soon."

"After Rainsford returns," Will suggested. "The lady will be visiting her cousin until then."

The lordling didn't appreciate that, but he put on his high top hat and cloak and walked out. With a sigh of resignation, the older fellow did the same, cutting Will without a word of greeting. Bastards, after all, could be ignored by toplofty gentlemen.

"Gentlemen like that often do not bother to pay, and there is naught I can do about it." The innkeeper said, watching them ride away.

Will had a lot of opinions on wealthy aristocrats who never paid their bills but expected the honor of their custom to be sufficient recompense. He didn't express them aloud.

His lips curled in amusement as he finally noticed the ladies shouting in the back parlor. Someday, he would like to understand the intriguing Lady Aurelia, who appeared to have more acute hearing than his dogs, but bastards weren't welcome in the parlors of duke's daughters.

A STAGECOACH dropped off passengers a half hour later, signifying the road was open again. Aurelia eagerly escaped the increasingly noisy tavern for the silence of the road. She watched the enigmatic Mr. Madden with fascination as he arranged her entourage without speaking more than a word here and there.

How had he silenced her suitors? She had known the instant they'd departed the building. Some men jangled restively simply by existing. No wonder she could hear nothing in their presence.

She knew that her fascination with an itinerant dog handler was most likely due to his indifference and her boredom. Still, she had to wonder why other gentlemen couldn't be as noiseless as he was.

The rain let up as they drove south, and they arrived at Alder Abbey without further incident. Eager to see her cousin, fearful of the bedlam Mr. Madden had warned about, Aurelia leaned out the window to observe Bridey's new home. She frowned as they traveled past the impressive entrance and down a side lane. Studying the medieval stone walls they passed, she realized this had once been an actual abbey with a cloister and a village of its own outside the walls. She could hear the shouts of children and the low chatter of voices inside beneath the closer sounds of the carriage horses. From the cries of excitement, she thought someone had seen them.

The landau rolled beneath a stone arch and into a paved courtyard apparently added in more modern times. Judging by the mixed sounds, Bridey did not have a large household. Aurelia could hear people and dogs in a growing roar as they approached, but she wasn't overwhelmed. Did the thick abbey walls muffle them a little? Or perhaps their happiness did not cause the pain of anger. Or unfamiliarity reduced her ability? She really must study the phenomenon more—should she ever leave the castle again.

Recognizing her cousin running from one of the low stone buildings, Aurelia breathed a sigh of relief. Bridey had been married to her first husband when Aurelia was still playing with dolls, so they weren't close. But she knew her cousin had been an unhappy countess and widow before meeting Sir Pascoe. Bridey had always been tall and strong, but now she looked radiant. Her cheeks and her rich auburn hair glowed in the last light of sunset.

A footman opened the carriage door to assist them down. Aurelia glanced around but could see no sign of Mr. Madden. Feeling oddly disappointed, she stepped out and embraced Bridey. Caught up in the emotion of the meeting, Aurelia was better able to pay heed to her words.

"I cannot believe your father let you leave his castle," Bridey exclaimed. "I had to see this with my own eyes. Will is not exactly the persuasive type, so this must be a momentous occasion."

"A sad one, I fear," Aurelia said. "We've brought you a patient I don't think even your herbs can heal."

Like the duke, Bridey had medical training. Her expertise was with women and children, though. She really was Mrs. Crockett's only hope.

Her more worldly cousin sent her a look that practically spoke aloud: *And you could not send her with servants?* But thankfully, she was too polite to say it. Aurelia couldn't have explained her decision to herself.

Bridey took charge, directing the footmen to carry the unconscious patient into a newly-renovated infirmary. A tall gentleman strolled out in the company of twins slightly younger than Rose. Bridey's husband was an Ives, Aurelia knew. He vaguely resembled Mr. Madden, bearing the same square jaw, deep-set eyes, and angular cheekbones, but there the resemblance ended.

Dark-haired, lean, and elegantly garbed, Sir Pascoe-Ives held out his hand. "You must be Lady Aurelia. Call me Pascoe, please, it's simpler than the explanations Will hates to make."

Unable to recall the relationship between the men, Aurelia accepted his hand while cradling the crying infant in one arm. "Pleased to meet you, sir. Bridey looks happier than I've ever seen her, and I assume you must be the reason."

He looked pleased as he watched his wife return to the carriage to take the babe.

"Oh, the poor thing," Bridey cried, unbundling the infant. "He's starving, but he looks flushed and healthy. You've done a wonderful job keeping him warm. Now let's see if we can find him some milk. Pascoe, why don't you take Aurelia into the house?" She glanced down at Rose, clinging to Addy's skirt. "Would the little girl like to go in with the twins?"

"She's deaf," Pascoe explained. "Will's already informed the nursemaid and asked if she could bring her puppy inside. As if he had to ask," he said with a laugh, gesturing at the deerhounds loping out to join them.

"Then go inside, Lela. I'll join you in a little while, after I examine our patient." Bridcy waved them off.

"Mr. Madden is an exceedingly elusive gentleman," Aurelia said as she took Sir Pascoe's arm and lifted her skirt to cross the rain-swept cobblestones while Addy followed with the children and the puppy in its basket. "And yet, he performs miracles without being noticed."

"Will, elusive?" Pascoe snorted in a manner resembling Mr. Madden's. "With his size, he has to work hard at being unobtrusive. Since your brothers are so far apart in age, you may not have noticed how males learn to communicate. But we were all brought up in a nursery that was little better than a puppy kennel."

Aurelia considered her father's kennels. "You fought for every crumb thrown your way?"

"And wrestled for the upper hand when there was naught else to do," he said with a tone of amusement. "Will was younger than most of us, but he could still lay Ashford flat on his back if he was angry enough. Laying the Earl of Ives on his back was frowned upon by the staff, even if the rest of us thought it was great entertainment. As the eldest, Ashford is a bit of a bully."

The Marquess of Ashford was a power behind political reform, a wealthy man with his fingers in more pots than her father. She'd not met him, but she'd heard he was large. A young lord with wealth, power, name, and older than his brothers would not appreciate being overpowered by a boy with nothing. Aurelia recognized it was the nature of the beast.

"So Mr. Madden learned to disappear from the pack," she concluded.

Pascoe shrugged as they entered the rear door into a towering hall.

The noise of the household washed over her, but she was too fascinated by Sir Pascoe's tale to let it affect her.

"Will isn't much on book learning, so he couldn't hide in the library. He chose to hide with the animals. And unlike the rest of us, he had a mother part of the time, so he could vanish as often as he liked, and we never knew where he was."

A mother who ran a village inn and had no doubt taught him to be silent and courteous, as servants must be. Aurelia began to understand.

"If he grew peeved with us," Pascoe continued, "he'd take a horse and ride out on his own, from Surrey to Yorkshire. The first time he did it was at the tender age of nine, if I remember correctly. He's been traveling ever since."

Pascoe introduced her to the housekeeper to take her to her room, so Aurelia didn't have time to question more. She was enthralled—and appalled—at the idea of a man who picked up and went where the wind blew him.

Traveling and meeting other people was more enlightening than she had expected. The distraction of learning new surroundings apparently allowed her to dismiss extraneous noise with greater ease. Of course, it helped that she was interested in these particular environs—and also the silent gentleman who *didn't* fling himself at her feet. That was quite perverse of her.

Dinner in the abbey's towering medieval dining hall that evening was equally educational. The children sat at a small table with their nursemaid instead of in the nursery. From the larger, adult table, Aurelia could hear them clearly, but the distance was such that she assumed the others only heard their childish murmurs.

But more interesting yet, she was seated across from Mr. Madden—a man who would never have been allowed to sit down at her father's table. That it was expected he sit with his family seemed normal, but she suspected he did not usually consent to dine with them. Vanishing was more his style.

He wore a loose country tweed, a decent embroidered waistcoat, and plain white cravat. His perpetual bristle had been shaved, and someone had trimmed his hair so it no longer brushed his neckcloth. His manners were more impeccable than the gruff country squire that he appeared.

She could also practice her dinner table manners and speak when spoken to for a change. The children seemed to be communicating in silence and did not overload her senses. The Pascoes apparently didn't employ many servants, and she could scarcely hear them from the bowels of the distant kitchen. She was accustomed to the usual drips and clangs of a household. To her relief, she could actually follow the present conversation.

"I fear Mrs. Crockett's infection is from her wounds, and her general weak health will make healing difficult," Bridey was saying. "I'll have to send for Emilia."

Mr. Pascoe and Will were discussing dogs, so Aurelia could focus on her cousin. "Emilia?"

"Lady Dare, one of Lady McDowell's brood. She is a botanist who has just published a pharmacopeia. But she also has a gift for healing, if we can keep her from overdoing herself. She's with child, so it's a delicate situation."

Aurelia recalled the McDowells from her last trip to London— more of her distant Malcolm relations. "Healing would be such a useful gift," she said wistfully.

"Because of her gift, Emilia couldn't hug her own family," Bridey corrected. "She could feel all their pains as her own. And if someone is truly ill, she is compelled to heal them, to the detriment of her own health. She's still skittish about touching, but her husband's weak lungs are teaching her how to manage the discomfort. We all need experience to work with our gifts."

"Experience?" Aurelia said cynically. "I have had ears all my life but no amount of experience in listening will teach me to be deaf."

Bridey frowned, and Aurelia suddenly realized the men had quit talking. She winced and studied the food she was supposed to be eating.

"It hurts you to listen?" Bridey asked tentatively.

"It's not a subject for the dinner table." She sipped her soup but didn't taste it.

"Bridey cannot open her inner eye without inviting evil spirits," Pascoe said cheerfully, as if his wife's gift was a jest. "I can smell fear right now and not have a clue from whom, although my experience with people tells me it's from both you and Will."

"Not fear," Will said, also tasting his soup. "Your nose stinks."

Aurelia tittered and hid it behind her napkin. Will lifted that lovely eyebrow at her. It made a perfect point, like a triangle, when he did that, causing her pulse to race.

"My undiplomatic husband is saying that it's not just experience with your gift, but experience with *using* it, that makes a difference. I have learned to test for spirits before looking at auras. Will and Pascoe are Ives, so they barely even recognize their gifts as such. They simply employ them in their daily life, and in their male arrogance, just assume they're better than anyone else."

"Mr. Madden has a gift?" Aurelia glanced across the table to see him addressing his food as if he were starved.

"The dogs," Pascoe pointed out helpfully. "He talks to dogs."

"Dogs don't talk," Will said, unhelpfully.

"Thank goodness. I don't need any more voices in my head." Not knowing how to take this extremely odd conversation, Aurelia set down her spoon and looked around for a footman to take away her bowl. There were none. She breathed a little easier that no servants could overhear them.

"You heard me call last night?" Mr. Madden asked warily.

"I couldn't say precisely that it was you, but I thought I heard my name, and I. . ." She sighed, unable to explain what she had never tried to explain before. "Is there another word for *emotion*? That is not quite what I mean, but it's all I have. Voices raised in. . . emotion. . . carry far."

His ears reddened, and he tore a piece of bread as if he studied a subject of vast importance.

"Imperturbable Will, shouting with. . . *emotion*?" Pascoe asked in amusement.

"If I were closer, I'd kick you under the table." Bridey rang a bell, and a footman appeared to clear the soup bowls, while a maid hurried to serve the next course. Then both servants melted silently into the shadows of an anteroom.

"One would have to be made of stone not to react to finding a dying woman and baby," Aurelia said in defense of Mr. Madden. "I cannot hear him at all most times, unlike other people."

"Apparently because he lacks emotion," Pascoe said in amusement.

"Please excuse my husband," Bridey said in exasperation. "Now that he needn't be diplomatic, he's releasing a lifetime of rudeness. Lela, explain, please. We've never had time to talk much, so let us use this moment judiciously."

"We have not had time to talk because I cannot sit in a room full of people and think at all. It's like being swept away on waves of noise. The more emotional conversations in the background often overwhelm, while the people who are talking directly to me go unheard. And if there is also music and dancing and laughter and horses in the street. . ." Fearing she'd gone too far into her weirdness, she shoved a piece of bread into her mouth to shut herself up.

"You can hear people in the house even when you're in the garden?" Mr. Madden asked with actual interest.

She blushed. "Let this serve as warning—I can hear a great deal more than people would like me to hear. Mostly, though, I let all the babble wash over me and just don't listen."

He snorted and she thought she saw a look of appreciation in his eyes. He had seen her in the garden with Lord Clayton. He had to have known that Clayton was proposing. She hadn't been listening, because she'd heard it all before. And she hadn't been interested in hearing it from Clayton, who didn't ring true even when he said *hello*. So she'd simply let the noise wash over her.

Pascoe and Bridey waited for explanation. Aurelia refused to say more. Mr. Madden looked up with surprise when he saw that they waited on him.

He pointed his roll at her. "Every man in existence falls on their knees when Lady Aurelia walks into a room. They spout poetry and songs and beg her to marry them. One can't walk through the garden without stumbling over the louts."

"Now I see why he doesn't talk. He's very bad at it." Pascoe turned back to Aurelia. "What is he trying to tell us?"

"That I don't hear them," she said, blushing even more. "I'm listening to the birds and my sister's piano and my father shouting at Rain and an amorous couple in the shrubbery, and I just don't hear their poetry and proposals."

Bridey snickered. Pascoe grinned. Mr. Madden nodded as if he'd known it all the time.

"The half-wit look," he said, before digging into his beef.

Seven

DELIBERATELY distracting himself from the memory of last night's dinner with the gossamer-beauty of Lady Fairy and her enchanting spells, Will hummed a tune stuck in his head and studied Bridey's deerhound pups. He chose the one with the least amount of white in his coat, not because of its color, but its mind. Deerhounds were difficult to train, but the full gray responded to his humming. It had a more focused mind than the others, one he could work with. A normal deerhound would leap happily all over strangers, then race after an animal they thought they could bring down. A *trained* deerhound... Will hoped for the best. If nothing else, he could breed the dog later for the traits he needed.

He had been relieved last night that his annoying family had focused on Lady Aurelia and hadn't turned the conversation to his own peculiarities. Bridey had been right. He'd never thought of his *gift* as peculiar until he'd heard the Malcolm ladies discussing their own abilities. Until then, he'd thought he'd been paying attention where others didn't and prided himself on his one accomplishment.

It made him uneasy to know he was even more odd than he'd thought.

It made him even more uncomfortable to understand that the perfect lady had her own problems. She'd always been so distant that he'd just assumed she was arrogant or half-witted. Now that he grasped some of her difficulty, he was in danger of becoming as enthralled as her other idiot suitors. She'd made *him* witless. Malcolm women were well beyond the reach of a landless bastard, and the duke's daughter was on the furthest pinnacle. He needed to move on soon, before he made an ass of himself.

He lifted the pup, let him eat from his hand and learn his smell. The wee ones had so much potential, it was exciting to watch. He really needed to build that kennel soon. It was a nuisance to keep traveling back to Iveston when he had a new pup. The Cotswolds were nicely central.

Feeling someone watching, he looked up to discover Rose

lingering in the courtyard. How had she fled the nursery?

Hearing the laughter of Pascoe's twin escape artists, he rolled his eyes. Of course she'd bolted. The twins had taught her how. The little lass wasn't stupid, and she was older than the privileged brats.

He'd had to remove her dog from the nursery so the children weren't too rough while he healed. So he carried his puppy over for her to pet. She smiled in delight and rubbed its head with one finger, which the puppy attempted to nip.

They were in the courtyard where the women's voices carried through unglazed windows from the infirmary. Pascoe intended to have the windows glazed before snow flew, but Will supposed these things took time. Feeling incompetent to take care of children, he started across the stones with the child at his heels.

Bridey's warning carried clearly through the window. "Be prepared to take Emilia's arms as soon as she starts swaying. That means she's going too deep."

"Touching her helps?" Lady Aurelia asked.

He probably shouldn't be listening, but the lady had admitted to listening to private conversations no one could know she was hearing. This one didn't seem precisely private.

"If spirits take me over," Bridey explained, "I need Pascoe or my brother to bring me down by holding my hands. I'm hoping we can do the same for Emilia."

"Hush," a third feminine voice said. "Let me concentrate."

Will considered looking in the high window but thought that went a shade too far. He stopped outside the infirmary door and leaned against the wall to let the child play with the pup. From the sounds of it, her mother was still among the living. He prayed Dare's wife could work miracles. Mute Rose wouldn't fare well in an orphanage.

The silence on the other side of the wall was disturbing. He knew what to do with women in bed, but outside of it, they remained mysterious creatures whose minds he couldn't read. Well, some of them were simple enough to read, but ones like Lady Aurelia. . . required far more attention than he possessed.

"She's stirring," Bridey said in muffled excitement. "It's time to bring Emilia back."

Rustling, a low moan, and then hurried whispers. It ought to be safe to enter now. He knocked.

Lady Aurelia answered, looking flushed and excited and so appealing Will had to resist hugging her. He would crush her if he did. He'd best stop to visit Miranda before returning to the castle.

The lady saw Rose at once and lifted the girl. "Mrs. Crockett is waking up! Emilia did it!"

"She also wore herself out. We need to pour some hot broth into her," Bridey called.

"I'll fetch it," Will offered, "if you'll look after the child. She's wandering loose. The twins probably are too."

Bridey glanced his way, noted Aurelia holding Rose, and nodded. "The devil children will be with Pascoe. Rose might be useful here."

Emilia, Lady Dare, rested on a stool against the wall. Tall and slender, dark-haired where most Malcolms were light, she laughed at Bridey's description of the twins. "I could eat a side of beef, right now, if you'll tell the kitchen that, please."

Comfortable with a serving role, Will acknowledged her request. "One side of beef coming up. Tea for everyone else?"

"Hot chocolate for Rose and broth for Mrs. Crockett, please," Lady Aurelia requested, looking so winsome Will almost didn't hear what she said.

He was a master of detachment, as Pascoe had alleged. What on earth was wrong with him today? Will loped off, found a servant, and passed on the requests. He needed to take the deerhounds out for a run, not play handmaid to a duke's daughter.

He needed to return to the castle and finish training Ajax while the lady wasn't there, he concluded a while later when he noticed a contingent of city people riding for the abbey—and the first thing he did was worry about their effect on the fairy princess. He couldn't afford to lose his direction when he was this close to buying land to house his kennel. Perhaps he ought to write Miranda... Well, writing wasn't his strength. He'd ride to see her first.

Time to tell Pascoe that he was leaving.

CROSSING THE courtyard, Aurelia winced at the shouting carrying from the main residence. It had been so beautifully peaceful here, she'd been hoping she could stay and learn to be useful. She couldn't imagine how since she had no medical training, no bookkeeping skills, and a gift that was worse than useless, but she was pondering possibilities as hard and fast as she could.

The shouting prevented any thought at all.

YOU ARE NOT A MEDICAL HOSPITAL. YOU CANNOT. . .

*We'll see you in **court** if you. . .*

Shh, we'll be quiet like little mice. . .

Arf, arf, arf. . .

Shh, Rascal, go away. . .

Where's my daughter?

How did normal people deal with people talking all at once? Did she run to the infirmary to see what Mrs. Crockett needed? Look for Rose? Find out what the twins were up to? Or see if she could help Bridey with her shouting visitors?

Or just hide in the library, because realistically, she could do nothing except feel her head spin.

Since she had just left the schoolroom where she'd been helping Bridey's secretary prepare lesson booklets for the would-be midwives arriving the next week, Aurelia stopped at the infirmary first.

The young wet nurse Bridey had left with her patient looked up with relief at her arrival. "I don't know what to do with her, m'lady."

Mrs. Crockett struggled to sit, anxiously picking at her blanket, and watching the door. Emilia's gift had really and truly facilitated healing. Aurelia thrilled with the knowledge that for once in her life, she had been able to help someone, in however small a way.

She assisted the patient to sit up against the pillows. "Rose is fine. I'll fetch her. Do you have a name for your baby boy?" She gestured for the wet nurse to bring the babe over.

The patient touched the swaddled infant uncertainly. "He lives?"

"You are a heroine," Aurelia assured her. "You delivered a healthy infant all alone and kept him warm until help came."

Wonder crossed her face as she admired tiny wriggling fingers. Then immense sadness took its place, and she said urgently, "You must find him a home."

Aurelia exchanged an appalled look with the wet nurse. What did one say to that?

With the argument in the main house escalating, she couldn't think of any good response. In her head, Bridey's replies were growing increasingly angry, blending with irate males and the overall household cacophony. Aurelia resolved not to run and hide, even if she didn't know what to do.

Giving up on thinking, she acted on instinct. Taking the well-fed infant, she walked out of the infirmary. She discovered Rose hovering at the back entrance to the residence, one hand holding her doll and the other holding her puppy. The little girl smiled up at Aurelia's arrival and happily followed her. She must feel as lost here as Aurelia did. She would send the child to her mother shortly. Right now, she had to focus on the argument in the library.

It had grown so loud that she wondered if Rose could hear it. From the pucker on the child's brow, she thought maybe the child heard the vibrations, although she most likely didn't understand the words. The child tucked her doll under her arm and clasped Aurelia's hand, tugging her back with fear as they drew closer.

Understanding from the rising argument that Bridey's visitors were from the hospital in Harrogate, Aurelia entered the library carrying an infant and dragging a deaf child with a wriggly puppy. She might not entirely understand the dispute, but she knew when men were harassing women.

She had learned as a toddler how to diffuse angry men. She offered a blinding smile.

The dark-coated gentlemen stood intimidatingly around the bookshelf walls, holding their hats and yelling, but as each one noted her entrance, they fell silent.

Standing behind a library table, refusing to sit so the gentlemen couldn't, Bridey glanced up to see what had silenced them. Aurelia thought her cousin winked, even though she was evidently in warrior goddess role.

"Cousin, these gentlemen were just leaving," Bridey said with a dismissive wave. "They are from the hospital in Harrogate and seem under the misapprehension that I am competing with them."

She turned to the black suit-coated gentlemen. "Sirs, this is my cousin, Lady Aurelia Winchester, the eldest daughter of the duke of Sommersville. She is holding two of our so-called *patients*. Lela, they think our *patients* belong in their facility, that we are unqualified to care for them."

Aurelia continued smiling mindlessly. Now that the argument

had stopped, she could think a little more clearly—and maliciously. Her father and brother were true physicians, ones who cared about their patients. They would have immediately checked on the infant and child first. These men merely looked nervous and angry, without once looking at the children. Fine then.

"You have a charity hospital?" she asked in her sunniest voice. "That is so wonderfully progressive of you! I commend your good work, sirs. The babe has no name and is in need of a wet nurse." She plunked the newly-soggy babe into the arms of a tubby man of middle age.

She turned to a younger gentleman with side whiskers who could barely keep his eyes in his head as he watched her. Merrily, she shoved Rose in his direction. "This is Rose Crockett. She is a deaf mute. She would benefit from a full examination. Her mother is deathly ill at the moment and cannot care for her."

The third gentleman was older and frowning ferociously. Beaming, she curtsied before him, fluttered her eyelashes a little, unsettling even his wary cynicism. "Mrs. Crockett has no husband and no funds. She is recovering from childbirth and serious injuries from being very badly beaten. If you deem it safe for her to be transported to your facility, we'll provide a carriage. Bridey is really not set up to be a hospital and only took my guests in as a service to me."

"Your father supports this. . . this consorting with the lower sorts?" the older gentleman demanded with incredulity.

The lower sorts. If he wasn't twice her size, she'd smack the hair off his face.

"My father is in London, but he supports my cousin's good works," Aurelia replied, hiding her ire. "As I am sure she has told you. He will be pleased to hear you have opened a charity hospital. He will most likely wish to visit when he returns."

"We are *not* operating a charity," the older man said curtly. He tore his gaze from Aurelia to glare at Bridey. "Had you simply told us the circumstances, we would not have bothered you, Lady Pascoe. You may keep your. . . your. . ." He wrinkled his nose at terrified Rose and the infant, who now smelled of dirty linen. "Your *beggars*. But under no circumstances are you to set yourself up as a physician or a hospital for women or we will take you to court."

"Oh, my, how very rude," Aurelia said in her sweetest voice. "I shall have to tell Papa you said that. He is most fond of Bridey, you know." She removed the smelly, soggy infant from the startled physician while Bridey took Rose's hand.

"Good day to you, sirs," Bridey told them. "My servants will see you out. I must see to my. . . beggars."

Tall and strong, with a glorious head of auburn hair, Bridey looked like a Viking sweeping from the room. Aurelia felt like a child in her wake—but at least the shouting had stopped. The angry grumbles continued as the gentlemen left, but for a change, the argument had not left her head pounding.

Bridey was laughing by the time they reached the courtyard. "You were marvelous! I never thought you had it in you. I'm so sorry I underestimated you. You look like a piece of delicate china but my word. . . You felled them like a lumberjack. I'm not certain they know what hit them."

"I am glad that I have helped, but truly, I did nothing. Men live with overblown philosophies blocking reason. They need to be reminded of reality with simple gestures." Entering the infirmary, Aurelia happily handed the now-crying babe over to the wet nurse.

Emilia had returned to hover over her unconscious patient with concern. "She really should be awake by now. Her fever has fallen."

Having seen the woman awake and surmising her to be faking, Aurelia lifted Rose onto her mother's bed.

Mrs. Crockett immediately opened her eyes and smiled at her daughter, who flung herself into her mother's arms.

"Simple gestures," Bridey said with interest, nodding at their patient. "Like that one? What made you bring the children to the library?"

"I couldn't cope with the shouting. It's been so lovely and relaxing here, and they were hurting my head."

"Who hurt your head?" Mr. Madden demanded from the doorway. "Those would-be nabobs? I thought Pascoe meant to heave them into the cistern."

He was dressed for travel, with his valise in one hand and the deerhound puppy in a canvas carrier over his shoulder.

While Aurelia stared at him in dismay, Bridey laughed. "I told Pascoe he would do no such thing, that I would manage my own business. I'll let you know if I need help."

Mr. Madden didn't look at Bridey but at Aurelia. He frowned, then apparently accepted what was done, since he didn't argue. "I need to finish Ajax's training. Let me know if there is more I can do for Mrs. Crockett."

"You could not wait another day or two until we decide what to do with her?" Aurelia asked, trying to hide her dismay. Returning home alone, without Mr. Madden's presence at the inns. . . She really needed to stand on her own, but the thought was dismaying.

"I want to be certain Mr. Crockett hasn't returned, in case she must go back there." Mr. Madden said.

"I cannot go back," their patient said adamantly, startling them all. "I am a danger to everyone."

"Do you have a place to go?" Mr. Madden's tone displayed anger more than comfort.

Aurelia glared at him, but Mrs. Crockett spoke before she could.

"Nowhere, or I would not have let him find me a place," she said wearily, but also with ire. "Even if I go to the workhouse, he will find me because of Rose. But if you hide the babe, he'll leave us alone. He has what he wants."

Tears streaked down her cheeks. Rose patted them, looking worried.

"Explain." Will entered the low-ceilinged infirmary, filling it with his masculine presence.

The woman shook her head. "I will not return your favor with evil. Please, can you find a place for the babe? He will be better off anywhere else than with his family."

Emilia lifted the now-dry babe from the wet nurse and hugged him, looking appalled. "I'm sure we can find an unfortunate couple who cannot have children who would love him, but. . . to give up a *child* after you did so much to save him. . . You must think on it while you recover."

The patient's dark hair whipped back and forth as she vehemently shook her head. "No, take him away now, please, before I become too attached. It is the only way he has a chance to live. And if anyone should inquire, say I died and the child with me."

Aurelia jumped when Mr. Madden placed his big hand at her back and shoved her in the direction of the door. "Leave. All of you leave. I would have a word with Mrs. Crockett."

Mr. Madden's hand on her back so startled her that she forgot to protest. And when she caught the look Bridey sent her, Aurelia realized—*Oh, yes,* if she concentrated hard enough, she could hear everything they said. She didn't need to be in the same room.

Eight

WHEN THE stubborn termagants packed up and left without argument, taking the wet nurse and babe with them, Will knew they'd understood his command. Were he a religious man, he'd worry that he'd just fallen under the spell of a coven of witches, but he was a pragmatist. And so were the Malcolm cousins, when it came right down to it. They needed knowledge to help their patient, and they would take it any way they could.

The invalid looked wary and buried her face in Rose's cloud of dark hair.

"I gather that your name is not actually Crockett, and the man who rented the cottage was not your husband," Will said, pulling up a stool so he didn't tower as intimidatingly.

When the woman said nothing, he continued. "I appreciate that you are protecting the ladies by concealing your identity. They are strong, but they are part of my family, and we dislike seeing them in danger."

He preferred that other men hold this part of the conversation. He probably ought to summon Pascoe, who was far better at explaining and pacifying. But Will had the uncomfortable notion that this badly mistreated woman would not respond well to Pascoe's particular brand of elegant diplomacy. She needed blunt honesty.

He thought the woman looked a little relieved. It was a pity he couldn't read her mind as he read a dog's because she still didn't speak. He hunted for words. "Is there any chance that the man who beat you might beat other women?"

That brought a reaction. She pushed up against the pillow and hugged Rose tighter. "I don't know," she whispered. "He hates me. He has no reason to hate other women." She looked a bit frightened, as if she'd realized she hadn't thought that through.

"People who hate are generous with their vitriol," Will warned. "I have fished a woman out of a pond who did no more than disagree with her husband over dinner. I have tracked a man who beat his children for speaking when they'd been told not to. One of the children died."

She looked horrified, then bewildered. "No, I am the one. . . Crockett. . . wants gone. He won't harm a lady without reason."

Will heard her hesitation and began to doubt anything she said. She was hiding more than the man's name. "Real men do not beat women, *ever*, lady or not. Anyone who would do what this brute did to you cannot be trusted with so much as a small animal."

He cast a meaningful glance at the puppy who still limped, most likely from having been kicked by a brute. "I don't want this Crockett around any woman I know."

Troubled, the woman glanced at the puppy in Rose's arm. "The man who wants me gone is my brother-in-law," she said with the hesitance of one sorting through words to find safe ones. "He will have no interest in us once he thinks my son is dead. If you could hide us, then perhaps. . ." She let the promise trail off into uncertainty.

Will didn't need an imagination to grasp the problem. The babe was heir to someone or something, and the villain wanted him out of the way. "I assume Crockett is not your real name."

She bit her bottom lip.

Will wanted to shake her. Instead, he said calmly, "Tell me who beat you. It will take me longer if I must track him, but I *will* find him. My family covers the breadth of the kingdom. There is nothing we can't uncover. We'll not let an abuser of women go free."

She was back to looking alarmed, damn it. He'd have to call in Pascoe.

Rose wiggled out of her mother's hold, leapt down from the bed, and handed her puppy to Will. Then the child clung to Will's leg. He was amazed that she had overcome her fear of him and had no idea what she expected him to do now. He scratched the puppy's head, but a dog couldn't give him names or even a clear picture of the man who had kicked him. Maybe he could have the ladies question Rose in writing, but how much could a child know?

"She trusts you," the patient said in wonder. "She has not trusted any man since. . ." Again, she bit off what she meant to say.

Another piece of the puzzle confirmed. "She didn't trust me at first. Children learn from example. You will teach her to grow up in fear."

She bit her lip but shook her head. "If you will just let us go, we will not use my husband's name in the workhouse. Under any circumstance, Rose will have a hard time. She must learn to fight back. You cannot change that. Once we are well away, I will send you Crockett's real name."

The lady was a damned good negotiator. She was telling him that the sooner he found her a safe place, the faster he could have the name. He didn't like it, but he stood up.

"I have no idea how long that will take," he said. "He could be out there courting some young innocent now, while beating any other woman who crosses him. That will be on your head."

She continued to look defiant. He hoped that meant the scoundrel wasn't after women, just the inheritance. But he wouldn't be happy until he knew.

He handed Rose the puppy and picked up the child. "I'll take this one back to the nursery. If you could return openly to your family, would they help her?"

She didn't answer, and he left her to think on it.

The women were waiting for him as soon as he entered the house. As he suspected, they didn't even bother questioning him—because Lady Aurelia had conveyed every word. She looked at him as if he'd set the moon and stars in the heavens—making him itch under the collar.

That was the problem with women—they wanted heroes. He was just a man who did what he had to do, then went his own way.

And now that he knew Lady Aurelia and her cousin could be in danger, he would be sucked deeper into Malcolm coils than was good for his sanity.

He wished he'd escaped the abbey when he had the chance.

"SURELY NO *gentleman* would have hidden a woman with child and beat her, even if she was just his mistress," Aurelia said in horror as they gathered in the parlor after settling Rose in the nursery. "It has to be some brute from the village. Why else would he have hidden her in that pathetic hut?"

Bridey and Emilia had dragged Pascoe into their discussion. They'd settled in the salon as far from the nursery and kitchen as it was possible to go inside the house. That lessened the household noises to a low roar. The conversation was too important to be distracted by childish shouts, rattling pots, and howling dogs.

Mr. Madden stalked up and down the length of the room, obviously irritated and restless, providing a lovely visual distraction. He was still wearing his traveling clothes, and his leather breeches and high boots held her fascination.

"Any man might settle an unwanted wife or mistress in the hut because he has no money, and he wanted her where she couldn't ask for help," Sir Pascoe corrected. "Don't be a snob and assume he's of a common class simply because he's an animal. He could very well have been at your house party."

Appalled, Aurelia could only stare. She'd lived a truly sheltered life if this was true. She couldn't imagine a single gentleman of her acquaintance who would lift a hand to a woman or child. What more didn't she know about the world most people occupied?

"If we assume the infant stands to inherit something a grown man wants, it doesn't necessarily follow that it's a title or fortune," Bridey argued. "Men would beat up women over a pig."

Mr. Madden snorted, apparently in agreement. "How long before she is well enough to be moved?"

He had a way of commanding the room simply with his presence. Aurelia tried to picture him in a gentleman's tail coat and breeches and couldn't. He belonged in the larger spaces of the outdoors. Even his gestures and voice were too large for the pretty salon.

"She cannot be moved until her wounds are healing," Bridey replied, "and she is able to care for herself. Where would we move her?"

"As long as she is here, she's a danger to all of you. It would only take a few inquiries to know we were the ones to remove her from the hut. We need to stage her death and remove her under cover of darkness," Mr. Madden insisted. "And I need to take Lady Aurelia home immediately."

Bridey, Emilia, and Sir Pascoe instantly fell into a discussion of possible safe places and logistics. Aurelia twisted her fingers and tried to tell herself that she really did need to go home and look after her sisters. They might have let a dangerous man into the house once already. He could return. And she had no purpose here.

But she had helped this afternoon, a little bit. She had let Mr. Madden talk to the invalid and relayed his information to the others. He could have done so himself, but taciturn fellow that he was, he might only have told Sir Pascoe. Leaving the planning to men would have been a bad idea.

The argument escalated inside her head. More outside noises intruded. Horses whinnied. The infant cried. The cook shrieked over a grease fire. The world was telling her to go home, where she belonged. But she had *helped*. She knew she had. She didn't want to be a useless ornament any longer.

With a deep inhalation of determination, she fought back the distant din. "Are there any schools that work with deaf children?" she asked, interrupting the heated discussion.

They turned to stare at her. The blessed silence returned the distant noise level to bearable.

"Not that I'm aware of," Emilia said. "None of the wealthy families of my acquaintance have deaf children. My family scours workhouses for able women and children to train for service, so I have some idea of the working poor. There are not so many deaf among them to start a school, or enough knowledge to help them even if they could."

"But if Rose wasn't with Mrs. Crockett, she'd be less noticeable. She said as much herself," Mr. Madden pointed out, catching the direction of Aurelia's thoughts. "If she believed Rose was safe and happy in a school, she might be more cooperative."

"We'd be taking both her children from her," Bridey argued.

As a woman who'd had difficulty bearing children, her cousin understood the sadness of losing them. Aurelia clenched her fingers into fists and tried to imagine how the patient would feel, but it was difficult. "We would return the children as soon as the abuser was caught. The babe won't really know the difference."

"And the babe might inherit a pig," Sir Pascoe added with a laugh.

Mr. Madden cuffed his uncle on the shoulder as he stalked past his chair. "Or the patient could be gently bred. Don't be such a prig, Pascoe. Appearances aren't everything."

Ignoring this byplay, Aurelia turned to Emilia. "Could your family take Mrs. Crockett if we stage a pretend funeral? If she disappeared into training for service, she wouldn't be easily found without the children."

"And we would know where she is so she couldn't wiggle out of telling us the name of the bastard who hit her," Pascoe said. "She wouldn't want to lose her safe position."

"Or Rose," Bridey added. "We would essentially be holding her children hostage until the culprit is caught."

Mr. Madden made an ungentlemanly snort and helped himself to Pascoe's brandy. "You're trusting that she actually wants them back and won't run."

Aurelia headed for the door. On the way out, she cuffed the dog trainer's muscular arm the way she had seen him do to his uncle. Startled, he nearly dropped the decanter.

"Rose has just left the nursery and is undoubtedly looking for her mother now. She was not raised by a woman who doesn't care for her." The room erupted in laughter as she departed. She almost felt smug that she'd been able to shut the big man up.

She felt even prouder still that, despite the noisy argument, she'd caught the confusion from the nursery when Rose had disappeared. The nursemaids would have found her eventually, and Rose was in no danger in the abbey, but Aurelia so seldom sorted out the noises in her head, it seemed a worthy accomplishment.

The patient looked up worriedly when Aurelia arrived. The ever-present puppy Tiny was under the bed. Rose was sitting on top, showing her mother a piece of paper covered in alphabet letters. Bridey's very pregnant secretary, Miss Thomas, glanced up from her bookkeeping. The wet nurse and babe were nowhere in sight.

"Miss Thomas, why don't you take a break from nursing duties for a while? I'll look after Mrs. Crockett and Rose." Aurelia settled into a comfortable chair. Bridey had been feathering her nest lately. The cold infirmary would soon look like a parlor.

Appearing intimidated by Aurelia's presence, the very young Miss Thomas bobbed a curtsy. "Thank you, m'lady. I'll be back shortly, if you please."

After the secretary left, Aurelia took Rose on her lap. "I do not even know your name, madam," she said formally. Then louder, she shouted in Rose's ear, "Can you write your mother's name?"

As Rose scampered down to take Miss Thomas's chair and pick up a pencil, the patient looked both amused and anxious. "The gentleman, he told you?"

"The gentleman wants to pack me up and haul me home

because of you. I don't want to leave. You must realize, Mr. Madden saved your life and that of your children. As he has told you, we have powerful families. We will see you safe. But if you betray Mr. Madden in any way, you will regret it for the rest of your days."

The invalid's sunken eyes widened. "You are scarcely out of the schoolroom and no bigger than a child, and you are *threatening* me?"

Aurelia beamed. "I suppose I am."

Rose returned and handed her a paper with BESS printed neatly on it. Aurelia hugged her and steered her back to her mother.

"Shall I call you Bess or Mrs. Crockett?" she asked. "I prefer to be polite to those I threaten."

"Bess," the invalid said, looking wary. "Why do you believe I will betray your Mr. Madden?"

"Because it is what I would do if terrified and not trusting anyone. We have discussed your choices and although some might offer safety, none will offer you and your children happiness. The only alternative is to risk trusting Mr. Madden and give him the name of the man who hurt you and them." She nodded at Rose. "Once the brute is eliminated, we can find you a place where you may keep your children with you. That is especially important for Rose."

"It is his word against mine," Bess said wearily. "I am no one. I was a tavern maid and B. . . my husband's mistress. When his wife died without giving him an heir, I was carrying Rose. So he married me in hopes of finally having a son." She choked. "He died before he even knew I was carrying a second child."

Aurelia pursed her lips, understanding the difficulty. Her father had taken on the task of magistrate these past years when all the other gentlemen in the area had died off or lived elsewhere. She'd deliberately listened to many of his cases, which often involved two parties claiming the other did them wrong, with no evidence on either part. Judgment often came down on the side of the person her father trusted, which wouldn't be a tavern maid and woman of loose morals, unless the person she accused was of even lower moral fiber.

"You lived respectably as husband and wife for at least six years," Aurelia said. "That must count for something."

Bess looked sadder still. "Fairy tales do not exist in real life, my lady. I married him to stay out of the poor house. He married me for a son he didn't receive. Worse yet, Rose was a sickly child, always catching fevers and colds and crying. He said I babied her and refused to waste coin on a physician. When I took her to an apothecary, he said she had infection in her ear which destroyed her hearing, and there was nothing he could do. I blamed my husband. We fought continually. He found another mistress. His family blamed me for driving him to drink. No, you'll find no sympathy for my plight. I brought it on myself."

"I think more than one party was involved," Aurelia said dryly. "And absolutely none of that excuses him or whoever beat you."

"But neither does it solve my dilemma. My children are of decent family. They are not bastards. They deserve a good life, but I cannot offer one. The most I can hope to do is to take Rose with me to the workhouse. I can keep her alive until she is strong enough to go out on her own."

"You sound educated," Aurelia reminded her. "You have more opportunities than that."

A fleeting smile crossed her thin face. "My mother was a vicar's daughter and a teacher who fell for a pretty face and a silver tongue. Does stupidity run in families? If so, Rose's deafness may be her only salvation."

Aurelia was starting to understand how a woman could be so foolish as to fall for a handsome face, but Mr. Madden lacked the silver tongue, she decided in amusement. Or, in her case, perhaps it was the *lack* of silver tongue that was an enticement. Either way, he would be as foolish a choice as Bess's. Her father and brother would no doubt see him transported should they think she favored a poor bastard over the earls and heirs they selected.

"I refuse to believe we are doomed for life because of poor choices we made when young." Not that Aurelia had ever given the subject much thought, but it seemed reasonable to her. Rose had obviously been raised in love. She had to believe that Bess could care for her best. "Everyone ought to have a second chance and be given the education or training needed to take advantage of it."

The patient leaned wearily into the pillow and closed her eyes. Rose curled up beside her and slept. Tiny lay his head on his paws beneath the bed.

"He will kill us all if he finds us," was the only reply Bess made.

Nine

AFTER LADY Aurelia returned to the salon and explained the ugly predicament she'd persuaded out of the patient, Will paced in agitation. How had he involved the duke's damned daughter in this disaster? The duke would hold him responsible if anything untoward happened. He'd never wanted responsibility for more than himself and his dogs! And now he didn't know whether he was more worried about the lady or the duke cutting off his head.

"We cannot take chances," he argued when the lady opened her pretty mouth to protest his decision one more time. "Ashford is ready to leave Wystan and return home with his wife and new babe. No one will think twice if my brother and his family stop here to visit."

Since Pascoe was their uncle, the abbey was an obvious stop on his family's long journey back to Iveston in the south. Pascoe frowned in thought but nodded his agreement.

"The nursemaid can carry out both infants wrapped in a single blanket, and a wet nurse accompanying them makes perfect sense. No one expects a marchioness to nurse her own child," Bridey added reluctantly. "I hate it as much as you do, Lela, but the men are right this time. If this would-be killer is so desperate, we cannot risk keeping Bess and her children here."

Will tried to ignore the pink rising in the lady's cheeks. He'd always considered her to be a delicate piece of porcelain whose sole purpose was to adorn the castle, and it had been simple to admire her from afar. If he were in her company much longer, he'd have to see her as a real woman. For the sake of his kennel and the secure future he planned with Miranda, he *needed* the lady to remain a gilded ornament.

Just being in the same room with her stirred visceral hungers he had difficulty suppressing. Long ago, he had promised his mother he would *not* sink into animal behavior just because he could think like a dog. Licking milk out of a bowl and gnawing a bone had brought on that particular demand, but Will understood better than most the depths to which he could sink. He *needed* to work alone.

Lady Aurelia, unfortunately, remained adamant. "A workhouse cannot possibly be good for an invalid and Rose. I simply cannot countenance them being treated that way." She rubbed her temple. "They must come home with me."

"They will do no such thing." Will didn't think he roared, but the lady winced as if he had. "Your father would have my head. He may do so anyway for involving you in this."

"Will's right," Pascoe said. "From the tale you tell, the patient could easily be the widow of a man of stature. If so, his family apparently wants nothing to do with her or her children, or we'd have heard the hue and cry at their disappearance. With her past history, they'll refuse to believe the infant is any relation. It's best this way."

"Rose needs a chance," the lady pleaded. "She's already paying for the sins of her parents. She will have no means of survival in a workhouse."

"Lela's right, too," Bridey acknowledged. "What if we put Rose and her mother in a cart and send them to my brother in Northbridge? He's never home and has no family to endanger. His housekeeper is elderly and could use extra hands."

"You don't fear Bess will seduce Fin?" Pascoe asked wryly.

"More power to her if she does," Bridey said with a laugh. "My brother lives with his head in the clouds."

Will heard the sadness behind her laughter. Lady Aurelia apparently did too because a line crossed the perfect smoothness of her white brow. The women with their soft hearts didn't want to separate the mistreated family. Will refused to care. Bess had made her choices and now must live with them. Once the babe was safe, Bess would give him the name of the brute and action could be taken. That was the best he could offer.

"That's settled then," he announced. "Ashford should be here in the next day or two. The deerhounds are already trained to patrol. I'll have them take turns walking the abbey perimeter until we stage the mock funeral. A few guards around the infirmary, keep the children inside, and you should be safe. I'll stay until Ashford arrives. How soon can the patient be moved?"

He didn't want to stay. He wanted to hit the road, ride over to toss Miranda into bed, then return to work. By spring, he'd have enough coin to buy the kennel. He had training schedules to maintain across half the kingdom over these next months. He didn't need to be twiddling his thumbs here.

Still looking dissatisfied, the duke's daughter drifted from the parlor.

Once he was satisfied she was out of the way, Will stalked out, intending to set the deerhounds loose. He'd like to have Ajax here as well, but it was too late now. He should have realized the duke wanted a trained guard dog for a reason.

"How will you go about looking for Bess's family?" Lady Aurelia asked, waylaying him in the corridor and catching him by surprise.

Her scented soap aroused animal instincts he had to fight. He didn't know the name of perfumes, but hers reminded him of the kitchen on baking day. He'd have the urge to nibble her slender neck if he didn't watch out.

"I hadn't intended to look for them," he said gruffly, tugging his tweed coat over his crotch. He wasn't fit for her company. "If she'll give me the brute's name once we have her settled, it will save time and effort."

She wrinkled up her perfect nose. "I think we need to start making inquiries into Bess's situation. Our families are widespread. Someone will know the gossip if her husband was a man of substance."

"You think she won't give us a name once she's safe?" he asked warily, because that was his fear.

"I don't think the babe is heir to a pig," she said dryly. "This brute went to great lengths to drag Bess and her child to an outpost of nowhere. He beat her severely enough to kill her and the babe. We must assume murder was his intention. One does not go to those lengths for a small inheritance."

"Then we must call him incompetent and stupid as well as a brute and a killer," Will retorted.

He'd never spoken to a lady in such a manner. The animal was raising its ugly head.

Lost in her own thoughts, she didn't seem to notice his growl. "He finds his courage in drink, I should imagine."

Will grimaced. "So we need a list of all the drunks in Yatesdale that night."

"For several nights before," she answered in a small, unhappy voice. "And a list of our guests, which nearly doubles the possibilities. I really hate thinking we invited such an animal. They all seemed perfectly respectable."

He knew he didn't have to remind her that appearances were deceiving. She was talking to *him*, after all. Of course, the innocent lack-wit probably thought he was a gentleman simply because of his father's name. "And what will you do with such a list? Send them polite letters asking if they beat a woman almost to death?"

The abbey did not yet have gas piping. Even in the dim light of a candle, he could see the sadness in her long-lashed eyes.

"My sisters know more of society gossip than I do. I will ask them to compile a list of our guests and ask if any of them are anticipating an inheritance. When I have the list, I will send it to all my relations and ask if any of them know the families and relate the story Bess told me. If you would give the list to Ashford when he arrives, he could expand the search."

Will probably knew more people on Bess's level than his aristocratic half-brother. But Will didn't write letters, and the people who might know Bess often couldn't read them. Still, he followed the lady when she entered the library and lit candles from the one she carried. "I'll send a groom with the message to your sisters. It will be faster than the post."

He should leave her there. He had the dogs to see to. But the fairy lady looked so fragile and alone sitting at that huge table, Will couldn't tear himself away. Or so he told himself.

He hated libraries. To hide his discomfort, he spoke. "You must know the names of your guests. If you could give me the names of a few, I could start now. Who were the three at the inn?"

"Lords Clayton, Baldwin, and Rush," she responded instantly, finding paper and pen and ink in the table drawers. "Lord Clayton is apparently up the River Tick as Rain says. But his father is a wealthy earl. Lord Baldwin is something of a bookworm and not much on fisticuffs. Other than knowing he likes lavender scent and is older than the others, I don't know Baron Rush well."

She looked up with a start, her eyes darkening to azure. "That night, there was a bit of conversation. . . I try to shut out private talk, but when they're very intense, I can't avoid them."

Will waited, his gut unreasonably knotting as she seemed to disappear inside her head.

"I only caught pieces," she said, rubbing her temples. "I cannot recall more than a man's voice asking *And Rose*? Since rose is such a very common thing, I did not think he might be asking of a person. He seemed agitated, which is why the question stood out from among all the other voices. My gift is more annoying than useful."

"Not if it means you heard the brute in your house that night." Horrified, Will tried to think of some other reason for men to have conversations about a rose and could think of none. The abusive scoundrel had been in the *castle*?

"But if he was asking after our Rose, then he was not the one who let her wander the moors." He tried to temper his fury with that rationalization. It didn't work.

Her eyes widened. "I had not even thought. . . A gentleman might have *hired* someone to do his dirty deeds. He could have been talking to a valet or groom or almost anyone. We don't have a chance of finding him this way!"

"If he hired someone, he is as guilty as the perpetrator. Keep writing," Will ordered, then bit his tongue. He had no right to order about the daughter of a duke.

But she returned to scratching her lovely script across the paper as if what he said mattered. He wasn't much given to introspection, but he had to wonder why he was surprised that she listened. Even his arrogant titled brother listened to him. But Ashford knew him. The lady didn't.

"You have family in London, don't you? You could write to them," she suggested.

He panicked. *This* was why he was surprised when strangers, particularly educated ones, listened to him. "When you have a complete list, Ashford can give it to Erran. My barrister brother will pay more attention to Ash than me."

She sighed and continued writing. "I want a magic wand. I want it all to happen yesterday."

"If you had a magic wand, it wouldn't have happened at all. I should let the dogs out." He had to escape the library. "Send someone to me with your letter when it's done."

"I only need to blot it." She hunted in the drawers for what she needed.

He almost said *Already*? It would have taken him an hour or more to compose such a letter. She scribbled it off as if it were the alphabet.

"Take a look and make certain I've asked all the right questions, please." She handed it over after she'd blotted it. "I don't want to alarm my sisters."

"I'm sure it's fine. Just seal and address it so no one else is tempted to open it." He handed the paper back to her as if it were a hot potato.

"Rain always tells me I leave half of everything out." She looked uncertain as she dug out the sealing wax.

"You realize your brother is a perfectionist who can never be satisfied, don't you?" He shouldn't have said that, but he was so relieved that she'd accepted his suggestion without argument that he felt compelled to offer what reassurance he could.

"That's probably my fault," she said sadly. "He blames himself for little Alan's death, but I was the one who was too late."

Why didn't he simply bang his head against a wall? It was sheer torture to hear and see the lady's sorrow and be unable to do anything about it. He could set dogs on thieves, but dogs couldn't solve grief. Will took the letter she handed him, tucked it in his pocket, and thought to make a run for it, but to his own shock, he heard himself asking, "Alan?"

She rose in a rustle of crinoline, her halo of ivory hair shimmering like jewels in the candlelight. "I'm sorry. I don't mean to bore you. Alan is the reason Father keeps us home if he's not about. You were probably at school when it happened. It was quite a sensation at the time."

Will doubted that he'd been at school unless it happened well over a decade ago. He'd probably been in rural nowhere, attending to his dogs and paying no attention to gossip. "You might as well tell me the story now that you've started it."

She took his arm, reminding him that he should have offered it. Her full evening skirt brushed his legs, and he recalled why he had not offered his arm. In her presence, he was a lust-riddled oaf.

"Alan would have been about fifteen now, I think." Her voice was soft and sensuous, even though she spoke with sorrow. "I was only about six and he was an infant when he died."

"You had a brother who died?" Fifteen years ago, he'd been a grubby little boy hiding in kennels. Will itched to move this story on and escape her delicious apple-pie scent and proximity.

"Rain was the heir, Alan was the spare," she said with rueful wryness. "The entire household was positively giddy to have another boy after three girls. I remember it well. I couldn't understand why I wasn't next in line since I was next eldest. I didn't understand the excitement and was just a bit resentful."

Will chuckled at her tone, relaxing a little as he related to her childhood. "You would not have fared well in Iveston. We beat up each other regularly on the basis of who was most fitting to be heir— not to the title, mind you. Titles are irrelevant to childish minds. We wanted to be heir to the horses and dogs and the pond and anything our small minds could claim."

She sent him a grateful smile that nearly brought him to his knees.

"Then you'll understand a little of why I was so angry with Rain when he didn't listen to me. I told him that Alan was crying and that the nursemaids couldn't find him. He brushed me off, and I thought I'd show him, I'd find Alan myself, and then I would be the hero and the heir."

Will didn't think he liked the direction of this story, but he couldn't walk away either. He'd spent the last decade rambling the length and breadth of England—the better part of that time had been spent pursuing tragedy. "You don't have to explain," he said, hoping she wouldn't.

She halted at the foot of the stairs leading to the upper stories. She released his arm, but now she faced him in the brighter light of the foyer. Shadows haunted the enchanting fairy face that was meant to be wreathed in happiness and laughter.

"It's all quite predictable, I know," she said. "My six-year-old self took off after the footman I heard yelling at Alan, who was wailing. I was mad and meant to kick him hard on the shins and tell him Alan belonged in the nursery with the other *babies*. But I was too late. I was in the house, but I was hearing them from that copse of trees at the far end of the property. My legs were too short. I arrived only to see him ride off. By then, I was much too far away to call for help."

"If Rain was only twelve, even if he'd listened to you, he couldn't have caught a kidnapper." Will thought he might suffocate from the turmoil roiling in his chest. He needed to be outside, away from her sorrow, away from his need to hold her and tell her that life was hard and people were cruel. Rescuing the lost was a heartbreaking and impossible task most days, as he knew too well. "Did your brother not believe you heard distant voices?"

"It's hard to say. We were both too young and raised too far apart to communicate well." She looked at the floor rather than at him. Will had the urge to lift her chin so he could see her eyes—or kiss her. With the fear of his animal instincts instilled in him, he resisted with all his might.

"We still don't talk much," she admitted. "By the time I ran back to the castle, crying, everyone knew Alan had gone missing. Rain was already on his horse. My father wasn't there, so Rain ordered all the grooms in the direction I told them. But it was too late. Alan and the footman were long gone. I believe the ransom note must have arrived that evening. I only overheard some of the tale when I was older. I played no part in whatever happened over the next days. As a child, all I knew was that Alan didn't come back, the house was draped all in black, my mother couldn't stop crying, everyone talked in whispers, and no one would play with me anymore."

"The blame lies solely on the kidnapper, you do know that, don't you?" Will asked, watching a sparkling tear fall from her cheek. He didn't dare look lower. Her gowns were often modest, but his thoughts weren't.

"I don't ever want to have to live with that again," she said weakly. "Alan's death tore the heart out of my entire family. I could not face it happening again."

"Which is why you agree to being sealed behind castle walls," he said, finally understanding.

"And I should never, ever have allowed my sisters to invite men of whom Father didn't approve. But they were too young to remember what happened. They don't understand our isolation, and I feared their resentment would lead to disaster. Besides, I could not see why being poor should keep young men from our door, since we all have dowries. So I agreed to the house party."

"And now you are blaming yourself for inviting a brute?" he asked in incredulity.

"If it was one of our guests who did that to Bess. . . I could not live with myself," she cried.

And then, to his utter shock, she fell against him, weeping.

Ten

WEEPING AS she had not in years, Aurelia soaked poor Mr. Madden's linen. He had no choice but to wrap his arms around her. Cocooned in all that muscular warmth, she felt safe to express her terror and anxiety. She tried so hard to be the calm one, the reassuring one, the older sister, but she *wasn't*. She was an hysterical lunatic with no ability to help anyone, anywhere. And poor Bess and her children would suffer for her ineptitude, just as her family had.

Hard arms tightened and rocked her as if she were a babe—or a dog. And that was when she realized she didn't want to be a pampered infant anymore. She wanted to be a whole woman, one who could be held by a man in a normal way, without hearing the scolding voices in her head of countless nursemaids and governesses and family.

And right now, with Will, she didn't hear anything but *him*. Wrapped in his arms, all she could hear was the beat of his heart.

It was such a relief that she reacted to an instinct as old as mankind. Standing on her toes, Aurelia kissed Will's whiskery chin, missing his mouth. He corrected that instantly, cupping the back of her head as he angled his mouth and bent to smother her lips with brandy-flavored excitement.

She'd never been kissed. She had no idea where to put her tongue or teeth, but he had no such uncertainty. He growled low under his breath and took her mouth hard. Then, at her wobbly reaction, his lips softened, nipped, caressed, until her insides softened like butter and her legs grew wobbly.

She parted her lips on an exhalation of pure desire. He braced his legs apart and lifted her to deepen the contact. His big hands on her bottom reduced her spine to hot oil, shaking her down to her very soul.

His tongue licked, and she thought she might go up in a tower of flame. How had she never known. . . ? And then their tongues touched, and she almost climbed his legs to be closer to this intoxicating new experience. She wrapped her arms around his manly neck, dug her fingers into his rough tweed, and hung on while her head spun. He was all bristles and strength and heat. . .

He abruptly crushed her sleeves, tugged her off, and set her an arm's length away. A vast chill rushed between them. With the lamplight gleaming in his burnished gold hair, he appeared an angry god.

"Don't taunt me with what I cannot have, princess. I will not write you poetry." He released her and walked away, vanishing down the dark corridor.

He would not write her poetry? She had just experienced the most bone-melting, thrilling event of her life, and he talked about *poetry*? Had she missed some lesson by not being more socially skilled? Did the gentlemen who wrote her awful rhymes expect to be paid in kisses? She couldn't ask Bridey. That would be too humiliating.

Holding her melted midsection so she didn't slide to the floor, she pondered. . . life, men, and misery. Wiping tear streaks from her cheeks, Aurelia stomped upstairs to check on the nursery. Rose had smuggled Tiny inside again. The pair lay sleeping on a cot next to the twins—who both had deerhound puppies with them.

That at least gave her something to smile about while returning to her lonely room.

AFTER A RESTLESS, sleepless night, Aurelia summoned the courage and determination to demand that Mr. Madden explain himself. She didn't care that Sir Pascoe said his nephew never explained. That was specious nonsense. She had *felt* something last night, something she had felt for no other man, and she thought surely he had felt it too. But for some obtuse reason, he wouldn't admit it.

They were playing with the pups, miss. . .

*Rose? Where is **Rose**?*

The frantic note caught Aurelia's attention as she descended to the breakfast room. It sounded like Bess. Why would she be worrying about Rose?

Rascal wants out!

She tried to filter out the cursing from the stable and the bustle in the kitchen and the newlywed couple's amorous murmurings in their bedchamber as she dashed down the rest of the stairs. Whoever was with Bess wasn't excited enough to be heard clearly from this distance. Instead of going in to breakfast, she re-directed toward the door leading to the courtyard.

Mr. Madden pushed in, carrying Edward, one of Pascoe's twins. "Take him to the nursery. Lock him up while I search the grounds. Kick Pascoe out of bed and tell him the dogs saw an intruder." The boy cried and kicked his feet.

Swallowing hard, Aurelia took the sturdy four-year old. She staggered beneath his weight.

"Edward, hush, where's your sister?" she asked, remembering Bridey's tales of the twins talking to each other without words.

"She's scared," he wailed. "She's *scared*. I gotta go."

Aurelia's stomach plummeted, remembering her own childhood disaster. Surely this was not the same! Still, she must listen to the boy as no one had listened to her.

"We'll look for her," she murmured to the terrified child.

"Take him to his parents," Will ordered. "Let them see if he can tell them anything."

Heart beating too fast, Aurelia murmured more soothing words as she hauled Edward up the stairs. Emma was scared? What about Rose? Thankfully, a worried nursemaid met her at the main floor so she needn't climb another set.

"Mr. Madden says to lock the nursery. Are the girls there?" But she knew the answer before the maid could give it.

"No, m'lady, we can't finds them anywhere. They took the pups outside to wee and went to see the kittens in the stable and no one's seen them since." The maid was almost weeping. "We thought they'd be fine with the grooms and all."

"Wake Sir Pascoe and his lady," Aurelia ordered. And then having an awful thought, she asked, "Where's the infant and wet nurse?"

"They's fine in the nursery, m'lady." She took the squirming, complaining Edward.

Aurelia drew in a deep breath to ease her spiraling panic. *Not the baby,* thank all that was holy. Who would want to take the girls? Surely, the naughty pair were playing a game.

"I think you'd best take Edward to Sir Pascoe. Tell him Mr.

Madden says there was an intruder. If the girls return, lock them in the nursery. I'm on my way to the infirmary." She didn't wait to see if the maid obeyed.

If there was an intruder, she needed to see to Bess, and Pascoe needed to protect his son.

Where would two little girls go if they were hiding from an intruder? Aurelia couldn't let herself think past that to the worst. Recalling her awful childhood memories last night had awakened old fears.

Outside, Mr. Madden had one of the deerhounds on a leash and was searching the various derelict buildings surrounding the courtyard. Aurelia ran straight to the infirmary.

Bess was sitting up in bed, looking pale enough to faint. The gash on her face had scabbed over, but the pink halo of infection still marred it. She'd lost too much blood to even sit straight—and she was trying to stand. The maid who had been left to tend to her hovered anxiously.

"Where's Rose?" the patient asked the moment Aurelia entered.

The whimpering terrier sprawled on the floor answered all her questions. His wiry hair was coated in blood. Aurelia fought down her nausea and screamed, "Willllll! Will, come quickly."

He shadowed the open doorway in seconds. Aurelia backed into the courtyard so he could see Tiny.

His curse was obscene as he dropped to his knees to cover the wounded puppy with both big hands. "Call Jack from the stable. He'll have to deal with this." He glanced up at Bess. "Did anyone visit you last night?"

Looking terrified, Bess shook her head of wild black hair. "I slept the whole night through. And then the pup crawled in this morning. *He* did that. He's got my Rose, I know it."

"Who?" Aurelia demanded, gesturing for the maid to run to the stable.

Bess started weeping, covering her mouth with her hands as she watched Mr. Madden use her basin of water to clean the dog.

Aurelia waited for him to speak, but he didn't. She didn't know anything to say. The missing girls, the injured dog. . . She wanted to weep too. But this was too important to dither in helplessness.

"Bess," she said sharply, mimicking a tone she'd heard her mother use long ago. "Rose is missing. So is Lady Pascoe's daughter.

If this mysterious *he* took them, what do you think will happen?"

The woman rocked back and forth, hugging herself. "He doesn't want Rose. He kicked her and the pup out. He tried to kill my baby."

"And he thinks you'll trade the boy for Rose? That's a trifle mad, isn't it?" Aurelia asked while Will applied padding to Tiny's wound.

"I don't know, I don't *know*!" Tears poured down her weathered cheeks. "But who else would do that?"

"You have to tell us who he is," Aurelia pleaded. "We can search if we know who to search for!"

Bess only wept hysterically. Had Aurelia been Mr. Madden's size, she would have shaken her. She had to give the gentleman credit for patience and restraint.

The groom rushed in. Mr. Madden waited until the other man had the dog's bandage pressed down before he took something from the dog's mouth, stood up, and walked out. Aurelia rushed after him, prepared to demand answers.

She didn't have to. He started speaking as soon as she was beside him.

"Tiny relates the intruder's smell to the same man who hurt him before." He showed her a torn scrap of cloth. "The dog bit him hard enough to draw blood. I'm giving this scent to the deerhounds. Pascoe needs to send for reinforcements. If they have Emma, this is no longer just about Bess and the babe. You and Bridey need to arm the household, bring everyone inside."

He said nothing more but let his long strides carry him ahead, in the direction of the stable, expecting her to follow his orders.

Aurelia ran toward the house, mind racing. Bridey met her at the door, and Aurelia spilled all the information in her possession while running for her chamber. Bridey threw commands as they ran.

"What do you think you're doing?" her cousin asked as Aurelia called for Addy and began stripping off the pretty gown she'd donned in hopes of seeing Mr. Madden at breakfast.

"I should be able to *hear* the children," Aurelia reminded her. "If the dogs follow the scent and Mr. Madden comes close, I can hear them and the kidnappers. . ." She had to stop a keening a sob at admitting the dread word. "*I cannot let this happen again.* I cannot do this to you and Pascoe. I *have* to help."

"We don't know for sure that they've been taken," Bridey said uncertainly. "The twins hide. It could be a game."

"I *listened*," she cried. "I cannot hear the girls anywhere! And they most certainly did not knife a puppy. Did Edward have anything to say?" Aurelia pulled on her silk pantaloons and her riding skirt while her maid helped her into her lace-trimmed cambric shirt.

"He says they all went out to play with the kittens, but he heard the hounds crying because they were penned up in one of the stalls. He left the girls with the kittens to see why the dogs were upset, and he tried to calm them down. But they smelled strangers and ran out, barking. He wasn't looking for the girls, just following the dogs."

Aurelia buttoned her jacket and rummaged in a drawer for her riding crop. "How long ago was this?"

"Probably at dawn," Bridey said in resignation. "Children rise early. The maids are accustomed to them running to the stables as soon as it's light."

"An hour ago, then? Were the kittens in a different part of the stable from the dogs?" Aurelia let Addy tut-tut and tie on her riding hat.

"I think so. They were in the loft the other day, but the mother cat could have carried them anywhere. So Edward went one way, the girls went the other. . . I want to go with you but. . ."

"You can't. Even if you weren't carrying a child, you can't," Aurelia insisted. "Ashford is arriving with his infant *heir*. They needed to be guarded at all cost, and you and Pascoe must take charge here. Lord Dare will send aid if you request it, won't he?" Emilia and her husband lived not too far away.

Bridey closed her eyes and swayed. Addy caught her and helped her to a chair.

"I'm all right." Bridey shook off the maid but sat. "It's just too unbelievable. I need to search the house, simply to be certain they're not hiding. They may have fallen asleep somewhere. Yes, we'll send for Lord Dare and find men we can trust. Take a groom with you to relay messages, please. The duke will kill us if anything happens to you, but they're *children*. . ."

"Exactly." Aurelia hit her crop against her skirt. "I am no longer a child. I can look out for myself. I can hear trouble coming from miles away." She said that brashly, as if she'd ever done such a thing. "We just need to find their hiding place. Don't worry. Mr. Madden and I are *magic*."

Which was a silly flight of fancy, but enough to cause Bridey to offer a watery smile and make plans as Aurelia pulled on her boots. Maybe the dog hadn't been knifed. Maybe it had caught on something sharp and the girls were sleeping in the hayloft and this was all for nothing. Anything was possible.

Except she trusted Mr. Madden to know what he was talking about. If he said the dog had been knifed, he'd no doubt been looking into the dog's mind. As soon as she had her boots on, Aurelia lifted her long skirt and raced for the stairs again.

The men were already in the courtyard, saddled and shouting orders. Aurelia ran to the stable, found Bridey's sturdy mare, and instructed the lone stable boy to heave on the saddle. She could hear Pascoe and Mr. Madden directing men to ride north to guard Ashford's coach, to Harrogate and Leeds to men they trusted to provide help, and setting guards around the house. By the time she'd seated herself and rode out, only Mr. Madden, Sir Pascoe, and one of the older grooms remained at the courtyard entrance.

Mr. Madden was pocketing a pistol and sliding a musket into a strap on his saddle. He scowled as Aurelia rode up. "You are not leaving the house."

"Did Bess give anyone a name?" she asked, ignoring his command.

"Not the one we want, I suspect," Sir Pascoe answered. "She said he calls himself Crockett, which we already knew. She claims he's about my height, with brownish hair, a long nose with a bump in the middle, and pock-marked skin. He does not sound like any noble I know."

Aurelia looked up at Mr. Madden. "I do not hear either of the girls, even though they should be in a panic and screaming loudly. I could hear Rose crying from a long distance last time. He must have done something to quiet them."

Mr. Madden looked as if he'd like to strangle her. But even if he would not say so aloud, he *had* to admit that she could be useful. She'd proved it to him before.

"Thank you, my lady," Sir Pascoe said. "My daughter is more precious than gems to me, but you are equally precious to your father. Be careful and listen to Will. He is experienced in tracking children and villains." He tipped his hat and rode toward the front drive as if he had completely expected her to join the search.

Left with an angry Mr. Madden, Aurelia experienced a small frisson of fear. She had gone out alone with him once and been completely safe. But that had been on her father's property. Riding down a public road without her sisters and with only an unfamiliar groom in accompaniment made her feel vulnerable and exposed.

"Your uncle trusts you implicitly," she offered, hiding her trepidation by attempting to appease Mr. Madden's anger. "Which way do the dogs say?"

Apparently, this morning's four or five sentences were the most he meant to utter. His jaw tightened, his eyes shuttered, and he set the deerhounds loose. The animals raced through the unbarred entrance of the courtyard, down the drive, and took the south road toward the village. Mr. Madden galloped off after them, leaving her in his dust.

Aurelia didn't ride often. It required too many grooms and usually half a dozen suitors and her sisters. The noise alone would be enough to drive her home. With Mr. Madden, she'd discovered, it was different. As she gave her horse free rein, she heard the hooves of numerous horses scattering in all directions. She heard a farmer cursing in his field and a woman calling to her neighbor, but the sounds were muffled in a way she could not explain other than to think of Mr. Madden as a padded wall between her and the world.

She hoped she could still hear the girls' cries. She'd heard Rose, even when she'd been riding directly beside him. She simply needed to concentrate. And pray.

Eleven

WILL HAD TUCKED tiny shoes the girls had worn into his pocket. He gave their scent to the dogs along with the scent of the intruder from the scrap of cloth. Even so, he knew his task was futile. If the girls had been stolen, instead of wandering off on their own, they had to have been taken away by horse or wagon. Holding a squirming, kicking child on horseback was impossible—unless the wretch had treated them the same way he had Tiny.

Just the possibility of violence to those children had Will's blood seething. He clenched the reins too hard and his horse reared in protest. He had to fight for his own control, but having the responsibility of Lady Aurelia complicated his difficulty.

Knowing the hounds would soon lose the scent was the only damned reason he'd allowed the lady to travel with him. If she respected his oddity, he was forced to respect hers. That apparently meant keeping noise away from her so she didn't go addled and blank, which meant he couldn't surround her with a troop of guards.

As the hounds started running back and forth across the road, hunting the increasingly elusive trail, Will prayed they were close enough for Lady Aurelia to hear the children.

He had *kissed* her. He had held heaven in his arms and nearly mauled her last night. His hunger had been so desperate that, had she not conveyed her inexperience in every single action, he would have hauled her off to bed. But for that single moment of glory, he would have willingly died a hundred times over.

He just *might* die a thousand deaths being this close and not able to have her, Will decided as he listened to her silence. He didn't court ladies. He bedded willing women. That was the limit of his experience, and he had been happy that way. He meant to marry Miranda once he had the kennel, if only because it made life simple, and he'd have someone to cook for him while he tended his dogs.

Lady Aurelia did not fit those parameters in *any* manner. And the duke would no doubt kill him if he learned Will had so much as kissed her.

"I don't hear them," the lady said plaintively, riding up beside him as they approached the village of Alder. "How does one silence children?"

Will could think of several ways, none of them pleasant enough to mention. "Rose can't talk and Emma seldom does," he said instead. "Perhaps they're busy and happy and playing with dolls."

"And perhaps the moon is made of green cheese," she retorted.

Well, so the lady was weird, not stupid. He'd known that. "Alder has no inn," he told her. "I need to go in the tavern and ask questions. I can't take you with me. Lady Dare's retired housekeeper lives just down this lane. I'll leave you and Pascoe's groom with her."

He prayed she had the sense to stay where he left her. Most Malcolm women were inquisitive nuisances who never did as told, but this one had reason to be painfully aware of the world's dangers. Cursing himself for three sorts of fool for bringing her, he introduced a duke's daughter to Mrs. Wiggs and left them taking tea in a small cottage where no one would think to look.

When he returned not long after, Lady Aurelia was waiting in the garden, holding a delicious-smelling bundle while the groom led her horse to a mounting block. Her fashionable riding attire belled around a narrow wasp waist. The tight-fitting coat emphasized the swell of her bosom, and the deep blue of the fabric darkened her eyes to mysterious pools. Will was so fascinated, he didn't reach for the bundle, even though he was starving.

He didn't help her mount either, not while he was in this state. She shoved the bundle at him until he was forced to take it. He settled on glaring at her for disobeying his orders.

"Did you intend to ride out without me?" he asked as she gained her seat with inbred grace—revealing silken knickers beneath her skirt. He thought he might expire on the spot. If their task wasn't so urgent, he'd not be able to think of anything else but those lacy pantalets.

"I heard you coming and assumed you learned the same thing I did—that Farmer Thorne's wagon rolled through the village at dawn, with a stranger at the reins." She leaned over, opened the linen bundle, and helped herself to a still-warm bun. "I wanted to be ready so I didn't slow you down."

That she'd asked the same questions as he had except from a woman's perspective startled him more than it should have. He'd known she was intelligent. He just never expected women to be logical.

Will took a bun, shoved the bundle into his pocket, and tore off a bite of sweet bread rather than reply. He snapped his fingers at the dogs to make them heel, and wheeled his mount in the direction indicated.

The lady trotted up beside him and handed him an old shirt. "Mrs. Wiggs' sister takes in mending. This is Farmer Thorne's."

"I have the direction," he muttered ungratefully. Her crestfallen look hit him harder than if she'd used her hand. "But it was a good thought," he added.

She shot him a baleful look and rode ahead, nibbling on her bun. He'd finished his in two bites. He noted the groom's pocket bulged with another bundle he wasn't sharing.

Will wanted—needed—Lady Aurelia to stay safely ensconced with the motherly housekeeper while he and the groom rode out to question the farmer. But the wagon had turned in the direction of Thorne's place. If there was any chance that the girls had been in that wagon, the lady had to be there to find them. Pascoe's hounds were trained for guarding, not tracking. He tapped quickly into the one sniffing the road.

Horses. Hunger. Rotting flesh, ummm.

In disgust, Will jerked away again. Smelling dead skunk and thinking *ummm* was too jarring.

They met Lord Dare and a group of men half way down the lane. Will remembered Emilia's husband looking pale and weak the last time he'd been this way. Family gossip said he'd been dying until his Malcolm wife discovered the source of his illness. The viscount looked hale and hearty enough now as he reined in his horse.

"Have the children been found?" Dare asked without waiting for introductions.

"We're tracing a lead to Thorne's place," Will said. "Do you know him?"

Dare's riders inched closer, ostensibly to hear, but Will noted their heads swiveling toward the silent lady doing her best to look stick straight and unapproachable. Given her delectable curves, she failed miserably. They'd all be panting if he didn't move on.

One of the men spoke up. "Thorne married a widow woman and

moved up to town. His son is running the place now, I reckon. He's a right sort."

Will desperately wanted to leave the lady with Dare, but watching her grow more tense and stiffer, he realized that hearing just the voices of these few men—and possibly half the village for all he knew—was painful to her. He couldn't leave her without her permission.

Reluctantly, he turned to her now. "My lady, I cannot in all good conscience ride up to a stranger's house with you in tow." At her look of protest, Will held up his hand. "I know we need you. But would you accept an escort to wait behind, out of sight of the house?"

Dare's expression lit as he realized who she was, but Will had no intention of introducing a duke's daughter to this group of strangers. As it was, they were vying to see beneath the hat veil that did little more than entice. Will blessed the viscount's silence and wished for a stave to beat the rest back.

He could tell she didn't want an escort. Beneath the veil, her rounded jaw set in determination, and she turned to look in the direction of the groom who had been accompanying them. Surely she could see that the man was jockey-sized, not someone who could stand up to a fight. With a sigh, she nodded. "One more person."

"Take Mapleton," Dare suggested. "I'd trust him with my life, and he's the quiet sort."

Apparently Dare's wife had imparted some of Lady Aurelia's disability to him. For once, Will blessed the Malcolm ladies' unceasing chatter. When a solid young man rode up and tugged his forelock, Will looked to Lady Aurelia for approval. She set her small chin and nodded once.

With a final exchange of greetings, Dare led his group on toward the abbey.

Will led his growing entourage between hedgerows in the morning chill, until they reached the rutted drive Will had been told to look for. He dismounted and leashed the dogs. "Is there a copse where the lady can be hidden?" he asked Mapleton.

Lady Aurelia rolled up her veil and looked as if she were biting her tongue and would like to bite him as well. She shot him a dagger glare, then tilted her head at her escorts. Will mentally smacked himself for stupidity. She wished to say something but wouldn't talk about distant voices in front of strangers.

Mapleton nodded. "Just around the bend, sir, there's a stream behind some willows."

"Go there and see if it's safe, take the groom, and if all is well, send him back to lead the lady there." Will watched the lad and groom ride away, then steeled himself to look at his companion. Seeing her fear, he put a damper on his lust. "What do you hear?"

"A woman telling someone he's a useless lump of coal. A man grumbling, almost as if he's in pain. I would be too if I had to listen to the harridan." Her lovely features grew vacant, but she continued. "There may be a maid or a daughter—too old for our pair. She's shouting about a shoe. There are two men talking to each other, possibly in a barn or stable since they mentioned oats and stall and I can hear a horse whicker."

"That's three men and two women," Will counted. "No children?"

She frowned. "I hear what sounds like animals snuffling. But the clanging pots and pans are louder. It was quieter on the moors."

"They may have gagged the girls, or they could have fallen asleep. Or the wagon could have gone elsewhere. I'll take the dogs behind the buildings, see if they catch a scent. Will you feel safe with young Mapleton?"

"I don't feel safe anywhere," she said flatly. "It's one of the hazards of my position."

AURELIA KNEW she shouldn't have said it the moment she saw Mr. Madden's jaw tighten. She couldn't take it back—she'd spoken the truth, after all. But now she'd laid all that guilt and worry on his shoulders. She wouldn't blame him for leaving her behind.

So she took herself off after her escort and left Mr. Madden to do what he did best—talk to dogs.

Blessedly, the young man Lord Dare had chosen to guard her remained silent while they waited for a signal from Will or the groom he'd taken with him. Aurelia strained to hear what was happening. A man capable of stabbing a puppy was capable of anything. Will's firearms didn't make her feel any more confident.

The mare beneath her nickered and stomped restlessly. Without

Mr. Madden to distract her, all the rustlings in the hedges as well as the distant calls of birds and cattle grew increasingly louder. She pressed her temples and tried to concentrate on Mr. Madden's progress, but she could hear her escort's breathing better. The wretched dog trainer was a vacuum of silence.

He'd had more than enough time to walk around a barn ten times over before she caught a sharp sound that was so alarming she almost toppled from the saddle. That had sounded like a *gunshot*.

She couldn't bear it any longer. What was the point of existing if she could never *do* anything? Without consulting her companion, she kicked Bridey's mare and trotted back to where she'd left Mr. Madden.

It wasn't hard to discern the path he and the dogs had taken, but the rising discord in the distance caused her to throw caution to the wayside. She spurred her horse into a gallop across open field. Mr. Mapleton didn't dare grab her reins to stop her. All he could do was follow.

She focused on the strangely muffled cries and sobs. They were almost indistinguishable beneath the harridan's nagging and other noise from the farm house. The thumps and thuds and now, curses, seemed to be in the same direction as the sobs—past the barn where two field hands did their chores, oblivious to the distant noise only she could hear. She saw no sign of Mr. Madden, his horse, or the groom.

But those were definitely the dogs growling in the distance. Aurelia swallowed hard and slowed down as they reached the crest of a hill. The rocky slope descended into a shadowed dale. At the bottom was a crude stone hut built into the next hill.

Mr. Madden's horse had been tied to a fence rail. The rifle was still tied to the saddle. The dogs leaped and scratched at the hut's only door, growling but not barking. Normally, Bridey's hounds howled at anything that moved. Was Mr. Madden mentally silencing them? Why?

Well, she knew the answer to that—to keep her from knowing he needed help. The fool man meant to do everything himself. If she knew any rude words, she'd use them.

She spurred the mare along the crest, looking for the groom who was supposed to act as messenger. Mr. Mapleton started to speak, but she held up her hand. Was that a groan?

The hut door crashed open and two men tumbled out. There was no mistaking Mr. Madden's large form pounding his fist into a man wielding a wicked knife. The dogs finally started howling, and Aurelia kicked the mare into action, with Mr. Mapleton hot on her heels. It didn't matter that she had no weapon or strength. Numbers had to count.

The clatter of hooves on stone caused both men to glance up. Mr. Madden was faster to react. Grabbing the knife-wielding arm, he twisted until the knife fell, then rolled his heavy weight on top of his opponent.

Aurelia could almost swear she heard bone snap before the man shrieked in agony. The dogs rushed to jump on the prostrate kidnapper while Will shoved up, grabbed the knife, and ran toward the hut.

"The window!" Aurelia cried, pointing. "There's one going out the back."

Mr. Mapleton spurred his horse around the hut while Will dashed inside. Aurelia rode to the open front door, heart thumping in terror. She still could not hear the girls clearly, even though they had to be hysterical.

She clenched her teeth as she rode past the man curled on the ground in agony. The hounds pranced on him as if he were prey, holding him down. They didn't appear to be biting. She wished she could tell them to snap off the rogue's nose.

The hut had no mounting block. Not seeing the groom, she disentangled her skirts and ungracefully slid down, thankful for the fashionable riding undergarments concealing her stockings.

Totally out of her element, she was practically shaking in her boots by the time she stumbled for the door. Mr. Madden still wasn't making any noise, but whoever was inside the hut was howling as loudly as the dogs. As sheltered as she had been, she never went anywhere alone, but she could not just stand here waiting for someone to show up. She shoved at the door.

Inside, she had to let her eyes adjust. She could see a small window framing Mr. Madden at the rear. His bulk effectively blotted any light inside, but she decided he tangled with the scoundrel trying to escape and wasn't in any danger. Neither man appeared to be wounded, so the gunshot must have gone astray. She hoped.

Attuning her hearing to the muffled sounds, and holding to the wall for guidance in the gloomy interior, she edged toward what might be a wardrobe. With the dogs baying, one kidnapper cursing and crying, Mr. Mapleton shouting outside, and what was apparently a second kidnapper screaming in fury, it was a wonder she didn't sink to the floor or run for the hills. She trembled all over, but she clenched her teeth and held her course.

The wardrobe was locked. An ornate iron bolt held two wooden doors together. If she had an axe. . . she might split heads or chop off a hand. She needed a key.

Mr. Madden apparently won the battle of the window. Clasping the back of the man's coat, he tugged him back inside and flung him toward the center of the dirt floor. Now that he wasn't blocking the light, Aurelia could discern a ramshackle table and chairs before a crude hearth. The kidnapper hit one of the chairs, toppling it. Silver gleamed in his hand. She shrieked in horror.

With the muffled cries of two little girls ringing in her ears, she couldn't think, only act. She grabbed the remaining chair and slammed it down on the knife-wielding hand of the kidnapper. He went down again in a cry of pain and fury, and the weapon flew into a dark corner. Before he could rise again, Will stomped his big boot on the arm she'd smashed. The stranger screamed like a baby.

"The key," Aurelia shouted at Will when he bent to grab the man's shirtfront.

Shooting her what appeared to be an angry look in the dim light, he lifted the struggling man up, slammed him the against a wall, and rifled through his coat pocket.

Having an awful thought, Aurelia raced out the front door just in time to see the first man run for the hills, holding his broken arm against his chest, the dogs at his heels. There wasn't any way she could gain her saddle fast enough. "Stop him!" she shouted.

To her amazement, the dogs instantly raced after the escaping rogue, bringing him down, face first into a pile of rocks. Mr. Mapleton was a little slower reaching him since he'd been on the other side of the hut.

"Look for a key," she called to him.

"The groom needs help," her escort shouted. "He's around back."

Grown men had to take care of themselves, Aurelia decided, returning inside the dark hut. The children came first.

Mr. Madden was trussing the tall, lanky kidnapper with his neckcloth. "I searched his pockets," he told her. "No key."

His captive began to curse, and in one effortless movement, Mr. Madden cuffed his jaw with a big fist. The man slumped in his grip. Tightening the binding of his linen around the villain's wrists, he let him drop to the floor. He stood there in in open shirt, looking like a woodcutter more than a gentleman.

He'd routed two kidnappers without killing himself or them. She didn't know whether to be astounded or faint. "I don't know if Mr. Mapleton needs help, and he said the groom is hurt," Aurelia said, standing there in shock, feeling helpless.

Will glanced out the door. "Mapleton is doing fine. The groom had the breath knocked out of him. He's chasing his horse now." He gestured for her to move away from the wardrobe. "Stand aside."

Bracing himself, he slammed his shoulder against the old wardrobe. The wood cracked.

The muffled cries on the other side escalated. Oddly, Aurelia couldn't distinguish a single word, but she knew the girls were in there. She looked around for a fireplace poker or anything that might help but the hut had apparently not been lived in for years.

She glanced out to see if Mr. Mapleton might have the key yet, but he had apparently fetched a rope from one of the horses and was tying up the injured wretch. She assumed that meant no key. Surely there had to have been a key to lock the door.

With nowhere better to look, she start searching the stones surrounding the hearth. Mr. Madden slammed into the door again. The crack widened.

"Damned sturdy chest," he muttered, rubbing his shoulder.

"Wood rot hasn't set in. Do you think there's a third man who has the key?" she asked.

"Let's hope not." Will favored her with a disgruntled look at the thought and returned to pounding the door with his shoulder.

She supposed he was upset that she'd disobeyed his orders, but she didn't care. She might be shivering in her boots, but she was done being helpless. Aurelia tugged at stones, until one fell loose and tumbled from the hearth. She cried out her surprise, then searched the opening with her gloved hand. "I found it. Oldest trick in the world."

Rubbing his shoulder, Mr. Madden stood aside so she could do the honors. She studied the ornate iron lock in dismay. There was no keyhole.

The girls were whimpering in terror. Mr. Madden muttered a litany of curses beneath his breath.

Feeling dwarfed next to his muscled bulk, Aurelia took a deep breath and shouted loudly enough she hoped even Rose could hear. "It's just me, girls, we're looking for a lock. You'll be out soon."

Recalling an intricately carved medical cabinet in her father's study where the keyhole had been hidden behind a sliding bolt, she removed her glove and began pushing the carving, hoping for movement. "There!" she said in satisfaction as the metal gave way.

The bolt slid to one side, revealing the keyhole. Biting her bottom lip, she poked the key at it until she finally found the right position and it slid all the way in. The lock was rusted and wouldn't turn.

Impatiently, Mr. Madden grabbed it, shoved hard, twisted even harder, and broke through the obstruction. The door fell open. Aurelia breathed a sigh of relief—until she realized the wardrobe was empty, and she panicked.

"We need light," Mr. Madden said, not sounding as hysterical as she felt.

His assurance gave her time to take a deep breath. "They're in there. I know they are." With no fire and no candle, Aurelia had no means of creating light. Instead, she stepped inside the narrow, dark closet and began slamming her hands against the back panel, until it moved. She grasped the edge and tugged, nearly falling back out the door in the process.

Mr. Madden caught her waist and lifted her free. His scent of male sweat and bay rum caused her to close her eyes and simply inhale while she tried to quiet the jumble in her mind. He held her a moment too long, as if he might be enjoying the moment too. *She'd known it.* He'd enjoyed their kiss. The wretched man simply wouldn't admit to having *feelings*.

"Let me remove the backing," he murmured near her ear, still holding her.

She could *hear* the children. They were safe, she thought, just trapped.

She prayed that she might have arrived in time to be useful.

Not allowing herself to feel jubilant yet, she steadied herself on

Mr. Madden's big body, enjoying the masculine scent of his skin. Hearing the pounding of his heart mixed with the muffled cries of the children, Aurelia backed off. The children needed him now. She had to be strong on her own.

While Will ripped at the wardrobe panel, Mr. Mapleton returned, dragging the wretch with the broken arm, who had mercifully passed out. He threw his prisoner down with the other and helped to lift the panel clear of the wardrobe doors. The cries were less muffled now—two of them, she felt certain.

The men were too large to look into the small dark hole behind the panel. Aurelia had to get down on her hands and knees and crawl into the opening to pull the girls free. "Root cellar," she called, rejoicing as she found Rose's small foot and helped her wiggle out. Rose's arms were bound and her mouth gagged. Tears streaked her dirty cheeks, but her eyes widened in recognition and relief, causing Aurelia to finally weep. She'd done it! This time, she'd arrived in time to help save the girls. She wasn't utterly useless.

Tears of joy rolled down her cheeks.

Will lifted Rose out so Aurelia could reach Emma, who had been similarly treated. She, too, was tear-stained but wide-eyed as Aurelia handed her over for the men to free their bonds.

Rose flung her arms around Aurelia's legs the instant she was free. She had to kneel down before she toppled. Crying in her jumbled words, Rose buried her face in Aurelia's shoulder and wouldn't let go. She hugged and rocked the child, glancing helplessly to Will, who had his arms full of weeping four-year old.

"Bbbddd mmmnnn," Rose kept repeating. Then finally catching sight of the bound men on the floor, she shoved free of Aurelia's arms and ran over to kick one on the thigh. "Bbbbbdddd, bbbdddd."

The man groaned and tried to kick her away. Rose fled back to Aurelia's arms.

Holding Rose's sturdy body, watching Emma clinging to Will, Aurelia thought she'd never been so happy in her life.

Unfazed by Will's large size, Emma was covering his bristly face with kisses. He didn't look the least uncomfortable with an urchin clinging to him. He'd obviously rescued people before, Aurelia realized. This was what he did—saved people. It must be amazing to hold the power of life and death in one's hands.

"What should we do with the rogues, sir?" Mr. Mapleton asked.

"Question them," Will answered curtly. "Once the groom catches his horse, the two of you can tie the scoundrels to your saddles and lead them towards the abbey. We'll ride ahead with the children and send men back to meet you."

"Shouldn't we question the farmer?" Aurelia asked, setting Rose on her feet and taking her by the hand.

"I'll do that, if I might," Mr. Mapleton said. "I know Roger. I don't think he was involved. I'll leave these two with the groom and just go round and ask about the tenants."

Will looked to Aurelia—she had to think of him as *Will* now. She felt closer to him than to her own father. She even knew what he was asking with his look.

"I think he's right," she told him. "Nothing I've heard says otherwise, and the lot of you made enough noise to wake the dead." She would tell him that the farmer was currently complaining about barking dogs and about to come over the hill with a pitchfork, but that would set tongues to wagging later.

Will inclined his head in acceptance. "Then we'll see how well you balance on a sidesaddle with a six-year old on your lap."

Since Rose refused to free her grip on Aurelia, that seemed the best solution. Remembering the bundle of buns she'd tucked into his capacious pocket, she reached in as if she had every right to be so familiar with his person. The bundle was crushed, but she opened up the linen to offer the girls food. They fell on it as if starved.

"Big breakfast for everyone when we reach the abbey," Aurelia said, daringly winking at the man who had forsaken his meal for two little girls.

She thought Will's rough jaw might actually have reddened just a little. But a moment later, he swung Emma to his shoulders and jogged out. "You said the magic words. C'mon, girls, let's see if we can race the lady home."

How easy it would be to love a man who understood children! After their horrifying experience, the girls needed reassurance that life would return to the normality of breakfast and adults who would take care of them. Aurelia wiped Rose's face with her handkerchief and led her out to the horses, feeling fulfilled for the first time in forever.

Twelve

ONCE BACK AT the abbey, Will left the women to fuss over the girls. He needed to distance himself from Lady Aurelia and the hug she'd shared and the bold wink that had nearly knocked him off his feet. The best way to return his boots to the ground was to take a decidedly grim Pascoe back down the road to meet the culprits. Dealing with challenges was his reality, not the feminine enticement of tears and winks and hugs. The lady would melt his spine to putty and expose his worst instincts.

While he waited for Pascoe to finish hugging Emma and his wife, Will tested one of the scent identifiers he'd thoughtlessly squirreled away in his pocket a couple of days ago. He offered both hounds a whiff of the drunken lord's handkerchief. Linking his mind, he couldn't scent any recognition in theirs. That didn't rule anyone out. It just didn't identify anyone. He fed the hounds extra treats and returned to his horse when Pascoe stomped out, looking like court executioner. They rode silently in the direction of the lane where Will had left Dare's men with the injured scoundrels.

"The duke's been acting as magistrate since the last one died," Pascoe finally said just before they reached the men hauling the kidnappers. "Even if he appointed me, I'd have to abstain or I'd have the rogues transported this minute."

"You can burn them at the stake for all I care," Will said callously. "I just want to know who sent them and why."

"Dare is a viscount. Let's nominate him as acting magistrate, take them to his place, away from the women, and pretend we're objective for a little while."

"What about Lady Dare?" Will had to ask. He could tolerate the *duke's* reasonable daughter. Lady Aurelia seldom made demands except when others were at risk. But city-bred, over-educated Emilia was a nag like her Malcolm mother—and a healer. She'd peel paint off their hides if she saw the condition of the rogues.

"Emilia is tending to Rose's mother and Bridey's impending hysteria," Pascoe said with a dark chuckle, understanding the reason for Will's question. "There'll be none but us to interrogate them. Although looking at their conditions," he added as they rode closer, "I don't think we need do much more persuasion. What the hell did you do to them? Take them apart and put them back together wrong?"

"I think I only broke one bone," Will said in indignation. "Maybe cracked a few ribs."

"We can give the cads to Harrogate physicians to fix later, but we'll talk first. A little pain should speed the process." Pascoe didn't look the least objective or diplomatic as he said that.

"It's a good thing you left the king's employ, old man. You'd be starting your own Inquisition with that attitude."

"You'd be amazed how bloodthirsty one becomes when your own flesh and blood is harmed. I'd strangle them with my bare hands if I could." Pascoe kicked his horse to a trot and joined the groom and Mr. Mapleton, directing them to Dare's abode.

They sent the groom back to fetch the viscount for the illusion of objectivity and fairness. But by the time Dare arrived, Pascoe and Will had the information they required.

"We was just arter the bitch," the villain with the broken arm protested as Will flung him toward Dare's farmers. "If she'd a'come when the brats started cryin' and the dogs hadn't howled, we'd of let them alone."

"They's just whelps," the larger of the villains whined as Dare's men prepared to haul them to Harrogate to await trial. "It ain't as if we hurt nothin' val'able."

Will rolled his eyes as his diplomatic, educated, sophisticated uncle plowed his fist into the lack-wit's jaw, probably knocking out what remained of his teeth. The nit slumped in the hold of one of Dare's grooms.

"Payment on Emma's nightmares," Pascoe muttered. "What hole do creatures like that crawl out of?"

"Better yet, how do creatures like Crockett find them?" Will asked. "Crockett was there. He's the one who stabbed the puppy, even if he didn't lay a hand on the children."

"And got clean away, *again*," Pascoe added in disgruntlement.

"Do you believe them when they said Crockett meant to exchange them for his son?" Will asked, troubled by the varied information obtained from the mind of dogs, children, and villains.

"First off, we don't know that Crockett is his name, since Bess disavowed it," Pascoe replied. "Second, we don't know that whoever hired the scoundrels is actually the boy's father. Third, I don't believe anyone would have walked away alive if Pseudo-Crockett got his hands on Bess and her son. A man who beats a woman heavy with child doesn't strike me as the polite sort to leave witnesses. I'm just irritated that no one knows how to find this bane on the rump of existence so I can hang him from a high limb." Pascoe was practically foaming at the mouth.

"Well, whatever you do to find him," Will warned, "it has to wait until Bess and her family are removed from the abbey. Word spreads fast in a village this small. Once the infirmary is empty and you spread the rumor that the infant and his mother died, your family should be safe. Then you can hunt your villain."

Hunting a lord, if that's what Crockett was, was better done by his city family. Will was ready to return to Yatesdale, finish his task of training Ajax, and move on.

As much as he had enjoyed Lady Aurelia's kiss, he knew it had only been because she needed comfort, and he was a lust-addled reprobate. He couldn't take her bit of familiarity with any seriousness, even if he'd enjoyed having her feed him buns and rooting in his pocket. Thinking of a duke's daughter was madness, and he was above all, sensible.

So he'd return the lady to her sisters, train Ajax, stay well out of the way until the duke came home, and then return to his schedule. His next post was in Scotland.

While Pascoe hurried to join his wife and children, Will rode to the stable to return the horses. His brother's enormous traveling carriage had arrived, and he grimaced. Then remembering he'd wanted to send his new pup back to the kennel at Iveston, he headed for a side door that would take him to his chambers. He'd have to pretend he was civilized long enough to ask the new parents to add the deerhound puppy to their baggage cart.

Seeing Lady Aurelia hurrying down the hall in his direction, Will almost fled back out the door. When those beautiful sky-blue eyes lit with expectation, he knew he was doomed.

AURELIA SIGHED in relief at finding Will so easily.

The household rang with the cries of the *very* loud marquess and his party. There were now two infants wailing in the nursery, and the staff had more than doubled. The marquess did not travel lightly when escorting his wife and new heir.

Will's blessed silence muffled all that. "I need you to go to London with me," she told him, keeping the plea out of her voice by using her best duke's daughter tone.

Will looked at her as if she'd just asked him to turn into a dragon. She would swear the solid bronzed jaw that had taken blows without bruising now paled in distress.

"*London*? Why?" he asked, stepping backward and acting as if she'd asked him to stop by Hades. "If you've taken a sudden desire to visit the city you said you hate, Ashford can take you. I need to finish training Ajax and return to my schedule."

"I need *you*," she admitted bluntly.

She had thought they'd developed a familiarity over this past week that left her comfortable enough with him to be honest. The morning's events had given her confidence. Had she been too bold? Too hasty? She was fairly certain her conclusion about Will's presence was correct. She'd read about such things in Malcolm journals. Perhaps she placed too much hope in ancient writings. At the very least, though, she needed to experiment.

She winced when he still glared at her in disbelief. "Somehow, you help me hear," she said, willing him to understand. When he only narrowed his blasted thick-lashed eyes, she offered the best image she could summon. "Have you ever stood outside after a heavy snowfall when all sounds are muffled? No bird calls, no wagons creaking, so that the church bell in the distance rings with perfect clarity?"

Encouraged that he seemed to be listening—or at least hadn't fled—she continued, "You are like that snowfall for me. Your presence blankets unnecessary noise and lets me concentrate on the important sounds. Do you have any idea what heaven that is to me?"

Instead of appearing pleased, his jaw ticked angrily. "You need me to be your *wet blanket*?" he asked in incredulity.

"Wet blanket?" Perhaps the unholy racket in the kitchen prevented her from hearing right.

"Wet blanket," he repeated. "The ones people throw over the heads of horses to keep them from spooking in case of fire."

She opened her mouth, but she couldn't rid herself of the image. She'd been thinking lovely blankets of snow, and he was thinking dirty soggy horse blankets and fire?

"I will not be your wet blanket," he declared adamantly. Without another word, he stomped back outside.

What had just happened here? Now that she knew she had some chance of joining the real world, she had been counting on him to help her. She hadn't expected flat rejection. No one had *ever* refused her requests—and certainly not behaved so rudely. She *needed* the wretched man. He hadn't even given her time to explain why this was so important to her.

Stupid tears sprang to her eyes. She might be hopelessly unskilled in communicating, but he was being deliberately obtuse in understanding. He *knew* what she meant. He had to. Why wouldn't he help her?

"That's the wrong tactic to take with Will, I fear," Sir Pascoe said from a doorway behind her.

Flushing that this humiliating argument had been overheard, Aurelia swung around. Her host was leaning one shoulder against the door jamb of the cluttered abbey office. She wanted to flee and hide her tears and frustration, but she couldn't help asking "Why?" with a plea that made her cringe.

"First, you need to understand Will. It's not as if *he'll* tell you anything." Pascoe nodded toward the office, gesturing her in.

With any other man, she'd be nervous when he closed the door behind her, but Bridey's husband was a diplomat who knew how to create privacy and a sheltered space where she might have a chance to think straight.

She could still hear the shrieking argument in the kitchen and the nurses soothing the infants along with the rumble of all the other voices Will had muffled, until he got angry, anyway. But the journal-lined walls at least dulled immediate sounds, and she gratefully accepted the chair he offered.

"What is there to understand?" she asked in puzzlement. "He's helped me until now. What did I say wrong?"

"Until now, he's been *rescuing* you," Pascoe said, pouring her tea from a steaming pot on the desk.

"He has not," she said indignantly. "He's been rescuing Rose."

He shrugged. "What you just asked had nothing to do with Rose. You asked him to be your tame lap dog."

"I did not," she said in outrage. "I would never think of him that way." Lap dog, indeed! A man who could knock down and truss up kidnappers, tear down doors, and still carry a child with tenderness—*lap dog*? Never.

"That's because you're not seeing through his eyes." Taking a seat, Pascoe pressed his fingertips together in a steeple and studied her over them. "First, I must point out that if you are not interested in Will, in particular, and simply need a protective companion, then there is no reason to discuss this further. My nephew is a man with a mission, and I will not help you distract him from it if all you need is company to keep you amused."

A man with a mission. Aurelia swallowed. She'd never met a man with a mission before, although she supposed her father and brother came close, but she sensed Pascoe was correct. Will meant to save the small pieces of the world that touched him—as she could not. Still, she did need Will in *particular* for protection. How could she explain that? Will certainly hadn't understood. And if Pascoe had overheard their conversation, apparently he did not either.

"I do not understand," she admitted. "I apologize, but it's hard to think with so much noise."

Now that Will had apparently left the vicinity, Ashford's bellows echoed down the stone corridor, and the twins squealed in mock horror loud enough to sound as if they were in the room.

She winced, and Pascoe immediately looked concerned. "I apologize. I sometimes forget what Will calls your *disability*. Let me restate this. You are accustomed to every man of your acquaintance falling all over themselves to do your bidding, are you not?"

She wrinkled her nose in distaste but nodded. "Although I usually only ask them to do things so they'll go away," she said honestly.

His mouth curled up at that. "But you don't want Will to go away? Why is that, do you think? And if you give the wet blanket explanation again, I'll tell you the same as he did."

She rubbed her temple and tried to think, but the answer wasn't in her head, it was in her heart. She simply didn't want to admit it. "Because I can hear him," she said in a whisper. "He hardly ever speaks, but when he does, I *hear*. Only my father and Rain can reach me like that."

He sat back in surprise and studied her. "You are hearing me now, aren't you? How is that different?"

She rubbed her temples and tried very hard to concentrate. "Because what you are saying is important, I think. If the noise grows any louder, or you start mouthing platitudes, I may start turning you off at any minute. But not with Will. I hear every word he says, no matter the circumstances, just like normal people must."

She couldn't admit how refreshing and wonderful that was, because she couldn't exactly say that was the only reason she enjoyed his company. She craved his presence for many reasons, few of which she could say aloud.

Pascoe grinned. "You could have any nobleman in the kingdom at your feet with the wink of an eye—and you are interested in a man who trains dogs because you can *hear* him? Or because he says what you want to hear?"

Aurelia laughed wryly at that. "He seldom says what I want to hear. We argue as often as we agree." And then she lit up with excitement. "Because he *argues* with me! No one but Rain and my father will do that."

"Malcolm perverseness," he said with a chuckle. "But if you're telling the truth and honestly want Will, then you'll have to change your approach. My nephew will never fall on bended knee and do your bidding. In fact, he will run as fast as he can in the opposite direction. He is probably packing right now. I fear if you must seek this misalliance, *you* will have to pursue *Will*."

Shocked, Aurelia nearly spilled her tea. Steadying herself, she sat back and sipped while she tried to comprehend what he was telling her. When she thought she did, she didn't know how to respond. Pursue Will? As her suitors pursued her? Was a *misalliance* what she wanted?

She certainly hadn't considered it until now. She shouldn't consider it. Her father would kill her. Or Will. Or Rain would join in, and they'd both die.

"It never occurred to me that a lady might pursue a gentleman," she murmured, stalling for time as she thought about it.

She had thought she only wanted his company. Did she really want Will in *that* way? It was a truly shocking notion, but perhaps not as shocking as it would have been before their kiss.

"Let's look at it from this angle—Will talks to dogs, not people." He looked at her expectantly.

She frowned. "I don't understand. He talks to me."

"Exactly," he said in triumph. "And that's the reason we're sitting here now—he talks more to you than any other person I've ever seen. He's interested in you, and he doesn't want to be. Which interests me." He added more tea to his cup while he formed his next words. "It may not seem like it, but we Ives look out for one another. We have to. Like your Malcolm relations, we're too different to fit in anywhere as comfortably as we do with each other."

"Is that why so many of you marry into my family?" she asked, curiosity stirred.

Pascoe shrugged. "Possibly, but that's not the point. The point is, Will doesn't feel as if he fits in anywhere, not even with his family, which means he has no one to talk to at all. He's younger than all of us but Jacques. He had a mother for longer than any of us, which meant he had another home where he truly belonged, so he didn't have to put up with our depredations. Having another home made him painfully aware of the difference between the estate of a marquess and his mother's rural inn."

"Did the rest of you have wealthy mothers?"

He added a thimble of brandy to his tea. "Not particularly, no, but the rest of us were too young to be aware of status when we were abandoned in the dog kennel that was the Ives nursery. The difference didn't stop there, though. Those of us raised from infancy at Iveston were tutored from a very early age. We competed as fiercely in the classroom as the playroom. Theo learned to show off by naming every star in the sky. Ashford followed his father around and learned how to balance books and calculate the harvest before he could drink milk without spilling it. We competed on *everything*. If Ash excelled at Greek, I beat him at Latin. Erran learned both. Even baby Jacques, once he discovered the library, was reading at four and could quote Shakespeare at six."

"And Will?" she asked uncertainly, realizing she never saw him with so much as a news sheet in hand.

"Will couldn't read when he first came to us at seven. Although he was already as large as any of us, the tutors kept him in the nursery with baby Jacques while the rest of us went off to school. He seldom spent much time in the schoolroom even when we were there. Before his ninth birthday he was crawling out the window and down the vines. We'd find him training sheep dogs half a dozen miles away. His father, the late marquess, finally sent Will off to Harrow with me and Jacques just so he didn't have to track him down."

"Harrow?" she asked, simply because every man she knew had gone to Eton.

Pascoe shrugged. "We're the bastards. Ash and his legitimate brothers were at Eton. I'm the same age as Ash, so I didn't see much of Jacques and Will when they arrived at school. I daresay you haven't met Jacques yet. He doesn't look like an Ives. He's small and fair and clever. Will spent their first year at school breaking noses of the boys who wanted Jacques to fag for them."

"And getting sent down in consequence," Aurelia said, trying to grasp all he was telling her.

"On the contrary," Pascoe said with a laugh. "The threat of being sent down forced him to offer to study harder so he could stay and look out for Jacques. So he *can* read. He's simply slow at it. After a while, the school kept him on just because he excelled at all sports."

"That sounds perfectly normal to me. My little brother Teddy is more athlete than scholar. I don't understand."

He waved his teacup in dismissal of that comparison. "There's almost a twenty year age difference between your little brother and Rain. They don't have to compete. But in our household, we were all born within eight years of each other. Will was bigger than all of us except Ash, but in schooling, he simply couldn't keep up. Besides that, he talks to *animals*. He spent more time in the barn than in the house. None of us thought anything of it until we met the Malcolms, and Will realized he's not only big and dumb but peculiar."

"He's not dumb!" Aurelia cried in shock. "He is the very last thing from dumb that I can imagine."

"Dumb, as in non-talkative. But the fact is, Will doesn't *fit* anywhere. In no manner does he fit into your elevated society, so *he* will never pursue *you*. My suggestion is that you leave him alone and find another companion, unless you're truly interested in more. What do you want?"

Will. She wanted lonely misfit Will. And she shocked herself to the core to admit it.

Thirteen

WILL ACTUALLY liked his half-brother, the marquess, when they were working together in the fields—not when surrounded by the glitter of fashion in formal salons. Unfortunately, now that he had a wife, Ash dressed like a gentleman and spent more time in politics than the country, so they had less in common. Will felt like a peacock strutting into the abbey salon in his most formal coat and the wretchedly tight trousers that made sitting down a conundrum.

"Yonder, what light awaits?" Ashford called the instant Will entered.

Will assumed it was one of his brother's Shakespearian quotes and didn't even bother glancing his way, not when Lady Aurelia was bearing down on him.

While the others pointed out Ash's deliberate misquoting of the bard, Will feasted his eyes on the kind of dream he'd never been allowed.

Garbed in a shimmering gold-and-white gown, her white-blond hair stacked to make her look taller, Lady Aurelia had outdone herself this evening. Her gown belled fashionably above her dainty ankles, revealing high-heeled slippers. Will had to physically drag his lascivious gaze from her feet to meet her eyes, but the high globes of her breasts diverted him. He felt like the veriest schoolboy, unable to control his all-encompassing lust.

"You are just in time," she told him, enveloping him in a luscious scent of roses and leading him toward the grouping near the fireplace while he was too distracted to flee. "We have decided to send Bess north to Bridey's brother, but Rose is too distinctive. She will have to come with me."

Will wanted to protest that she was making herself a target, but her cloud of seductive perfume held him enthralled, and the brush of her gown against his damned tight trousers sent what brain he had into hiding. He'd have done better to take his puppy and ride straight to Iveston than to ask Ash for anything.

"Aurelia can ride with us," the marchioness promised before

Will could drag his gaze from the fairy princess to greet his sister-in-law.

Christie, Lady Ashford, was a beautiful, sturdy young woman who could stand up to Ash on his worst days. Childbirth had added a few pounds, but she carried them well. That was the kind of woman Will wanted—one who wouldn't break in bed. Except he didn't want one who expected castles and abbeys. Miranda suited—or she had, until he'd been distracted by a fairy princess.

"Rose will ride in the baggage cart," Bridey continued, as if Will were part of the conversation and not a fencepost. A slavering fencepost. "We're to have a pretend funeral for Bess and the babe. The abbey has its own graveyard, and they're digging a hole as we speak. We've locked the door of the infirmary and placed a funeral wreath on it."

"Then it's all settled," Will said with relief, finally grasping their charade. "I'll return to Yatesdale."

"Not quite, little brother." Ashford slapped him on the back hard enough to make most men cringe, but Will was used to it. He elbowed his bully of a half-brother to make him back off.

The elegant lady on his arm watched them with interest, and he was ashamed of his childish behavior. "What do you mean, *not quite*?" he asked, not because he wanted to know but because he didn't know what else to say.

Erudite Erran would have spouted a speech of protest and twisted everyone to his way of thinking. Will could only walk off, and he couldn't even do that right now. The lady had him pinned to the floor. He was more aware of her presence than he was of a dog's mind when he was inside it. Any more of this, and he would howl like a wolf and hump her.

"The Lords rejected the Reform Bill," the damned marquess said, as if that meant anything to Will. "The duke is staying in town a while longer to discuss strategy, which means Lady Aurelia and her sisters are still vulnerable to the cad who may have taken advantage of their invitation earlier."

"Assuming this Pseudo-Crockett, as Sir Pascoe calls him, is pursuing *me*, I must lead him away from my sisters," Lady Aurelia explained.

That woke Will with a jolt. He shook off her hand and glared at her. "That's ludicrous. The cad won't go near your father. He'll head straight to Castle Yates for easier prey."

"I plan to have a ball," she said, smiling so brightly she could eclipse the sun. "And you're invited. So are all the other gentlemen who were under our roof."

"The very best part," Bridey said, interrupting before Will could explode, "is that Lela will pretend to be overcome with a catarrh and be confined to her chambers in the townhouse, away from all visitors. Emilia's mother, Lady McDowell, will plan the ball without her. She has a daughter who is brilliant at designing ballrooms, so no one will question."

Will came down off the ceiling to regard the ladies with suspicion. "And what will Lady Aurelia really be doing instead of hiding in her chamber with a non-existent illness?"

"Well, we hope once Bess is safe, she'll send us the name of her husband and the man who attacked her," the fairy lady at his side said. "Although even if she doesn't, we can continue looking for a family situation similar to the one Bess described. We already have letters out across the kingdom, and I have given Ashford the guest list my sisters sent, so he might look into them."

"You can't do a thing even if you have the scoundrel's name!" Will roared.

Pascoe and Ash grinned at each other. Will wanted to smash their faces together. They were always plotting, and he was always the butt of their plots.

"The lady can *hear*," Pascoe reminded him. "And apparently, she needs your *help* to hear clearly. So as her suitors come to call with posies, the two of you can listen safely from another room while they're kicking up their heels in the salon, waiting to see if she'll come down for them."

"If you establish regular calling hours," Lady Ashford added with obvious delight, "one or the other of the family will be around to draw them out about their situations."

"Rain will hate it," Lady Aurelia whispered, before adding with a hint of mischief, "It will be good for him."

"You are all insane," Will said flatly. "I'll take the pup to Iveston on my own, then ride back to the castle to finish training the dog. The rest of you can play pretend magic all you like."

"I would go with you and read their auras, but my students and teachers are arriving this week," Bridey said as if Will hadn't said a word. "I need to stay here. We can't risk drawing Lela's suitors back to the abbey and the twins or to her sisters. London is the only way."

"If we had any way to lure them to our townhouse, I could test them," the marchioness said, "But it would look awkward for me to sit in the duke's salon, nursing Alan. So we have to reserve my abilities for the time we've narrowed our suspects, and Ash can invite them over."

The women's soft, insistent voices combined with their rustling silks and seductive scents to spin Will's head. He glared at his uncle and brother, knowing from their smirks that they'd planned every step of this. He could walk away. He owed them nothing.

"Please, Mr. Madden?" Lady Aurelia asked. "We've worked well together these past days. I don't know how to investigate any faster. We simply can't leave a murderer loose."

Will wanted to say the wretch hadn't murdered anyone, but it had been near enough. Next time, he very well could. And having children kidnapped. . . He had the urge to snap more bones.

"Didn't you receive a ransom note while we were looking for the girls?" Will demanded, his stomach sinking even as he opened the door to the preposterous scheme.

Pascoe produced a folded paper wrapped in a handkerchief from his pocket. "It simply demands his son back. The rogues we caught can't write."

"But it could be an example of the culprit's handwriting and might have his scent." Will snatched the linen-protected paper from his uncle, finally finding a reasonable side to this bedlam.

"You could train Ajax in the city," Lady Aurelia purred in a tone that was downright seductive for her, taking his arm as if he'd agreed to her insane proposal. "I'll send for her, shall I? Father will be most pleased to have a guard dog for my sisters when they come to town in spring."

Will clenched his molars. The duke's recommendations provided half his income these days. He didn't *have* to please him, but he preferred to. Would the duke be more displeased to find Will in his daughter's company or if he abandoned Aurelia and ran away?

Will didn't need the duke's opinion. He knew his own. Running away wasn't what he did, not anymore. "Does your father have a kennel in town? A stable of his own? I won't be prancing through a duke's palace with dogs."

Ash and Pascoe both smirked. The conniving marquess was the

one who spoke. "Pascoe's townhouse is unused. You and your new pup can bed down there. We're the same size. I'll have my valet clean out my wardrobe of last year's clothes so you don't look as if you just stepped off the farm with shit on your boots."

His wife poked him for his crudity. Will would rather smash one of the pretty vases on the mantel over his brother's head. The only thing keeping his—clean and polished—boots on the floor was the lady's hand on his arm. Well, and the knowledge that Pascoe's house, like that of his half-brothers, had limited staff with low expectations of a family who had been raised like a pack of uncivilized wolves.

Besides, training Ajax for town was an interesting challenge.

"I'm not sitting around salons sipping tea," he warned. "Wet blankets belong in stables."

AURELIA STOOPED down and let a tearful Rose hug her neck while Bess was spirited away in a wagon under the shelter of night. Emilia's miraculous healing abilities had helped Bess recover sufficiently to be moved when any other woman would have been dead by now. They needed to see that she stayed alive for the sake of her children.

Bess had stayed tight-lipped and unyielding, even while she was hiding after her mock funeral. Aurelia had to pray she'd keep her promise and tell Bridey's brother who her abuser was once she arrived in the north. Bridey and her brother had pigeons that could carry word even quicker than the post, if necessary.

Rose tapped her chest and pointed at the departing wagon. Aurelia thought her heart would break. She imitated the gesture in reverse, pointing at the wagon and then tapping Rose's chest. The girl smiled, apparently reassured that her mother loved her. At least, that's what Aurelia hoped she'd said.

"She needs to learn to read and write," Will said gruffly.

He'd come up so silently, that he'd startled her. From beside him, Ajax happily wagged her tail.

Holding Rose's hand, Aurelia stood to face him—or his loosened neckcloth. She had to tilt her head to study his expression. He'd gone to Castle Yates to fetch Ajax and deliver notes to her sisters and

Addy. She'd sent a message to her maid to follow in a baggage carriage with her trunks on the morrow and had expected Will to accompany them.

Will had evidently opted not to stay the night at the castle overnight. He'd apparently worked off his anger, though, and didn't seem quite as peeved with her as she'd feared.

"She knows her letters. I'm trying to teach her words," she told him. "But how does one sound out letters to make words if she can't hear?"

He wrinkled up his brow as if considering the problem. "Does she have to hear them? Can't you just write G-O-D and point at Ajax?"

She laughed at his interpretation of a dog's placement in the heavens. "I'm trying, but two words she can almost say are 'bad' and 'man.' If I point at you, do you want to represent all of mankind?"

"Better than representing all forms of bad, I suppose," he said with almost a smile.

Just the simple curve of his lip had her pulse pounding, and she realized he hardly ever smiled. She really didn't know this man. She had no idea what made him smile—and she was mad enough to *want* to know. She had to decide if her wishes were worth the trouble she would cause.

Aurelia hated to make him frown again, but she knew more about Rose than anyone here. Most would dismiss her as a child, at best, and a deaf and dumb one, at worst. But Rose was quick and clever—and a witness to her mother's beating. "Do you think there is any chance that the false Crockett might believe Rose a danger to him? Could the kidnapping have been a message to Bess?"

There it was, that formidable frown again, creasing his wide brow. The sun had lightened the strand of hair that fell in his face, the one he pushed back now as he studied the little girl. "Without knowing the man, it's impossible to say. But the fact that he hired vicious rogues willing to abduct children doesn't bode well. We probably ought to send her to Iveston and away from your suitors."

"She'd be surrounded by strangers. I hate to do that now that she knows us. The nursery is at the top of my father's townhouse. You can be sure my father's servants won't let strangers near it. We'll remove her the night of the ball, perhaps."

She could tell he didn't like it, but Rose could be the daughter of nobility. Besides, she really couldn't survive a workhouse or be abandoned with strangers, not any more than the infant could. If naught else, she couldn't allow a villain to inherit their rightful places.

"Bess could be lying about everything," he pointed out. "I don't want you to be hurt if Bess turns out to be someone's mistress out for revenge."

"I can't think like that. Rose is a clever child and needs special help and it doesn't matter who her mother is." She waited defiantly to see if he objected, but he merely nodded acquiescence.

"It should be entertaining hearing you explain that to your father, but I'd feel better if she was within our sights too. Do you know how far away I must be to. . . *muffle* your noises?" he asked with trepidation.

She wasn't very good at pursuit. She wanted to demand that he stay by her side, but she feared he'd flee if he thought they must be together continuously. She wasn't much accustomed to considering how others felt, she realized. She really had been wrapped in batting too long.

"I don't know," she admitted. "I don't wish to make you uncomfortable. Perhaps we could test it on our journey south?"

"You'll be in the berlin with Lady Ashford. I'll ride at different distances. Perhaps you could signal with your handkerchief out the window if the noise becomes too unbearable."

She nodded, dissatisfied with the distance he insisted they keep and her inability to attract this man as she did others.

She could lie, she supposed, watching as Will strode off on his own pursuits. She could tell him he had to be close. But what if he really wasn't interested in her? How much of a fool did she wish to make of herself? Worse yet, how much trouble would she bring down on his head with her silly fantasies?

Fourteen

WILL WAS accustomed to traveling with a simple change of clothes, his horse, and a dog. Normally, he enjoyed the road.

The journey to London with a duke's daughter, a marquess and his family, their assorted wagons, and servants was not normal by anyone's standards.

Ash's eyesight was recovering from an earlier misadventure, but he'd learned to enjoy riding with the coachman. That left Will in the company of the grooms. Lady Aurelia's maid and baggage wagon had joined them, and Rose was happily sitting beside Addy, the lady's maid, holding her recuperating terrier. Not wishing to exhaust the duke's young mastiff, Will let Ajax and the new deerhound pup travel with the baggage. That gave him the freedom to ride ahead, except then he couldn't see the lady's handkerchief if she waved it—which meant he spent a great deal of the day riding in the dust at the back of the train.

The best he could conclude was that she was fine as long as he was in sight of the carriage because the handkerchief never waved. Which actually irritated him. If he was to be made into a comforter to cosset a lady, he wanted to at least know he was needed and not enduring this nonsense for nothing.

By the time they reached the inn they meant to stay in for the night, he was too grumpy for engaging in idle converse. He took the dogs down and set out to scour the inn for the scent on Pascoe's ransom note. That was a task he understood.

Finding the inn clear of the villain's scent, Will bedded the dogs with the horses and headed for the main tavern and food. Before he had time to assuage his irritation, Ashford waylaid him in the corridor and dragged him into the private salon with the ladies. Being practical Malcolms, they hadn't changed out of their modest travel clothes for dinner, but they had washed in perfumed soaps and fixed their hair with ribbons and sparkles. Will didn't know whether to growl or turn tail and run.

"I haven't had time to wash up," he protested as Lady Aurelia and Lady Ashford looked up with smiles at his entrance. "I stink."

"Will adds that little extra that makes a dinner table special, don't you agree?" Ash said, pounding him on the back and shoving him toward a chair.

"We're writing lists." Lady Aurelia ignored the quarrel and greeted him with a smile of delight.

Will could bask all evening in the glow of that smile. He sat.

Lists were of no interest to him. But he ate, let them chatter, and just drank in the enchantment of the lady's excitement. In her home, she had always appeared aloof, as if she existed on a higher plane above mere mortals. He now knew that had something to do with her weird hearing. Apparently her lists and his presence distracted her enough from the inn's noise that she could be herself. And that self was a lively mix of laughter, mysterious smiles, and a rather wicked hint of humor.

"Mr. Ives-Madden, are you listening at all?" she asked as the servants cleared away the main course and delivered apples and cheese. "Does my hearing come at the cost of yours?"

He peeled an apple, sliced it, and handed her a segment. "I'll listen when you have something to say that I need to hear."

She perched there, a glistening golden bird on a bough far from his reach, but bearing the audacity of a hawk. With nonchalance, she addressed the powerful marquess who made Parliament thunder and grown men quake. "I know your brother is the son of a marquess and was raised to be a gentleman, but he's lived too long with his hounds. May I have your permission to swat him when he misbehaves?"

Lady Ashford choked on her apple, but Will's lordly half-brother merely sat back and grinned. "I'll give you the switch, shall I?"

"And I shall call him Will, because it is much too difficult to catch the attention of a hound if one uses his full designation." She bit delicately into the apple and regarded him over the table through laughing blue eyes.

Will wasn't much at flirting. He'd tried a time or two in his wayward youth, but he'd found it was just as easy to give women a smoldering look and let them do the talking. This lady didn't seem interested in smoldering looks or poetry or flattery, which was fine with him. So what the hell did she want?

"Does that mean I should call you Lela?" he asked warily. "Because you don't hear the full title?"

"He barks! I like it. Yes, please, call me Lela." She pushed a neatly scripted list at him. "This is all the information we have on Bess and her attacker. Can you add anything we've forgotten? Did Farmer Brown or the kidnappers give you any further description of Crockett?"

Will's gut clenched as he glanced down at the gibberish she shoved at him. If he concentrated hard enough, he could probably unweave the letters and make some sense of them, but handwriting was even worse than books. So he just followed her spoken lead. "They both said much the same. He's a tall man, lean, rangy, raw-boned, dark hair, wore expensive boots but didn't look or speak like a gentleman. I doubt he's one of your suitors."

Lady Aurelia—*Lela*, Will savored the name—took the list back and jotted more notes on it.

"We must look at grooms and valets," she said excitedly. "I couldn't imagine any of my suitors being so brutal, but his paid servant. . . That's a very real possibility."

"Gentlemen can be brutal," Ash admonished, speaking from painful experience.

The lady winced and glanced at him apologetically. "True, but the guests at our house party tended to be men who need my dowry or my father's support. They have titles, but they could not afford boxing salons or expensive stables. At most, they are politicians who spend their time in smoky clubs. At worst, they are dandies and not men who understand fists or weaponry, or so I thought, anyway."

"That's a very cynical vision for someone who doesn't even listen to her callers," Will chided, uncertain why he did so.

She shrugged her dainty shoulders, and he thanked the heavens that she wasn't wearing a revealing evening gown. Her generous bosom distracted him with the slightest movement. He was a dog.

"The number of men considered eligible for my hand is limited. I've known their families since childhood. Their advantages have been discussed endlessly by my sisters and friends. Just because I can't concentrate on their inanities when they speak doesn't mean I don't know who they are."

Will suspected she made lists of their advantages and disadvantages, if only to force herself to focus on such a momentous decision as marriage. He almost sympathized with her plight. Almost.

He turned to his brother, who knew every aristocrat in the kingdom. "You have seen her list of guests? Do any of them resemble Crockett's description?"

"You need to attend occasional social functions so you meet them on your own," Ash said, reaching for the last slice of cheese. "There's a whole younger lot of bachelors out there now. I don't know them."

And lately, Ash hadn't been able to see them well. Will swallowed a sigh of aggravation.

"I need to feed Alan," Lady Ashford declared, pushing back her chair. "I didn't grow up in Lela's circles and can't be much help identifying anyone either."

Ash leapt up to assist her from her chair.

"Would any of the grooms back at the castle be able to recognize him?" Lela asked.

Distracted by the question, Will cast his thoughts over the duke's stable hands. "I doubt they can read. I'd have to ride back and ask. But if this Crockett was acting as your suitor's valet, we'd also have to ask the house servants."

"I'll have my sisters talk to their maids and start making inquiries. It will give their idle minds some occupation." She made another note.

The door closed after Ash escorted his wife out, and Will was suddenly, vividly aware that they were alone. Lela's white-gold head bent over her endless list. Her seductive scent teased his nostrils. And he dared drop his gaze to the linen she wore tucked into her bodice to conceal the assets with which nature had blessed her. Envisioning the elegant white globes beneath, Will felt his cock stiffen, and he hastily shoved his chair back. "We'll be leaving at dawn if we're to make London by nightfall tomorrow. I'll see you back to your chamber."

She glanced up in surprise. "Oh, I didn't think we were attempting to make the city so soon."

They probably weren't, but Will couldn't manage another night like this one. "We still haven't ascertained how far away I must be so you can sleep easily." Knowing the etiquette but out of practice, Will strode to her side of the table and held the back of her chair, waiting for her to rise so he could move it out of the way.

Instead of rising, she sat back and smiled teasingly up at him. "It's impossible to wave a signal at you if you're out of sight."

He had all he could do to drag his gaze from the inviting temptation of moist pink lips. Was the woman insane? Didn't she know better than to taunt a dog in a manger?

He dragged the chair from the table without her aid. "I'll stand in the stable door and you can wave from your window." He grabbed her elbow and almost heaved her from the chair.

"My, we are in a hurry." She picked up her list, carefully folded it, and tucked it into a hidden pocket. Standing toe-to-toe with him, she tilted her head back to meet his eyes directly. "I've been told I can have any man I like, but that's not entirely true."

Will blinked and took another step backward. But she was still too close. He need only put his great clumsy hands around her waist and. . .

She continued as if his head hadn't spun off his neck. "Until now, I've only been able to choose among the gentlemen my family finds suitable. Their taste is evidently not mine. I intend to explore further afield, if I am able. Will you help me?"

Damn, but there was an opening big enough to run a bull through. And he couldn't take it. Wanting nothing more than to savor those taunting pink lips again, he offered his coat sleeve. When she didn't immediately accept it, he yanked her hand through the crook of his elbow, then opened the door so he could breathe again.

"No," he said coldly, unequivocally. "I am not your play toy, your servant, or your footstool. I am here to help you find a would-be killer, nothing more. Beyond that, you're on your own."

She ran to keep up with him as he strode toward the staircase. "You are an extremely thick-headed man, William Ives-Madden."

"I am a man gifted with strong survival instincts. Do you want your father and brother to kill me?" he asked in anger.

"I am of age," she said indignantly, stomping up the stairs ahead of him, if ladies as delicate as she could be said to stomp. "I have my own income. I could set up a house by myself, if I so wished."

"But it would have to be on an island so you wouldn't hear voices," he finished for her. "I cannot help you there."

"You could, but you have just refused. So perhaps I should start shopping for islands."

"I have a cousin who will gladly help you shop. He's a bit of a pirate and in the Caribbean now, but maybe he could recommend someone."

They reached her bedchamber door. She glared at him. Her heart-shaped face and long-lashed eyes weren't designed for glaring. She looked like a petulant toddler. Will fought a grin.

"I had wanted to find a husband who would let me be *useful*," she said in fury. "But now I see it would be far better if I learned to be useful on my own. Good-night, Mr. Madden."

She swung around and entered her chamber, slamming the door in his face.

Will thought he'd just been reduced from Will Ives, brother of a marquess, to Mr. Madden, the dog trainer again—where he wanted to be, right?

THE NEXT EVENING, the berlin took on fresh horses and traveled at a brisk clip to reach the gas-lit city streets before dark, leaving the slower baggage wagons behind. Will was torn between staying with the carriage or the wagons, ultimately deciding that he needed to take Ajax around the duke's property before he could be positive the lady and little Rose were safe.

Outside London, he took Ajax from the cart so they could travel ahead. At the duke's townhouse, he let the dog scent the kidnapper's note before walking around the circumference of the city-block-sized home. He let the servants know the berlin wasn't far behind so they could prepare the fires. He had the dog check all the shrubbery. While servants ran to help Lela and Rose from the carriage in front, Will headed for the mews and the duke's private stable in back.

The gaslights were lit and the duke was just emerging from the stable when Will and Ajax trotted down the alley. Tall, slender, with graying blond hair, the duke of Sommersville looked weary as he noted their approach. He removed his tall top hat and ran his hand through his still-thick mane, then petted the dog when they reached him.

"Is there trouble at home?" His Grace asked, frowning.

"Lady Aurelia decided to come to town," Will said evasively, not wanting to reveal anything the lady didn't wish to tell him herself.

"Ajax is such a smart animal, I thought it might be useful to take her training up another level."

"That's a diplomatic response," the duke said with a snort, heading for the back gate. "Come on in. We'll let Lela explain."

Going inside the duke's palace and listening to his daughter was the last thing Will wanted to do. "I'm staying at Pascoe's. If you'll tell me if you prefer the dog stay here or with me, I need to let his servants know I've arrived." Not that he expected Pascoe to have left anyone but his elderly housekeeper in charge, but Will wanted to establish that he had other places to go.

"Nonsense," the duke said dismissively, opening the back gate usually reserved for servants. "Ajax needs to learn the household. I'm eager to find out how you dragged my daughter out of her tower."

Descendant of one of the more eccentric Malcolm women, the duke was purportedly a healer, like Emilia. But the true mark of his heritage was that he disdained aristocratic formality for expediency, one of the many reasons Will liked working for him. Still, if a duke invited him inside, only a prince could defy him.

Gritting his teeth, Will entered the towering paneled corridor running down the center of the house. Unlike other mansions of this size, this one had not been created by knocking out walls of adjoining townhomes. It had been designed and built from the ground up as a palace fitting for a duke. Another of the duke's ancestors had been infamous for his architectural madness, but this place was of more modern vintage and even sported interior gas lamps.

Servants were bustling up and down the back stairs. They didn't look startled at the duke's arrival through the rear door but accepted his hat and redingote as if it were a normal event. They did appear a little surprised by Ajax but the duke was holding her collar. Will, they ignored. He looked the part of dog trainer in cap and tweed, and they didn't recognize him otherwise.

As they reached the front of the house, the duke asked a footman to find Lela, then proceeded into a book-lined study where he poured a brandy for himself and Will. Ajax settled happily on the warm hearth.

"Does this mean Ashford has returned to town?" His Grace asked, settling into his desk chair and gesturing for Will to sit.

Avoiding the upholstered wing chairs with delicately bowed
legs, Will chose a sturdy leather settee. "Your daughter traveled with
Ashford and his lady, sir. Ash is eager to take the bit again, I believe.
With your permission, I'd like to take Ajax around the perimeter of
the interior, learn who belongs here and who doesn't."

Perhaps he could escape before Lela came down. She'd have to
settle Rose in the nursery, and then dress for dinner or rest after the
exhausting journey. He couldn't drink the offered brandy on an
empty stomach, but he made a pretense while waiting for an excuse
to escape.

"Of course, of course, after dinner," the duke said with a
dismissive gesture. "We keep city hours here of necessity. The
sessions run late. I'm ready to hand the lot of horses' asses back to
Ash. I'm too old for this. I don't suppose you've ever considered
politics like that other brother of yours? He's good. We need more
men like him."

Will petted Ajax and tried not to swear. "No, your grace," he
said, reminding the man of their differences in station. "Erran is the
erudite lawyer in the family."

"Has a way with words, no doubt about it. But sometimes we
need men who can knock heads together, although I suppose that's
not your way. You Ives tend to be more cerebral. Ah, I think that's
Lela now." The duke stood at the soft shuffle of slippers in the
corridor.

Will thought the lady may have inherited some of her acute
hearing from her father. He'd only just caught her scent. He rose
too, wishing he could be anywhere else but here. *Cerebral*! He was
the one Ives who was anything but cerebral. Knocking heads
together was exactly how he liked to solve a situation.

Lela entered still wearing her travel gown, although she'd shed
her pelisse and hat. She flung her arms around her father and kissed
his cheek. "Well met! I feared you wouldn't arrive until late. I have
so much to tell you!"

She spun to greet Will. "Unless you have told him, of course?
You're doing an absolutely marvelous job of suffocating voices. I can
almost hear myself think!"

Will had no reply for that. He nodded and waited for the duke
to take the lead.

"Shall you tell me over dinner? Especially this bit about

suffocating voices," the duke asked, hugging her with obvious affection. "You must have just arrived."

"Will you stay?" she asked, looking at Will.

How did he say no? She was this shimmering field of pure light and energy, and he could no more resist than a moth could a flame. He couldn't even remember why he should say no. He did remember, however, that he wasn't dressed for a formal dinner. Sighing with relief, he managed to utter the empty phrases he'd heard his loutish brothers use as excuse, "I am still in my travel dirt, my lady. I need to retire to my uncle's home and raise the servants."

She waved her hand dismissively, as a fairy would her magic wand. "Don't be foolish. The baggage wagon is carrying your things as well as mine and won't arrive until morning. Ashford should be home now. We'll send a footman over to collect the clothes he promised you. I'll have Mrs. Brown show you to a room." She petted Ajax's head. "One where you can easily take out the dogs if you must, although we have servants who will do it for you."

She rang for the housekeeper before Will could open his mouth. Any of his brothers would have found a way out of this trap, but he'd never been quick with polite lies.

Since the duke appeared to approve of his daughter's suggestion, Will followed the housekeeper to his doom.

Fifteen

FEELING LIKE a conquering general who had just routed the enemy troops, Aurelia dressed triumphantly for dinner. She'd persuaded the very stubborn Will Madden to stay in her home! She probably ought to think about why she found this exciting, but no man had ever excited her before, and that was reason enough.

She checked to be certain Rose was settling into the attic nursery with a maid who claimed to have experience with little ones. They'd had to leave the puppies with the baggage wagon, and the child was sad about that, but interested in her new surroundings. Lela left her with a stack of picture books and dolls.

Addy was still with the baggage wagons too. This meant Lela's wardrobe choices were limited. If she were to take this quixotic journey of pursuing Will, she had to decide if she wished to continue overwhelming him with glamor—or let him learn there was more to her than appearance. Not a difficult decision.

The evening gowns she'd left here were from several seasons ago, but Will would never notice. Unfortunately, the only ones she'd left were the off-the-shoulder bodices because they were too chilly for Yorkshire, but she had a lovely shawl she could wear over the pink crepe. The skirt was only slightly belled and the drape very Grecian, so it was reasonably simple.

It showed her ankles, however, and she was vain enough to remember Will noticing the last time she'd worn the new style. So, she wasn't a Puritan. She wore her laciest stockings. He couldn't fail to notice her hemline, and she thrilled foolishly at the notion.

Perhaps Will wasn't a proper suitor, but she should be allowed to enjoy the same thrill as her sisters at the possibility of practicing her womanly charms. Dinners had always been a horrible ordeal before. The freedom to enjoy herself was invigorating.

She called in a maid to finish fastening her bodice and to affix bows in the curls above her ears, but she merely fixed the mass in back in a low Apollo knot fastened with a jeweled comb. She wasn't at all certain how a modest country lady dressed for dinner or if she wished to know. So she dressed to suit herself.

Amazingly, she was nervous. Once the maid left, Aurelia closed her eyes and tried to pick out the various voices forming a low background hum in her head. The maids who had seen Will were tittering in excitement. The footmen weren't very verbal unless they were flirting or complaining, which they didn't have time to do this evening. Her father was speaking to his valet in a low voice. She didn't know if he understood how much she could hear if she tried, but his tone was normally moderate.

What was so amazing was that the city noise wasn't causing the pain and disorientation she usually suffered. With Will in the house, she didn't notice the cries from outside, or any of the drama inside. She'd always felt miserably exposed, trapped by the four walls of a smaller house, surrounded by city streets on all four sides. Her chamber windows overlooked a quiet, tree-lined park, but it was usually filled with people. If she looked out now, she would see them hurrying to their destinations, shouting greetings or hawking their wares. But at the moment, the usual cacophony was bearable.

She didn't think Will understood what a miracle this was. Might there be other men who could do the same?

The dinner bell rang before she could gather her thoughts. Her eagerness to see Will and see how he would present their story to her father told her a great deal, but she would examine those feelings after she'd seen how Will behaved in her father's presence.

Unlike her usual suitors, Will wasn't waiting anywhere, ready to pounce on her for the honor of escorting her to dinner. She was almost disappointed, then realized in amusement that she probably ought to find him and lead the way. But she had confidence in his problem-solving and tracking abilities. Maybe he'd let Ajax lead him.

Entering the drawing room, she found Will and her father already there. Will held a snifter of brandy and leaned against the mantel, obviously wearing one of his brother's exquisitely tailored evening habits. The marquess had been wrong about their sizes. Will's muscles strained at the seams of the silk. He had no valet and so had merely wrapped linen around his throat, letting it drape to cover his shirt, and knotted a black band around it to hold it all in place. With an alluring hank of goldish hair dangling over his bronzed brow, he looked uncomfortably elegant.

Lela tried not to glance down at the form-fitting trousers, but she was a country girl. She couldn't resist. Mr. Ives-Madden was a supremely well-made man—wearing boots to dinner.

Will straightened, bowed stiffly, and did his level best to keep his gaze fixed on her face. She swung her skirt, and his gaze dropped to her ankles. She nearly chuckled at her newly-discovered feminine power.

Her father topped off his snifter and greeted her entrance with a nod. "There you are. I thought we'd have to dine without you. My man tells me you have installed a child in the nursery?"

That successfully opened the conversation. Lela took her father's arm into dinner, since Will didn't offer his. She did nearly all the talking. Will had said he did not like to explain himself, and he was true to form. He was a most—*ungentlemanly*—man, but she noticed he added quiet details that seemed important to her father when needed. And his imperturbable composure muted any drama in the servants' hall as well as the cacophony out in the streets.

By the time she was finished relating their reasons for being here, her father was looking to Will for solutions. She ought to smack them both for that, but it wasn't as if anyone had ever expected her to be useful before. They couldn't be blamed for overlooking her now.

"It takes weeks to plan a ball," her father said to Will. "Surely you'll find this monster before then. I don't see a good reason to use Lela as bait."

Will lifted his wine glass and tilted it in her direction, giving her the floor. She beamed at him. He actually sipped the wine. She'd noticed he normally didn't.

"We cannot wait helplessly hoping someone will recognize the cad or Bess's situation," she said in the tone she used to pull her unruly sisters into line. "Bess needs to be returned to her children, and they deserve to be brought up and recognized as their father's namesake. You really must meet Rose. She is adorable, courageous, and clever. If I cannot help her, I am a wart upon the face of the earth."

Will spluttered his wine. Her father grunted.

"This session is likely to drag into eternity. I suppose giving people an event to look forward to will keep everyone from falling asleep," her father said, grimacing. "You've certainly not cost me much in bringing you out over the years. If you're prepared to deal with the consequences. . ." He glanced up with more interest. "Is this what you meant by *suffocating voices*? You are no longer bothered by your headaches?"

"When Mr. Madden is about," she said demurely.

Her father raised his eyebrows to regard Will, who finished off his wine rather hastily.

"Interesting," the duke grumbled. "You should send for your sisters. They will be up to more mischief otherwise, although I shouldn't reward them for their abominable behavior in inviting those curs behind my back."

"All respects, your grace," Will objected, "but I'd rather not have to guard three ladies running about the shops at once."

"Is that what you're doing here?" her father asked. "Guarding my daughter?"

"Training Ajax to do so," Lela corrected helpfully. "Mr. Madden will eventually have to leave for his next position."

"Exactly. As long as that is understood. Give me a list of the reprobates invited to the house party. I'll have my man look into them." The duke gestured for the servants to clear the table.

Knowing she was being dismissed, Aurelia rose, curtsied her departure, and withdrew to the next chamber. She picked up a book she'd left lying about and sat down to listen to her father interrogate Will. She wasn't at all certain her father understood how well she could hear his conversations.

"I hired you because I thought my daughters would be safe around you," her father said.

Will's reply was impossible to hear, drat the man.

"Well, see that it stays that way. I've let Lela come out of her shell at her own pace, but now that she seems to be doing so, she needs time to gain some town polish."

Again, a murmur, probably of agreement, double drat the man.

Her father changed topics in a manner that indicated he was satisfied with Will's answer. "Did your brother say anything of his plans for bringing more of the backward asses to comprehend that we'll have a revolution if they don't give up their damned rotten boroughs?"

Triple drat the man. He'd probably reminded her father that she could hear every word he said if she put her mind to it.

How was she to pursue her interests if her father kept reminding Will to stay away?

How did she go about encouraging the insufferably stubborn man to act on his interest in her that he tried to conceal?

And should she? That fear left her nibbling her lip in indecision.

AURELIA DISCOVERED it was easier to hold Will's interest if dogs were involved. The day after her arrival, after consulting with Lady McDowell, Emilia's mother, about creating a ball in a short time, she had the afternoon to herself. She wouldn't establish calling hours until the invitations had been sent. That left her to suggest that she walk the dogs with Will around the homes of her various suitors.

"Just give me their direction, and I'll do that," he said gruffly over luncheon. "I don't want anyone recognizing you."

She could always count on him arriving for meals if invited. She thought he might have gone to his uncle's this morning—the noise levels had been particularly difficult while she spoke with the McDowells. He had returned wearing a coat that wasn't tweed, and a neckcloth that almost looked starched.

"Other than the men we met at inn, I doubt any of the gentlemen who were at the house party would recognize you," she told him. "So if I conceal my face and we wear servants' garb, no one will realize we're anyone at all. It will be exciting to finally see the city without feeling as if my ears will explode!"

"You've never seen the city? Been to the shops or parks?" he asked warily.

"I've tried," she said with a shrug. "I can only manage a few minutes at a time, though, before I go catatonic or stark, raving mad. I like concerts, though," she said, when he started frowning. "The music blends all the discord into a more harmonious hum."

He couldn't deny her after that, she realized with triumph. The poor man rescued *everyone*. Even from themselves. Her admiration for him knew no bounds.

Addy had arrived with the baggage, so after luncheon she had her maid create a costume suitable for walking the street in disguise. The crude wool skirt, coarse petticoats, and bulky bodice covered in an apron from the kitchen sufficed to hide her figure. An enormous bonnet with a long bill hid her face. And in exchange for a pair of Lela's old slippers, a maid gleefully offered up her old heeled work boots, thus creating an illusion of additional height.

She met Will in the kitchen garden, where he waited with Ajax and his own leashed pup. The young deerhound leapt all over her in excitement, and Aurelia sent Will a look of amusement. "Did you tell him to do that?"

She thought she almost detected a smile.

"We like the disguise," was all he replied. "You need a box of flowers to sell."

He'd returned to his tweed and buckskins with a crude cap pulled down to his eyes. With the enormous Ajax straining at her leash, Will looked the part of a rich man's groom out taking a dog for a walk—except he was much, much too large for a groom. He couldn't disguise who he was much better than she could.

"I had my father's secretary write out a list of addresses of the men at the house party." She handed it to him, but he didn't take it.

"I don't spend much time in London," he said, opening the garden gate. "I've enlisted one of your father's footmen to accompany us." He nodded at a tall young man in livery at the end of the mews. "Give the list to him, and he'll lead the way. We'll saunter along behind as if we've nothing better to do. I told him to take us through Hyde Park, though, so you can have a little less street noise."

So much for adventuring on her own. She may as well have brought Rose.

With deliberate provocation, Lela caught his arm and leaned intimately against him. "We'll be a newlywed gentleman farmer and his lady come to town, shall we? Show me the sights, dearest."

She could almost feel the shock rippling through him, and her spirits soared. She could *do* this. She could be a normal female flirting with her gentleman caller. She simply had to make the gentleman realize *his* part in her play.

Sixteen

WALKING WITH a duke's daughter through the streets of Mayfair to Hyde Park as if he belonged in the neighborhoods of the wealthy and powerful made Will's hide itch. Or it could just be Lady Lela digging under his skin. She was wearing the scent of roses again today, a more sensuous aroma than her innocent one of cakes baking. He tried to call up Miranda's face to replace the one at his side, but for the life of him, he couldn't even recall the color of her eyes.

The lady stood taller than usual in her ugly boots. The top of her head was at his shoulder, and he was irrationally aware that he need only bend a bit to kiss her. Indeed, if they were truly playing the part of newlyweds, he could do so now and she would have no right to protest.

He suspected she *wouldn't* protest. Will feared she was using her feminine wiles to entice him for reasons only she could understand. He wasn't an arrogant man, but he could think of no other explanation for her current behavior. He had to make it clear that despite the pleasure of working together, he could never be available as anything other than an escort for her safety.

Once they left the crowded thoroughfares to enter the park gate, Will pried her hand off his arm. "Yesterday's test of my usefulness showed that I could ride behind a few carriage lengths. We should see how you fare in the city. Walk ahead with your footman and the pup. Use your handkerchief signal if the clamor starts hurting."

Not that there was a great deal of noise in the park at this hour on a drizzly day, but carriages rolled, people talked, dogs barked, children played.

She regarded him with a miffed expression, but raising her adorably proud chin, she trudged ahead, walking his pup. The footman had been told to head straight for the nearest address and stay slightly ahead of them. Will wasn't too worried about the lady's suitors popping out of the shrubbery to molest her. But a woman alone was prey to more scabrous rascals. That's why Will had the dogs with them.

She stayed on the paths. He wandered further afield, always keeping her in sight but increasing the distance between them. He topped a grassy knoll a few hundred yards away without any signal. She was approaching a hedge near the Serpentine, when he noticed her hesitate, as if debating whether to pull out her handkerchief. He jogged down the side of the hill and realized the reason for her pause.

A large ruffian in rags had come between the lady and the footman, blocking her path.

Will slipped the knot on Ajax's collar and sent mental messages to both dogs. The deerhound on Lela's leash began yipping, causing the footman to turn. And the mastiff practically took flight across the field, howling in a far more menacing manner.

Instead of acting, the footman merely stared in horror at the two dogs and the ruffian. Lela wisely released the pup's leash and backed off. Running, Will couldn't hear if words were exchanged, but the pup went for the rogue's ankle—and the huge mastiff leaped on his back, tumbling him to the wet grass.

When the rogue produced a knife, Will almost had a heart attack. Both pup and Ajax were within striking distance of the weapon. Hurting one of his dogs would kill Will almost as surely as if the knife had been driven into his own hide.

To his utter shock and admiration, the lady kicked the knife-wielding hand with her heavy boot, sending the weapon flying.

Will crowed in triumph. He wanted to hug Aurelia for her courage and dance her around in relief. But his responsibility was to the animals first. He mentally ordered them to dig their teeth into the man's bulky coat sleeves. He didn't want to teach them to bite humans unless necessary, but this one needed to fear for his wretched life. By the time Will reached the little party, the footman had gained enough courage to approach and put his boot in the middle of the thief's chest while the dogs growled ominously.

With the scoundrel conquered and knowing no other way of expressing himself, Will scooped Lela up and hugged her. She flung her arms around his neck and clung, trembling. *Damn.* The incident had frightened her more than he'd thought, given the courageousness of her action. And it was all his blamed fault.

"You were marvelous," he murmured, encouraging her as he would the dogs when they'd acted as they ought. "You did exactly what you should have."

"I wanted to stomp his face," she whispered ferociously from beneath her hat's veil.

He chuckled. Her response was much better than a dog's. And she definitely felt better in his arms. He didn't want to set her down, but they were drawing a crowd. He kissed her cheek—as his assigned role allowed him to do. "No stomping in front of all these people. Give me a minute to leash the dogs."

Those blindingly blue eyes gazed up at him in awe for just a moment, making him feel like a giant, and then she released him and stepped away.

Will whistled at the dogs. They growled a little more but reluctantly released their victim. He ordered them back to Lela. Then, as the thief tried to gain his feet, Will nodded at the footman. "He needs to be taught a lesson. Grab his other arm." Will leaned over, caught one chewed coat sleeve, and hauled the wretch to his feet.

Ignoring the nearly incoherent curses from the drunken rogue, Will and the footman dragged him to the river and flung him into the reeds. The small crowd that had gathered cheered.

"Pretend I'm tipping you for your help and go on ahead. We'll meet you at the gate," Will told the footman, handing him a coin. The footman winked, lifted his cap, and strutted away.

Several gentleman were engaging Lela in conversation about the dogs. With his only goal to drag Lela out of here, Will tied Ajax's leash again. Even in disguise, she attracted attention.

"Sirs, my lady is shaken, that she is," he said in a rough country voice, keeping his cap low to conceal his face. "Let me take her back to our rooms. Thank you for all your help," he said, without adding the irony to his tone that the useless idiots deserved.

Catching Lela's waist, Will tugged her after the footman. "We can take the near gate and go down the street back to the house," he murmured as they left the crowd behind. "I should never have brought you out without an army around you."

"I don't want to go back to the house," she said in alarm. "I'm not hurt. The noise seemed to grow louder if you were at a distance, but not so much that my head aches. Let us go on! The dogs were marvelous. Did you do that?"

He almost stopped to glare at her but instinct said to keep moving. The thief's cries were growing dimmer. If the sot could manage to drown in three feet of water, the world would be a better place.

"You were just assaulted in the park," he argued. "You're still shaking. Are you mad?"

She punched his arm with the hand not wrapped around his elbow. Astounded, Will shook his head to clear it. The gentle lady had *punched* him!

"I have been sheltered from real life for too long," she said, almost angrily. "I had no idea thieves existed in Hyde Park! Call it part of my education. I didn't faint, did I? I wasn't harmed. I'm allowed to be a bit shaken. And I kicked a thief! I want to learn to be the protector instead of the protectee!"

"I'm quite sure there's no such word as *protectee*," he grumbled. He was no expert at arguing, and if it had been anyone else but Lady Lela, he would have agreed with her. "Your father will take off my head."

"I shall tell him I gave you no choice. Does your puppy have a name?" she continued, as if one topic had anything to do with the other.

"Deerhound." He knew he sounded surly, but he didn't like the position she placed him in. He was a dog trainer, not a security blanket for rebellious ladies.

"You don't name your dogs?" she asked, apparently not objecting to his tone.

"I train, breed, and sell them. What is the purpose of confusing them when they'll be named differently later?"

"Because they need to know who they are," she said indignantly. "I shall call this one Hero, to match Ajax."

Will hid his smile at the outlandish name for the useless pup. "Hero he is, then. We've arrived."

He nodded toward the footman waiting at the gate—and the man he'd asked to meet them there.

"All hail the conquering hero," Jacques called, striding toward them.

The lady snickered. "Hero and the Conquering Hero," she murmured.

Blond, shorter and slighter than any other Ives, Will's half-brother dressed the part of dashing man-about-town in caped redingote and beaver hat.

"Jones here says you're still up to your old pursuits, heaving villains into the drink." Without stopping for breath, Jacques bowed grandiosely before Lela, doffing his tall hat, and said, "My deepest condolences, my lady, on being reduced to the company of ill-bred dolts like my brother."

The lady glanced at Will with amusement curving her luscious lips.

Will rolled his eyes. "I will refrain from flinging the wretch into the nearest drain unless you request it," he said, hoping she might consider his suggestion. When she merely waited for explanation, he sighed. "Lady Aurelia Winchester, may I introduce Jacques Ives-Bellamy, my youngest brother."

"My pleasure." She offered her mitten-covered hand as if she were dressed in silk and standing in a reception line instead of looking like a ragged denizen of the slums.

"The disguise is adorable, my lady," Jacques enthused. "You need only a feather bobbing from the bonnet to divert attention, because no one with eyes in their head could believe you are any other than one of the finest ladies of town."

With a sigh, Will grabbed his brother's neckcloth and lifted his feet off the ground. "Stop slavering. I asked you here for a purpose. Get on with it."

The lady giggled, actually *giggled*. Will sent her a look of equal exasperation. "Don't encourage him. He hangs about too many thespians until he thinks he's one of them."

Jacques nobly waited to be returned to his feet before responding with a punch directly to Will's midsection—which didn't hurt Will at all but probably cracked his brother's knuckles.

Wincing, Jacques turned his back on Will to address Lela directly. "I have gone over your list, my lady, and marked those most likely to meet my clod of a brother's description of circumstances."

Lela glanced at Will questioningly. He didn't appreciate having to explain, but he owed it to her. "Jacques is a playwright. He knows everyone who attends the theater and everyone with coins enough to invest or fund his work."

"I know their financial status better than a banker," Jacques continued with relish. "And as Ash's relation, I'm granted access to all levels of society. I'm far more interesting than Farmer Will here. Shall I take you around and introduce you to more entertaining people than normally tread the hallowed halls of a duke's residence?"

Lela laughed and squeezed Will's coat sleeve. "I would love that, but only in Will's company. What can you tell us of the men on my list?"

Will fought an urge to swell with importance that the lady preferred his uncouth company to Jacques' far more polished presence. The lady was *using* him, he reminded himself.

Jacques' expressive features formed a moue of disappointment. "Know that I am always at your disposal, my dear lady." He pointed at the first name on the list, the one Will had ascertained as the nearest to the duke's residence. "Lord Rush lives with his mother the next street over, but you waste your time on him—starting with, *he lives with his mother*. He's a baron, near forty years of age, a fine supporter of the theater and several of. . ." He glanced at Will. "How would you like me to explain his predilections?"

"Illegal," Will offered succinctly. "And if he does not court ladies, let us proceed to the next on our list." He feared Lela would question him later, but she wisely held her tongue now. He liked that in a woman.

Jacques waved the paper. "None of the ones around Mayfair will be who you seek. We're assuming the man you want is short enough of coin to steal a babe's inheritance. That sort would be unable to afford this area. There are two names that might qualify, Clayton and Baldwin. Baldwin lives over in Richmond. It's a respectable area, but you'll need a carriage and a few hours to visit. Clayton has rooms in the City, where no lady should go. Neither of them have feathers to fly on. You should send Will and his mongrels to sniff them out."

"I have a carriage at my disposal," Lela replied eagerly. "I have always thought Kew Gardens charming and would love to explore Richmond."

Jacques sent Will a sympathetic look. "Sorry, old chap, I did my best."

So much for keeping the lady home. Will shrugged. "I appreciate it, thank you."

Lela smiled in delight, so that even Jacques looked stunned in her glow. "It was a pleasure meeting you, Mr. Ives-Bellamy. I shall be sure to send you an invitation to my ball so you may raise funds all you like. You've been most helpful, even if your brother is now growling like one of his mongrels." Lela made a full curtsy in her clumsy woolens.

Jacques laughed, offered more of the flummery ladies liked, and took himself off under Will's glower. The tall footman waited at the corner of the park, as instructed. Will was taking no chances with the lady's safety.

"I know I cannot go into the City," Lela said, following Will's lead in the direction of home. "I'm not sure taking Ajax there is wise either. But we can easily go to Richmond tomorrow. I don't wish to sit idly about, doing nothing."

The old City walls encompassed the Fleet Street and Whitechapel areas near the Tower, an all-male bastion of bankers, lawyers, and other criminals not welcoming to ladies. Will was heartily relieved that he didn't have to argue with her over going there. He would take Ajax to search for scents, but he didn't hold much hope of finding any in streets that crowded. "A visit to Richmond seems safe enough," he agreed reluctantly. "Although it might be simpler to wait until your family can report back on Lord Ballwin's situation."

"I can ask anyone about Lord Baldwin's family situation," she said with a shrug. "Except coming into a recent inheritance or having an older sibling who married badly is no proof of guilt. But if the dogs can recognize his scent, that would be proof enough to investigate further."

"It should be quieter in the countryside," he agreed. "And perhaps safer for testing distances between us. I haven't tried determining how far I can be from the dogs before I cannot speak to them, so that's another experiment we can work on.

She tugged his arm until he halted, then stood on her toes and pressed her delectable lips to his cheek. "You are a man among men, Mr. Madden, thank you."

He was a lust-riddled degenerate going up in a pillar of flames, that's what kind of damned man he was.

Will nearly carried the lady back to the house so he couldn't molest her.

LELA POUTED when Will didn't stay for dinner, but with her father nodding his approval of Will's leave-taking, she couldn't say a word. Instead, she inquired if the duke's secretary had had time yet to peruse the rest of the list of guests at the house party. A duke's secretary had information even the Malcolm ladies might not uncover.

Her father dismissed her request with a wave. "We're up to our necks in political quagmires. As long as you're safe now, it can wait."

There was a villain on the loose and Bess needed her children and her home, but Lela bit her tongue on the protest. Her father had the concerns of an entire nation on his desk. Hers would have to wait.

She had spent the early part of the evening with Rose, attempting to teach her the sounds of the alphabet. Picture books helped. Pointing at an image of a dog, then at Tiny, and then at the letters made a visual connection. And Rose happily hunted through books looking for the same letters elsewhere. But it was a slow process and required a patient teacher.

Since Rose could almost pronounce *bad* and *man*, Aurelia worked with those as well, finding an image of a knife-wielding pirate and writing Bad Man underneath it. Rose laughed and grasped the concept fairly quickly, running down the picture gallery later and assigning *Bad Man* to half Lela's ancestors wearing cloaks and swords.

She knew she should be satisfied with her day's work, but she was still awake late that night, watching out her window for some sign that Will might have returned. He had no reason to, she acknowledged. He had his own life, his own family, and probably a willing woman elsewhere.

Lela felt like Rose, locked in a world from which she couldn't escape, except where Rose's world was silent, hers was filled with cacophony.

She knew the instant Will returned, even though she couldn't see him. The distant din of arguments and drunken laughter gradually died away. Carriages rolled on cobblestones but their rattles were miraculously muted. She noted the time so she could ask him later how far away he might have been at that hour.

Relaxing for the first time since he'd left, she climbed into bed and wondered what it would be like to have him join her there—in every sense of the word.

And how in the devil could she bring about such an impossibility? Will was right in that—her father would kill him if she chose to lie down with a dog trainer.

Seventeen

"IT'S RAINING," Will stated flatly when Lela came down for breakfast the next day.

Lela noted her father had already left, so she was free to tease. Having the freedom to think clearly was such a relief, that she couldn't resist. "Let me see. . . The rest of that statement goes: *It's raining, we can't go to Richmond or you'll catch your death of cold,*" she suggested.

"It's raining and your coachmen will catch a death of cold," Will retorted. "And there isn't any chance of the dogs catching a good scent even if our villain just passed by."

She couldn't argue the point. But she had reason for wishing to be out of the house. "The ball invitations went out yesterday."

He looked at her blankly. "I don't believe I can complete that thought for you."

She laughed and fluttered her lashes just to see if he was in the least susceptible to her *wiles*, such as they were. She thought the bronzed skin stretched over his cheekbones might have become a little ruddier. He turned to the buffet to fill his plate.

"That means my guests will start calling," she informed him. "Today, we have assigned to accepting calling cards. I am not officially at home. So there will be no one on whom to eavesdrop. Tomorrow, I am to develop my catarrh, and Aster is to take my place in the salon, accepting callers. She often has interesting insights, but I do need to be in the house to overhear conversations."

He set his plate down on the end of the table furthest from her. She really wanted to kick the recalcitrant man.

"And so today is the only day you can go out and play. Did I finish the sentence correctly?"

She beamed. He applied his considerable attention to his plate, refusing to look at her. She hoped she wasn't being vain by counting that as a score in her favor.

"You are trainable," she acknowledged solemnly. "I've been told there is a teacher at an orphanage school in Battersea who is teaching her deaf daughter. How difficult would it be to travel there?"

He appeared to be considering as he chewed his bacon, then washed it down with coffee. "With the new bridge, it's less distance and safer than traveling to Richmond. Does your orphanage have a place where your coachmen can stay while you gossip?"

She wanted to roll her eyes and say they were servants, paid to stay with the coach in any sort of weather, but she realized that he was probably baiting her with their differences. "If it's not too distant, I can ride. I won't melt any more than my coachmen will," she retorted.

This time, she thought she detected a twinkle in the wretched man's eyes when he deigned to turn and notice her. "Find an unmeltable groom to go with us. Erran and his bride live in Battersea, and we can leave our horses in his stable."

"You have to work at being disagreeable, don't you?" She picked up her tea and ignored him for the rest of the meal.

She didn't know why the aggravating man fascinated her so, but she was inexplicably thrilled to be spending the day in his company—almost alone.

Other than wearing her veiled hat, she had no good way to conceal her identity in a riding habit, but Will didn't appear too concerned when she came down in her fashionable outfit with only a pelisse to conceal it. Rightfully so, she judged, as they rode into the heavy traffic crossing the Westminster bridge. Who would notice her in this mob?

They'd left Rose safe in her nursery and even left the dogs behind for fear of their being trampled. Surrounded by wagons, carriages, riders, and pedestrians, they rode down the main thoroughfare, following a direction Will seemed to know. She smiled as she realized he was humming as they rode along. Along with his muffling presence, the sound soothed her.

Lela had met Lord Erran on numerous occasions since his family and hers were related by politics as much as distant ancestors. His wife Celeste, however, was fairly new to London. A striking woman with skin tinted darker than most, lustrous dark brown hair, and spectacularly blue, almond-shaped eyes, she was the most exotic creature Lela had ever met. And she forgot Lady Erran's looks the instant they began discussing Rose and voices.

"To me, the world is music," Celeste said in her mellifluous voice.

"Siren music," Lord Erran claimed. "She can seduce the multitudes with her voice."

Will snorted inelegantly. "And you drive the multitudes to riot. Rose simply needs to make herself understood in a normal sort of way."

"I wish I could grant her some of my hearing," Lela said with a sigh. "But I am told the teacher uses a hand language that might aid in lessons."

"Aster claims your hearing is so acute that you can listen to people talking anywhere in the house," Erran said, warming his boot by propping it on an andiron at the fire. A typical Ives male, he had swarthy skin, high cheekbones, and thick black curls. "A pity you cannot be an international spy. Or even a domestic one, for all that matters."

Lela shrugged. "Will would have to go with me. Otherwise, I would go quite mad. I have been unable to visit London for any length of time because of the constant cacophony inside my head. For whatever odd reason, only Will's presence makes it bearable. Which is why I must do everything I can while I am here, before I'm forced to return home."

As expected, Lord Erran and his wife exchanged glances. Lela didn't care if they marked her a candidate for Bedlam or sympathized with her plight. She'd accepted her deficiencies. Her challenge now was to overcome them.

"Don't look at me," Will grumbled when his brother directed his gaze his way. "It is probably my empty skull that absorbs the noise."

Lela laughed. "At least you're not telling me it's all in my head."

"I have brothers like *him*." Will nodded at Lord Erran. "I know it's all in our heads. That doesn't mean we can change anything. We simply must test our usefulness."

A footman arrived with a reply to the message they'd sent out when they'd first arrived. Celeste passed it to Lela, who unfolded the formal stationery. "Mrs. Snowden says she cannot leave her post today but would be delighted to help if we could come to her." She glanced up at Will. "It is on the outside of town, but I can't think that Battersea is very dangerous."

"You need only follow the river road to find the orphanage. They've built some rather impressive mills and factories down that way," Lord Erran said, after taking the paper and checking the direction. "The shoe factory alone is ingenious. It's a pity we don't need boots in that quantity now that we're no longer at war. And the mill driven by air... well before it's time, unfortunately. I understand the maintenance was too costly to keep it running. I would have loved to see it. Battersea isn't London. You'll be fine. I have a meeting in the city or I'd go with you."

"And then we'd end up spending the day investigating musty mills and accomplish nothing," Will said.

Rising, Lela sent him a laughing look. "The curmudgeon speaks. We should confine him to *writing* his thoughts."

Erran cuffed Will's massive shoulder. "Dogs don't read, so Will doesn't write."

Lela thought Will flushed, but he shrugged off his older brother's taunt. "I leave the writing to those with naught better to do with their time."

He strode out, ordering up their coats and horses, leaving Lela to say their farewells.

She belatedly recalled the note Will had sent attached to Ajax. She had thought it the result of circumstance. Surely no expensive school would let a student graduate who could not write properly?

THE LADY'S silence as they rode east told Will she was ruminating over what she'd just heard. She would be asking him to write missives shortly, just to test Erran's idiotic jest. Will supposed if he wished to end her unwarranted interest in him, he ought to comply.

He hated the idea.

He was a man of action, not one given to philosophy, so he couldn't explain, even to himself, why he hated the idea of the lady losing interest in him. It was the only sane course, after all. Once she'd accomplished her purpose, she would return to her tower, and he would seek Miranda, as things should be.

In ways, she was as crippled as he was. That didn't make him feel any better.

"The mill and factory really do have quite impressive facades," she said as he rode closer on a wide curve. "It is quieter over here, even though I can hear machinery running."

"Perhaps the machinery provides a blanket of sound that masks other noises," he suggested.

"I should live by the sea, then, shouldn't I? We went once, and I remember the waves being very soothing, like your humming." She nodded at an unprepossessing building on a barren hill. "I think that may be the school."

"Does music have the same effect as the waves?" he asked out of sheer curiosity—and relief that she hadn't asked him about writing. He turned his horse down the rutted lane.

"It does. Lydia's constant practice on the piano is very helpful. I will miss her when she is gone. I would take up piano, except that doesn't help me accomplish anything, does it? One can't sit at a piano and talk to teachers. It sounds as if the children are at play."

Will heard the laughter and shouts in the distance, but he wouldn't have noticed unless she'd mentioned it. Even with his so-called *muffling* presence, her hearing was acute.

Uncomfortable in social settings, Will wanted nothing more than to follow the groom and horses to the rickety stable at the rear of the orphanage. But, as usual, he was caught between his two places in the world. As a gentleman, he had a duty to accompany the lady. He reluctantly let the groom take the horses, then followed Lela. A servant led them back to a tiny parlor so crowded that Will feared crushing stuffy old furniture no matter where he turned.

The teacher was nearly as stuffy and faded as her furniture, well-padded, graying, and standing stiffly until Lela settled on a chair that might once have been blue. An adolescent girl sat on a window seat with hands primly folded in her lap, watching them with curiosity.

Will chose to lurk in a corner by the fire. The teacher introduced herself as Mrs. Snowden and the girl as her daughter, Alicia. The girl stood and made her curtsy at a gesture from her mother, then made gestures of her own, directed at Lela.

"Do you speak French?" Mrs. Snowden asked. "She is spelling out letters in French to say she is pleased to meet you. We are trying to find simpler gestures for English, using words instead of syllables. It would be more crude, but faster."

"But that would mean everyone would have to learn this hand language to communicate with her," Lela said in obvious disappointment. "I was hoping for some means of communication so Rose could make herself understood to anyone."

"Once you establish a means of communication, she can learn to write," Mrs. Snowden reminded her. "Alicia's spelling is still atrocious because it's difficult for her to acquaint the sounds of letters with the words." She used her gestures to show her daughter what she was saying.

The girl made a series of signals. Mrs. Snowden translated, "She is saying that if there is just one other person in the room who can understand her, then they can speak to the rest."

"It looks so very complicated! How did you learn how to do this?" Lela asked.

Will could think of any number of ways a silent language might be useful, but none of them applied to little girls. He held his tongue and listened.

"A religious gentleman in France devoted himself to teaching the deaf. They developed this method of speaking, and it has spread to several deaf schools across the Continent. Unfortunately, we have none here. I had hoped that I might. . ." Mrs. Snowden shook her graying head. "I am too old. I will have to leave my dream to Alicia to accomplish."

Will could tell from the way her eyes lit that Lela was considering aiding that dream. He didn't want to discourage her, but she was inexperienced and naïve and Mrs. Snowden could be a fraud. He stepped in before she could make rash promises. "You should speak with your family, my lady," he warned. "They are accomplished in finding educators and people who need educating. As Bridey has shown you, it's not easy."

"True, I only meant to help Rose," she admitted. "But just imagine an entire school of silent people! It's almost too tempting and providential. I might finally be useful!"

"But you'll remember that Rose isn't silent. What if there are ways to teach her to speak normally?" Will found himself drawn into the discussion against his will.

Mrs. Snowden nodded knowingly. "There are schools that emphasize teaching the deaf to speak normally. If your child has partial hearing, those methods might be more useful to her. It is not an easy subject, and there is much argument among the community as to which is preferable."

"Why not have both kinds of teachers?" Lela asked excitedly.

She didn't even bother correcting the assumption that Rose was their child, Will noted. The lady didn't possess a bit of common sense, or arrogance. If he started looking at Lela as a real woman, and not an unreachable fairy princess, he'd be in true trouble.

The animal in him, the one his mother had warned him of, already considered her as his to protect. He had to quit living like a dog. He'd ask Miranda to marry him as soon as he could safely leave Lela on her own.

Until then, Will kept his distance and tried to behave like an invisible servant as Lela worked with the teacher to learn a few simple hand signs to teach Rose. They gave her a book Lela promised to have copied in quantity. But when he noticed the light from the window growing dim, he had to step in.

"It's late. If we wish to cross the bridge before dark, we must leave now."

Blessedly, Lela didn't argue. She donned her cloak and hat, thanked them warmly, left a donation for the school, and obediently followed him out.

"The old bridge is closer," she suggested, glancing at the gathering fog. "Once we're across the river, the mist won't matter so much."

The old wooden bridge was an unlit fire trap and dangerous when the Thames was high. But people had been using it for half a century. Should they risk footpads in the fog riding through the dark to the new bridge on the far side of town, or take advantage of daylight and crossing quickly to the gas-lit city?

"I wouldn't want to take a carriage across the old bridge, but we should be safe enough with the horses," he concluded. "Just don't stop for anyone or anything."

"I like that you listen to me and don't call me foolish," she said, riding close to him. "Most men want to pat me on the head and laugh."

"I don't pat people on the head," he said, sounding surly even to himself.

She laughed. "You don't come close enough to people to pat them," she said. "Is that because you understand dogs better than people?"

Will considered it. "Not so much, no. It's because dogs listen and people don't, unless I'm saying what they want to hear. So it's not just that men of your ilk think *you* are frivolous and silly so much as they consider themselves more knowledgeable than women and people like me."

In the fog and deepening twilight, he couldn't read her expression, but he caught the surprised turn of her head anyway. That's what he got for trying to explain himself.

"*People like you*? Hard working people? Intelligent people? In what way are you otherwise different from all the idle gentlemen with whom I'm familiar?"

He'd known better than to explain. "Other than bastardy," he said dryly, "I don't dress fashionably. I am not a book or math person. I cannot quote Shakespeare, don't play cards, don't know the language of flowers or fans, and have no interest in learning. I'm at most, a boring farmer who likes to put his boots up at the fire in the evening. At worst, I'm a servant who gets a little above himself upon occasion."

"And you assume because idle gentlemen consider you inferior, that you *are* inferior? Or that this is good reason to write off the human race?" she asked in a decidedly pert tone.

They were almost upon the bridge. Will had just about decided not to answer when Lela abruptly straightened and seemed to be straining to see ahead.

"That wicked, wicked man," she cried. "He's promising her fancy gowns and a choice of men!"

Will had to spin his brain around from their foolish argument to the real world and then translate it through her eyes—or ears, as the case apparently was. "Fathers promise their daughters such foolishness all the time."

"He's not her father. She sounds terrified. She's asking to go back to her mother. He's telling her he's taking her to a lady who has rooms for girls, and she'll be able to see all the sights of the city. He does not sound in the least savory."

That sounded like a pimp furnishing his brothel. The lady shouldn't know about such things. "Don't jump to conclusions," he warned, gesturing for their groom to approach. "Jack, remain with the lady while I ride ahead."

Will saw the Gypsy wagon on the bridge as soon as he traversed the next bend. He had his weapons with him, but he preferred not using them unless he had no other choice. What in hell approach could he take in a matter like this? He was wearing a gentleman's redingote and hat and expensive knee boots. He'd have to behave with the aristocratic arrogance of Ashford or Erran.

He rode up beside the rickety enclosed caravan. Dressed in a shabby cloak and cloth hat, the driver didn't even look up until Will rapped the footboard with his riding crop. "I say there, your door has come loose in back. You'll be losing your contents on those loose planks ahead."

The driver looked undecided about stopping, so Will reined his horse in front of him. He tried not to grimace at the sight of Lela and the groom waiting at the end of the bridge.

While the driver wordlessly climbed down, Will rode around to the rear and slid his crop under the loose bar holding the sagging doors in place. It slid from its rack and the doors fell open.

Will already had his hand on his pistol when Lela suddenly galloped her horse onto the bridge shouting, "He's hiding her in a carpet!"

Leaving the bar down, the driver turned tail and raced for his seat. Taking that as a confession of guilt, Will grabbed a door and swung inside. A muffled scream emerged from a threadbare old carpet on the floor. The knife-wielding old rogue standing over the carpet was of more immediate concern—that and Lela just outside the damned door.

Knife first. The wagon jolted into movement just as Will grabbed for the ruffian's wrist. The jolt set him off balance, and the blade sliced the side of his hand. He still had sufficient grip to twist hard enough to force the scoundrel to drop the weapon. Will kicked it out and grabbed the carpet, tugging it toward the still open door with as much force as he possessed, using the wagon's forward motion for impetus.

The screaming rug hit the bridge as the wagon jolted into motion. The furious pimp leapt for Will, and they both tumbled to the wooden planks. Lela added her frantic cries to the mix.

The groom's shout of "Look out, my lord!" caught Will's attention through the racket.

He'd had the breath knocked out of him with his landing, but he managed to look up just in time to see his assailant wielding a pistol so old, it was more likely to blow off the old codger's hand than hit any target. With his bleeding fist, Will smacked the rogue's arm backward.

The pistol exploded.
And Lela screamed.

Eighteen

AT LELA'S SCREAM, Will leapt for the railing as if he had the bounding abilities of Ajax. He did not. Before he could reach her, his fairy princess tumbled from her horse and over the side of the bridge, into the filthy rush of the Thames. Will howled his anguish and fury like the animal he was.

Without hesitation, he dived into the heavy current after her. His only chance was right now, when he might hit somewhere close before the river dragged her on.

Weighed down by heavy boots and caped coat, he sank fast. Hanging on to what breath he had left, he kicked hard to resurface.

Fighting his clothes and the current, he also fought despair. He didn't have any hope that a sheltered princess like Lela could swim. She was too small to fight the weight of her skirt and cloak. This was why he taught dogs to rescue drowning victims. This was one time he wished to be a dog.

Finally breaking through to the surface, he gasped for air. Flinging his hair out of his eyes, Will searched the night-dark river. He could barely see his own hands in the deepening twilight and heavy fog.

Lela had been wearing a light blue outfit—that was his only hope, light against dark. He fought panic and the deep desire to simply die of his inadequacy now rather than know he'd been the one to extinguish this piece of heaven. But for now, if there was any hope at all. . . He could die later.

A plank rammed his shoulder, and he flung one arm over it. Using the wood to stay afloat, bobbing with the swift moving current, Will hunted for blue.

He needed his dogs. He needed brains that worked instead of ones howling in panic. She had to come up again, didn't she?

Or had the bullet killed her? Anguish wrung another cry from him. If her hearing was acute, could she hear him and know he was near? Shouting, kicking, paddling, he fought the current and terror, not looking to save himself but to find a piece of summer sky in the filth of the river. Surely her cloak had to billow up from the water.

There! He gulped a mouthful of filthy water shouting in relief. A bit of blue—closer to the shore and not in the heavy tide in the middle. Clinging to the plank, Will fought the current, straining every muscle to kick and swim to the shallows. As soon as the blue came in reach, he grabbed a handful and tugged.

Another tug, another mouthful of water, and he had the lady in his arms again.

He held her head above the slapping waves with one arm, while steadying himself on the plank with the other. He wanted to weep but he didn't have time.

He couldn't tell if she breathed. Fighting the water and the drag of their clothes, he held her while he paddled with waterlogged boots. His arm muscles strained and ached as if he fought battles with a galleon. Strength flagging, he couldn't stop the current from dragging them further downriver from the bridge. He made wild incoherent promises to Whoever, while he fought to reach the shallows where his feet might hit bottom.

His boot hit a rock. Or a sunken boat. He couldn't tell. He shoved off the hard surface and pushed the plank with Lela draped across it nearer to shore. She coughed. He swore she coughed. *Thank you and praise be, she was alive.*

He may have wept then. He was too wet to tell. He fought on.

It took an eternity. Keeping Lela's head out of the water, moving against the current, Will was exhausted by the time he found enough solid ground to stand with his shoulders out of the water. In relief, he gathered Lela into his arms and staggered up the embankment.

She was shivering so hard that he feared dropping her in his exhaustion. The fog was thicker now. He could barely make out the shoreline. He just put one foot in front of the other and mindlessly prayed.

He nearly walked into a wall. "My apologies for what I need to do, my lady," he murmured, although he didn't think she could hear him. Wearily, he threw her over his shoulder so her head hung down his back. With his free hand, he felt along the wall, looking for a door, a window, anything. They needed shelter. Not that a little rain could soak them more, but the river breeze was icy.

She coughed harder and stirred. Will kept moving, more urgently now. He had to bring her inside, fetch help somehow. Had the duke's groom ridden back to look for them?

No one would find them in this murk.

Finding a broken window, he used his coat sleeve to knock out the remaining shards of glass and pried at the latch until it gave way. He thanked the heavens that it was a wide double frame that swung inward so he could fit through. Lela was digging her gloves into his coat, and he had to pry them loose to lift her over the sill.

She groaned as he lowered her to the floor. He scrambled inside. "Where are you hurt?" he demanded, terrified the bullet had hit her.

Before she could cough a reply, he stripped off his gloves and tore at her wet clothing. His own hand hurt like seven devils, but he needed to staunch her bleeding first. Women were frail. They died so damned easily. . .

COUGHING WITH every breath, Lela sensed Will's big fingers fumbling with the tiny buttons of her riding habit. As much as she'd once tried to imagine this moment, she felt as if she'd been battered by a herd of. . . fish, maybe. She was soaked to the skin and shivering so hard her fingers didn't work enough to help him.

She tried to recall what had happened, but her mind wasn't working so well either.

Taciturn Will muttered what sounded like prayers as he finally ripped off the rest of her coat buttons and pressed his hands to her shirtwaist, apparently searching for damage.

But it was her *head* that hurt. As much as she liked the heat of his big hands through her soaked linen, she tried to lift her arm to see if her head was properly attached.

"Your head?" he asked in horror, following her hand. "I can't see a bloody thing. We need a fire."

He probed at her skull. She could feel her hair dangling in filthy wet tangles on her face and neck. She'd lost her hat, of course. She winced and yelped as he rubbed a sore spot.

"I can't see a thing," he repeated in frustration. "You're wet all over. If you're bleeding, I can't tell."

She felt him tearing at his own clothes, then he pressed a soggy length of linen into her hand.

"Hold this to your head. I need to see where we are."

Coughing, head pounding, she couldn't think well enough to recall what had happened much less panic. She strained to hear anything, but there was nothing other than Will stumbling about in the darkness. That he was alive and well and with her was enough to ease some of her fear.

They had to be isolated for her to hear almost nothing other than the lapping of the river and the squeak of a few mice. She would shudder at the sound but she was already shaking from cold.

"I found a grate," he called. "There must be a chimney."

"Filled with bird nests," she protested through her coughs. "Do you have magic fire?"

"Better. I have lucifers wrapped in oilskin. The window is already broken to vent the smoke, if I can find kindling."

Lucifers? That sounded dangerous, but a man who traveled had to be prepared, she supposed. She wrapped her arms around herself, but she still shivered hard enough that her teeth chattered and bones shook. Her head felt as if river mud oozed out her ears.

"Books," he said in what sounded like triumph. She heard pages tearing and crumpling.

A moment later, she saw a flame. "You're burning books?" she asked, appalled.

"Old account books as best I can tell." Will's large form loomed out of the darkness, silhouetted by the few flames behind him. "We have to get you out of those wet clothes and I need to look at your head."

Just his presence warmed and reassured her. He lifted her as if she were made of nothing, when she felt heavy as lead. Against his solid chest, she felt safe, and she resisted being set down. She dug her fingers into his soaked waistcoat and snuggled closer.

He actually hugged her tighter, and she could swear her enigmatic dog trainer pressed kisses to her hair. But then he put her down in front of his odd little fire and moved away. Still too muzzy to understand much, Lela studied the tidy little flames. He had, indeed, found a stone hearth and an ancient iron grate. A large account-style book burned steadily above a bed of ashes presumably created by crumpled pages. She'd never been much of an account-book sort. She simply welcomed the meager heat and light.

Fabric ripped and Will cursed under his breath as a piece of metal hit the floor. A moment later he returned trailing a cloud of dusty material that had her coughing all over again.

"Sorry," he muttered, dragging the cloth away and apparently shaking it.

"Where are we? And how much destruction will we have to pay for?" she asked as she struggled to sit up and figure out how to right herself. Was that blood on her shirt front? She didn't feel injured. She patted her front and winced where her stays bruised her ribs, but nothing seemed to be bleeding. She coughed harder.

"Must be one of those old factories Erran mentioned. The place is mostly empty. I don't think they'll miss a few rotted draperies and ancient journals." He returned carrying heavy lengths of cloth over his arms. "You need to take off those wet clothes and get warm."

"Warm would be nice," she said with doubt. "Moth-eaten, flea-ridden draperies, not so pleasant."

He dropped his sodden jacket and sat down to tug at his boots. "Believe me, as the temperature falls, you'll appreciate moths and fleas." He leaned over to examine her head, touching the sore place with gentle fingers. "I feared you'd been shot, but this is barely bleeding."

"I have blood all over me," she protested, glancing down at her white shirt—which she would not take off, no matter how much she shivered.

He leaned over and ripped off her neckcloth and shirt despite her protest, exposing her stays and chemise.

"Will!" She swatted at his marauding hands, then realized why he'd been so clumsy with her buttons. She grabbed his big fist and examined it in the dying light. "You're injured!"

"I'll clean it as soon as I know you're unharmed. You cried out just as the pistol fired." He ran his hands over her, then threw more pages on the fire to raise the flame, adding another volume so it would smolder longer. "I don't see anything except the bump on your scalp."

The intimacy of his touch wasn't easing her trembling. She stopped his hand to examine the raw gash. "This needs to be cleaned! It's deep, and you've had it in the filth of the river. You'll come down with something awful. If you become fevered, we'll have to take you to Emilia."

"Anything but that," he said dryly, picking up the redingote he'd dropped earlier and rummaging in the pockets. He removed a flask from an interior pocket and offered it to her. "Drink. Once you stop shaking, I'll take care of the hand."

Lela grabbed the dreadful drapery and wrapped it around her near nakedness.

"Take off the skirts too," he ordered. "Or you'll be the one Emilia quacks."

"She's not a quack," she muttered, but she understood his reluctance to be hauled back to the abbey for healing. Draped in heavy fabric, she began wiggling out of her riding skirt. "Pour whatever is in that flask on your wound, right now."

"Not until you're warm. I don't know how much is in it." He shoved the flask at her again.

She grabbed the wretched thing and attempted a sip. Gagging, she handed it back to him. "Nasty. Now fix that hand or I'll do it for you."

"There's the high-and-mighty duke's daughter. You must be feeling more the thing." He took the flask and drank from it.

"Clean and wrap, *now*." She took her discarded neckcloth and handed it to him. "And the duke's daughter is cold, wet, and terrified out of her mind," she admitted. "I am so far out of my cocoon that I cannot fathom how anyone survives like this. If it were not for you. . ." She pulled the drapery closer around her. If it had not been for Will, she might not be alive at all. That didn't help her shivers.

"If it were not for me, you wouldn't be out of your safe house at all," he muttered. "This is all my fault. I'll do what I can to make it right."

"Don't play martyr," she said, almost angrily. "We're here because I wanted to do this. You didn't. And I went in the river because I have no experience and did something stupid, after you told me not to. And do not make my head hurt worse by spouting more silliness."

She thought he almost chuckled, but he sank into morose thought again as he poured the whiskey over his wound.

"If this is a Battersea factory, can we find the bridge again and walk back to London?" she asked, dragging information out of him. "Do you think the groom is leading our horses this way, and we might catch up with him?"

"No, no, and no." He wrapped linen around his hand. "The fog is too thick to see where we put our feet. And it's a long, long walk back among rural footpads and the likes of that wretch we left on the bridge. And you can't wear draperies down the road."

"Do you think the groom helped the girl out of the carpet?" she asked, now that he was talking and her head was working a little better.

"If he had any ounce of human compassion, yes, but only if he didn't have a heart attack watching you go into the river," Will said, still grumpy. "The duke will nail his hide to a door for losing you."

Still dizzy from whatever had grazed her head—the bullet?— Lela struggled with the simple task of removing her soaked woolen skirt, while clinging to the dusty drapery for modesty. Not that Will could see much in the meager firelight, but the situation was beyond awkward. Knowing her father wouldn't actually blame a servant for her transgressions, she concentrated on her current predicament and not the poor groom.

Part of her problem was giddiness at being this close to Will and seeing his big frame stripped to wet shirt and under-drawers. While she fought with her own clothes, he yanked off his wet stockings, and his big bare feet held her entranced. Had she ever seen a man's naked foot?

Giving up on her skirt, she worked at her boots, but they were wet and unwieldy, and she lacked the energy to fight. Before she could just curl in a ball and give up, Will loomed over her.

Stripped of all external identity, he was just a man, a large man who ought to be awkward handling her much smaller limbs. But he competently removed her sodden boots as if he did it every day.

To do so, he had to wrap his bandaged hand around her leg. Once the boot came off, his bare fingers lingered on her ankle. The intimate touch thrilled and warmed her more than any blanket.

With his bare hand on her bare skin, the whole world went away.

When he realized what he was doing, he jerked away. Lela boldly caught his arm. "I can't pull the skirt off. And your shirt is soaked. You'll catch your death of cold."

"I can't do this!" he roared, abruptly yanking from her hold and heaving another book on the fire. "I'm not made of wood! If I were, I'd go up in flames right now."

Startled, but just a little thrilled if she interpreted his cry correctly, Lela stood and returned to fighting with wet wool and ribbons. "And you think it's any different for me?"

"It's always different for women," he said in disgust, keeping his back to her. "Men are animals, driven to breed. Women are merely made to lure."

If she wasn't so scared and cold, she'd laugh. "Men are driven to hunt, not breed. I am only a trophy to be won."

He growled under his breath, turned, and snatched at the ties she fumbled with. "One doesn't do what I want to do with *trophies*."

The passion in his tone left her breathless. Will would never quote poetry or write sonnets, but he offered honesty. Lela decided she valued that far more than romance.

Her skirt slid heavily to the floor. They were both garbed only in damp underclothing—transparent linen and muslin that clung and did little for modesty. Lela suspected they both stank of salt and filthy water, but the urge for simple human warmth was compelling.

Words were useless. She simply placed her hand over the linen on his broad damp chest and lightning struck.

He shuddered, as if fighting a force stronger than he. Will was strong, but whatever was between them was stronger. With a groan, he wrapped his muscled arms around her and hauled her against his fierce heat, where she wanted to be more than anything else in the world.

Lela closed her eyes in sheer bliss at having all that heated strength and muscular hardness pressed against her. She'd always wondered what it might be like to linger in a man's arms—it was far more consuming than she could possibly have imagined.

With the blessed silence, she could *feel* more, focus on her hunger for more. When Will bent his head to press his mouth to hers, she responded eagerly, as if starved. She *was* starved, she realized, starved for a human touch, an acknowledgment that she existed as a real woman, and not a *trophy*.

His tongue touched hers, and she surrendered to sensation, wrapping her arms around his neck and holding on for dear life. It was an invasion of the senses, his whiskey taste, his masculine smell, the whiskery scratch of his beard, the toughness of his fingers pressing into her. Going up in flames didn't begin to describe it. She met his kiss and deepened it, savoring the passion.

Will tore his mouth away, gasping and cursing. Before she could protest the separation, he undid her chemise and pushed it down, baring the tops of her breasts above her corset and riding drawers.

"I will regret this either way," he muttered, swinging her around to remove her corset ties.

She moaned her delight at the removal of the stiff stays, then nearly fainted at the sudden rush of blood when Will's big hands reached around to cup her breasts.

He nibbled her ear, and her knees buckled until his arm supported her, with her back pressed to his damp linen and heated chest. She would have pondered the extraordinariness of the sensation, but her mind had ceased to exist. Desire flowed in a hot river from her breasts to the place between her legs.

He lay her on the velvet draperies in front of the fire. She could hear admiration in his voice as he stroked her, but she was beyond hearing words. She grasped his wet shirt and tugged upward, peeling it from his muscled torso.

He obliged, tugging off the shirt and flinging it in a dark corner. In the firelight, kneeling over her, he was a bronzed god. She was convinced no ordinary English gentleman could look as he did. In delight, she ran her hands over hard ridges and taut muscle. The bulge beneath the waistband of his drawers held her fascination, but even though her mind had sunk that low, she was not bold.

He kissed her again, a long, lingering kiss that tormented her beyond endurance because she wanted more, needed *more*.

Propping himself on his bandaged hand, he used the unharmed one to circle and lift and play with her breasts, until they were sensitive beyond measure. Her body hummed with lust. Lela caught at his arms, urging him on, even though she didn't know what she needed.

Then he bent and suckled at her aroused nipple and she was lost. Crying out, she tugged him down, covering his bristled jaw with fervent kisses until he groaned a desire that matched hers.

"We can't do this," he protested, even as he ran his hand from the curve of her waist to her hip.

She knew what he meant, but she didn't want to hear it. "Is it always like this?" she whispered, desperately needing to know.

"Not nearly enough," he replied, applying his mouth to hers again and taking her breath away.

She might find desire again, he was saying, in some distant

future. But why take chances when opportunity arose now?

"Don't stop," she murmured. "I couldn't tolerate it if you stopped."

He sprawled his heavy weight half on top of her, and she felt the thickness of his arousal pressed against her thigh.

She could have Will, she realized. Keep him forever. His honor would allow no less.

All she had to do was be bold enough to reach for that male part of him and urge him on.

Nineteen

WILL'S ANIMAL self warred with the part of him trained as a gentleman. He had heaven in his arms, bliss, relief—and a future he didn't want. One Lela didn't want either, once her head cleared and she realized their predicament.

Knowing he could never be the husband she deserved didn't end his desire, but it dampened his ardor sufficiently to resist her innocent seduction. He grabbed her wrist before she pushed him over the brink of no return.

"Please, Will. . ."

Her plea of protest almost undid him. Instead of pushing away, as he ought, he kissed her again. Her lips were fine silk pillows, she tasted of rich honey, and her delicate perfection ruined him for any other woman. He said a mental good-bye to Miranda as he sank into Lela's kiss, certain it would be the last he'd ever know. The duke could kill him now, and he'd die happy.

Heavy and luscious, her breasts overflowed his wide palms. He greedily shoved her inner chemise down to kiss the tightly furled tips, pink and wet in the firelight. Her moan was sweet music to savor for what time he had left.

His cock pulsed against her hip. Just the thought of the ecstasy awaiting him once he shoved inside her tight heat was enough to craze his mind. He had to do something drastic to end this *now*, but he couldn't abandon her at this point, leaving her dissatisfied and thinking she wasn't the most desirable female in existence.

Her hips rose imploringly, begging for a release she didn't know. *This*, he could do.

Will caressed Lela's beautiful breasts until she moaned and clung to his arms. Then he explored her willowy waist, rode his hand over the full curve of her buttocks, and memorized every beautiful moment for savoring over the loneliness of his future.

Fascinated by the transparent fabric concealing silken flesh, he explored the ridiculously lacy drawers clinging to her long limbs.

Will left his own drawers on as a damp reminder. He tugged the draperies over her enticing legs to keep her warm and prevent the temptation to explore more. But he left the core of her open for his touch. He located the opening in the crotch of her linen and tenderly caressed her lower lips. She shrieked softly and rose against his fingers, proving her readiness.

He rubbed a little deeper and she shuddered. He did too. She was moist and eager, but he couldn't take her like this, not in a million years, even if his cock turned permanently to wood. Any deeper intimacy was reserved for the security of a marriage bed and a gentleman who wouldn't split her in two. All he could do was teach her pleasure.

And so he did. He suckled her breasts, caressed her inner folds, found the bud swelling with desire, and stroked until she writhed and cried out, flung her arms around his neck, and shuddered in the throes of her first release. He lost control like a schoolboy, spilling into his already damp drawers. Having Lela in his arms like this. . . He would never have the words to describe the raw, animal beauty of her sexual discovery.

The dawn would bring the destruction of all his dreams, but it was almost worth throwing away his future for this blessed moment that he couldn't have dreamed of sharing a few short weeks ago.

LELA WOKE TO the comfort of a warm furnace pressed to her back. It was still dark, but she didn't hear rain. She didn't hear much at all. Her body felt languorous and aroused at the same time.

Will had almost made love to her—finally. She might expire of happiness simply thinking about it.

She knew he hadn't taught her the whole experience between a man and a woman. She ought to be relieved that she could honestly tell her father that she wasn't a ruined woman, but she longed to be ruined, to learn more of how he made her feel. She *wanted* to be forced to marry Will.

She was probably quite mad, but then, that's what everyone thought anyway.

If she could only learn to control her gift as the rest of her family did, she might survive without Will at her side. Maybe. She didn't know if she wanted to be parted from him, but she supposed she ought to at least try to be the lady she was raised to be, to help the needy, start the deaf school, do the things her father expected.

She could do none of those things as a dog trainer's wife buried in rural anonymity. It wasn't as if she hadn't lived like that most of her life. It wouldn't be difficult. She simply felt. . . unfinished.

Will stirred, and she felt his arousal pressing against her bottom. Temptation was at her fingertips. She could give up her futile search for usefulness and just be the wife he needed. . . Except he didn't much seem to need a wife. He apparently liked wandering the length and breadth of the kingdom with his dogs, saving lives, training others to save lives. He'd found his purpose, and it wasn't her.

"How do you read dog minds?" she asked, more to distract her wandering thoughts than because she wanted to know.

He grunted. Or maybe it was a chuckle. There was so much she wanted to learn about this fascinating man. Why couldn't other gentlemen be as appealing?

He stroked her bare breast, and the tingle in her middle came alive. Then he ran his hand down to test her drawers, abruptly pushed away, and took his heat with him.

"We should have set our clothes out to dry," he grumbled. He stood and fumbled in the dark, apparently looking for more books to sacrifice to the dying embers on the hearth.

"That meager fire won't dry them before morning." Shivering, Lela pulled the draperies over her shoulders and watched his shadow moving about. "I really am curious about how you can focus on a dog's thoughts. Ives don't leave journals for us to study, but from all I've read and heard, they have this uncanny ability to balance Malcolm gifts. Since you seem to shield me from noise, I thought there might be some connection with your gift."

She heard him crumpling paper and a moment later a flame caught, casting his big frame into shadow. Every particle of her longed to be in his arms again, but she knew his damned honor wouldn't allow it. He didn't even have to explain why he kept his distance. She understood. She hated the distance and wished it could be otherwise, but she wouldn't cause him harm just to have what she wanted.

"I don't know how it happens," he said. "I spent a lot of nights as a child, sleeping with my dogs in stalls. I often slept in the stable when I lived with my mother because she needed to rent out my room. So I was more comfortable in stables than in the fancy beds my brothers used. I started seeing and hearing things the way the dogs did. I didn't think it odd, since they heard and saw the same things I did. It wasn't until they sent me away to school, away from my dogs, that I realized the sharpness of my senses declined."

He was explaining himself to her! Letting her see his difference was a gift greater than any other he could have offered. She had to treat this revelation with the respect it deserved.

"I am trying to relate what you're telling me to what I suffer, but you apparently *like* the acuity and I don't," she said, trying to understand.

"It's not a matter of liking. It just is." He gathered their clothing from where they'd left it scattered across the filthy floor. "When I'm with the dogs, I can choose to stay inside my head or open to theirs. They can be trained to know my mental commands in the same manner they learn voice commands."

"I need to be trained," she said gloomily.

He laughed a little and dropped her still damp attire over her drapery blanket. "The question may be what is there about me that allows you to focus on immediate sounds instead of being bombarded by distant ones."

"You," she said promptly, sitting up and poking at her wet shirtwaist in disgust. Her breasts were daringly bare. Reluctantly, she wriggled into her damp chemise. "I think when I'm with you, I am *focused*, as you say, on you." She heaved her stays at a distant corner and wrestled with her shirt.

"And music, you said." He sat down on a crate and tugged the damp leather of his trousers over his drawers. "And the sound of the sea. If you can focus on a particular sound, would that block the other noises?"

Lela sighed, wishing there was more light so she could see him clearly. If this was the only time she'd ever. . . She couldn't think like that. She needed to *focus*.

"What good would it do me to concentrate on piano music? I might not go more mad from noise, but I wouldn't hear anything anyone said any more than I do now. And my governess would have tormented me for a month for such a circuitous sentence." With a grimace, she finished fastening her shirt and picked up her riding skirt.

"Your sentence made perfect sense to me," he said with a shrug. "If we're communicating what we want to say, why do we need to put boundaries and restrictions on how we say and write the words?"

"We are not discussing grammar. We are discussing my inability to live without you by my side," she said curtly. Now that she'd said it, she was glad of the darkness.

Her bold declaration silenced him. So much for expecting a proposal. She could hear him rustling in the shadows, wrestling with his clothes as she was with hers. They might as well walk out dressed in draperies. No one would believe their innocence after they'd spent a night alone together.

"You've lived for over twenty years without me," he pointed out. "What you want is to live *better*."

"I don't see how I could live worse." Now it was her turn to sound grumpy. "If you walk far enough away from me, I would probably hear my father's men shouting my name, hear half London shoveling coal into their grates, and a dying boar's screams in the forest, if there is such a thing. How can one *think* like that?"

"Whereas I need to have the silence of the country to better hear inside the heads of my dogs. Living in the city is worse for me."

He was telling her she was being selfish. Maybe her good deed was to let this good man go. She wanted to weep and kick her heels and throw a tantrum, but she would *not* force him to live as she did now, just so she could live better.

"Your gift could tell us if we're anywhere near civilization and lead us there," he suggested. "Your gift has its purpose, and I nullify it." He sounded more irascible than reasonable as he stomped his foot into his boot.

She didn't want him to *nullify* anything. She just wanted to be normal. She dropped the draperies to stand and put her feet into her riding skirt. "I need to learn *focus*. How does one do that?"

She took satisfaction in noticing his head swiveled as the drapery fell, exposing her near nakedness.

"By *wanting* to concentrate on something, I suppose. Do you want to hear your father's men on the river? Focus your attention on that." He stood and tugged his shirt over his head.

She could almost see the white of his bandage in the dusky light. Dawn must be close. She closed her eyes and tried to concentrate.

She'd never been much at book studies because concentration eluded her.

She heard Will's clothes rustling, mice scurrying, waves lapping. Those were all close and probably normal, sort of. It wasn't as if she had a good grasp of normal. She closed her eyes and tried harder. "I think I hear men calling. And that could be oars hitting the water. I'm unfamiliar with the sound."

"I'll go down to the riverbank, but the fog is still thick. I'm not sure I can see anything. Keep focusing. Maybe you'll hear better when I'm out of the way." He shrugged on his coat over his wet waistcoat and climbed out the window.

She didn't want him to go. But that was the problem, wasn't it? She had to let him go. She couldn't keep him as a pet forever.

Scowling, she tugged on her own coat while trying to listen to Will's footsteps walking away. More sounds intruded. She could hear birds twittering in what had to be distant trees. She didn't remember any trees growing along the riverbank where the mills and buildings were.

Concentrate on the river. It lapped more loudly now that Will was walking away. They never had measured how far he had to go before he lost his *nullification* ability. But if that came from her focus on him, then he needed to be in sight. She had to quit thinking about a man she couldn't have.

Think of her father's fear, of Rain's terror at losing another sibling. They'd be scouring the riverbank for her body. She couldn't allow them to suffer. If she could just hear the men looking for her and let them know she was alive. . . She knew her father would have sent men out from the moment he received word of her disappearance. She might be addled, but she knew she was loved.

Concentrate on their love, on their fear, on the men in the river. . .

She didn't know if it was because Will had walked far enough away or because she'd conjured the sound from sheer willfulness, but she could hear the calls clearly now. They were frantically shouting her name and Will's. Their emotions were so charged that she thought she almost recognized their voices.

And all the other sounds disappeared. She'd done it, she'd concentrated on just *one* sound.

Amazed and excited that she could hear only the one distant

sound, she wanted to run to tell Will. Tugging her coat around her, realizing her neckcloth was around Will's hand and that she looked decidedly wanton as well as shabby, she climbed through the window into the foggy dawn. Lifting her skirts, she concentrated on the despairing cries, using them to guide her down to the river. She couldn't see Will. She could scarcely see her feet.

The shouts from the river intensified. Did that mean they were closer or she was getting better at this? She wanted to curse her useless gift, but it was her own stupidity that was the problem. Stomping over the muddy bank, she began shouting back. Could they hear her as well as she did them?

Will stepped out of the fog to halt her. "Don't go too far. The bank is slippery. What are you hearing?"

He wrapped his arm protectively around her waist, and she wanted to melt into him, let him take care of her, be all that she was not. That was even more stupid. She straightened and stepped away.

"I can hear men calling our names. Can you not hear them?"

He didn't protest her retreat but tilted his head to listen. "No. I hear only the river. What else do you hear?"

"Too much," she said with a sigh, "and not enough. Now that I'm near you, the cries are more distant. But I'm sure they're out there. How do we signal them?"

"We wait until they're closer and start shouting, I assume. I don't know if I can make a torch of anything in this damp. It's hard to wave a burning book," he said.

"They should have brought Ajax. She'd smell us, I wager. Half the city ought to smell us," she added in disgust, pulling at her nasty coat.

"I don't think they'll be noticing our stench once they discover we're alive. They might drown us later for terrifying them," he admitted, touching on only one of her fears. "Ashford will be having tantrums and demanding the old bridge be torn down and the river paved over."

Lela giggled at this odd perspective of their fates. "That would be an amusing solution to the public sewer that is the Thames. I don't think shipping merchants will appreciate it though." She lifted her head, suddenly alert to closer sounds. "I do believe that sounds like Lord Erran. Do we shout at him or let him go on by?"

"Erran is better than Ashford. He's probably using his mob-inducing bellow. Shout away."

Lela cried, "Over here! By the mills! We can hear you! Can you hear us?" And then she realized if she was using her gifted hearing, that they might still be too distant. She mimicked one of her brother's curses under her breath. "They may be too far away."

"Keep shouting. I'll fetch a stack of books. And draperies. That ought to do it." Will stomped back up the bank, leaving her to halloo into the distance. The voices she heard clearly now did not sound as if they heard her. The desperation in the cries wrung her heart. She had not meant to cause so many people so much pain.

But despite the pain, she couldn't restrain her excitement. She was *hearing* them and not ten thousand other irrelevant sounds— because she needed to hear them. Because she was concentrating on hearing them.

She didn't know how she could apply this lesson to social situations when she really didn't want to hear any of the chatter, but that was for another time. She now knew that when she was desperate, she could concentrate.

She'd probably done that when she'd heard Rose crying in the wilderness and simply hadn't realized she was doing it. She really was quite stupid.

Will carried down a heavy load of books and fabric and laid them in a clearing that should be visible from the river. He crumpled book pages and used one of his lucifers to light them.

Lela kept yelling. She thought the voices were coming closer, but in the muffling fog, it was difficult to tell.

Once the fire flared into a beckoning beacon, Will took her hand. "After this night, I am yours to command. Whatever you need, you must let me know. I do not know how to say it more plainly."

If that was a proposal, it was a poor one. Unfortunately, she understood. It was so strange that this man, so different from any she knew, could speak to her as no other could. She squeezed his warm fingers. "I will be fine. My father is not an ogre."

He offered no reassurances but turned toward the river and added his cries to hers.

"They hear us," she murmured in wonder. "I can hear them shouting in excitement. They just haven't seen us yet."

Will bent and planted a hasty kiss on her mouth, one that had her knees buckling all over again. "You are a gem above all others. Never forget that."

She barely had time to recover before he straightened and waded out into the river, roaring at the top of his lungs. "We're over here, you lazy landlubbers! Where have you been?"

Lela laughed at recognizing his brother's voluble curses. The refined barrister knew how to use Anglo Saxon English to good purpose.

Twenty

ONCE THE BOAT reached the shore, Erran jumped over the side to hug Will, pounding him on the back in relief and probably annoyance. Uncomfortable with showing emotion, Will was still moved by his half-brother's embrace. He'd never felt quite part of his successful, aristocratic family, but it was good to know they might have missed him had he drowned.

He punched his brother's shoulder in acknowledgment, then turned to tighten the drapery around Lela's shoulders. Everyone stayed blessedly silent as he helped her aboard the small craft. To prevent them turning into icicles on the river ride home in these dawn hours, Erran insisted they both wrap in the dry fabric. Beneath the bulky material, Will held Lela close. She lay her fair head on his shoulder, possibly for the last time.

Will tried to fix the memory in his head of her flaxen hair falling over his shirt. He soaked up her scent as a dog might. But in his head, he recognized he was no dog and neither was she. Lela was far, far more than river stench and wet clothes, and he thought his innards might shrivel and die at knowing he must let her go.

At the duke's grandiose palace, Will was grateful for Erran's officious presence. Despite the early hour, the whole household was awake and frantic. The duke and Rainsford had left to organize the search in the dead of night, and there was no one about to limit the tears and cries as he and Lela straggled in looking like sorry fish.

But his lawyer brother was a no-nonsense sort who didn't suffer questions. Erran simply used his commanding voice to send servants hunting for the duke and Rainsford. Will gratefully hurried Lela upstairs where they could both recover, wash, and change into warm, dry clothes. Will had his hand freshly bandaged. It ached but the wound would mend. He didn't think his heart would.

It was past noon by the time Erran left and the duke returned to summon Will to his study.

The door knocker had been rapping steadily for half an hour or more with Lela's visitors, and footmen were informing callers that she was regretfully unavailable. As yet unaware of the prior night's events, society bumbled on as usual. As he strode down the stairs, Will noted bouquets and cards decorating the tables. In the wide foyer, he passed an eager suitor standing, hat in hand, at the door.

Will wanted to punch all society and rip the knocker off the door. But those fops were the lady's future, the kind of powerful gentlemen he would never be.

He could only be grateful that word hadn't spread yet about their disappearance. He feared that wouldn't last long. They needed to straighten out their stories for their families to spread.

The duke of Sommersville looked more gaunt than usual when Will entered the gloomy study. The day was still overcast, and a fire crackled in the grate, but no one had lit the lamps. His Grace wasn't one to imbibe heavily, but he had a brandy bottle at hand Will noticed. He could use a good stiff drink right now. The bath hadn't warmed his innards at all. But the duke didn't offer brandy or chair.

Will knew what was coming. He'd practiced his response as best as he was able. But no matter how he answered, his future was doomed.

"I wanted to die when they fished Lela's hat out of the river," the duke said bluntly.

Will bowed his head. "I nearly died when she went in. There are no words to offer in apology for what you must have suffered."

The duke waved a hand in irritation. "Your lawyer brother's tongue is as glib as rumor tells it," the duke said sourly. "He's convinced my heir that all is well because that's what Rainsford likes to believe—that the world turns fine without him."

"I believe your heir prefers to concentrate on what can be changed," Will said respectfully, puzzled by the change in topic. "Rainsford is a good man."

"He has no understanding of human nature. His mother was like that—removed from all messy emotion suffered by the rest of humanity. Good minds but no passion. As much as you pretend otherwise, *you* aren't like that. Neither is Lela. You wouldn't have gone to so much trouble to save a deaf child and her mother if you were. Tell me what really happened."

Will *wanted* to be like that. People were unreliable. It was safer to lavish affection on animals who returned it. But Lela was far better than most people, and his gut churned in anguish. He prayed he was strong enough to do what he had to do. "First, did the groom release the girl? Lady Aurelia will wish to know her fate."

"Jack left the tart on the bridge to make her own way home. He rode directly here and roused the household. This past night has been hell." The duke reached for the brandy, pouring a finger, then slammed the decanter on the desk. "I want facts, not whatever cock-and-bull tale your brother and Lela have concocted. I'm counting on your honesty."

"Lady Aurelia will tell you the same as I," Will asserted stiffly. "We stopped the Gypsy wagon. I should not have let her become involved. I'd hoped to resolve the situation peacefully and failed. In the ensuing altercation, a bullet grazed her head, and she fell in the river."

His Grace snorted ungracefully. "And Lela will tell me you were a conquering hero, and it's all her fault. I take it you dived into the river like a madman, hoping to haul her out. You're not one of your dogs, you know. You aren't trained to sniff out the drowning and drag them to safety."

This was not precisely the direction Will had expected this conversation to take, and he clenched his fists at his side, preparing for the blow. "I had no choice."

The duke drove his hand through his graying hair. "Exactly. Passionate idiocy. You'd rather die than let my daughter die. I respect that. That's more than any of those other young fops would have done in your place."

"To be fair, your grace," Will said dryly, "They wouldn't have been there in the first place. I'm the one who let her talk me into riding to Battersea."

"You have a brother there. It was a perfectly reasonable request. That Lela never makes such requests without you around is another subject entirely, and the one leaving me bewildered. Why is she suddenly riding about instead of hiding in her room, staring vapidly at her toes?"

Will twitched his shoulders inside the tight coat Ashford had given him. He despised explanations, but he owed the duke one. He sought words for the only explanation he understood. "She believes I help her muffle the noise in her head."

The duke nodded as if that actually made sense. "I love my daughter. Last night, I vowed if she was returned to me, I would give her whatever she wants."

Still puzzled, Will remained silent, waiting.

"Lela has always behaved as if she hasn't a ha' penny's worth of sense," the duke continued, tapping his pen against the desk. "Her governesses despaired of her. But she knows everything anyone has ever told her and more that they have not. She listens, when she wants to. You've made her *want* to listen."

"I wouldn't go so far as to say that, your grace," Will protested. "She has taken an interest in little Rose and her plight."

"But the moment you ride away, she'll go back to staring at her toes, won't she?" he demanded.

Will shifted from foot to foot, reminded of his own aching toes in Ashford's fancy shoes. "I can't speak to that, your grace."

"Quit bloody hell calling me *your grace!*" the duke shouted. "You're an *Ives*, with ancestry dating back to the Roman emperors for all I know. Your damned brother is a marquess! You have every right to call me duke or sir or stupid just as all the other young pups do."

Will liked the duke. He really did. But he couldn't see where this was going. "Yes, sir," he said, not belaboring the point of his mother's peasant ancestry.

"Very well, then." The duke sighed and settled back in his chair, studying Will as if he were a specimen under glass. "You're a gentleman. You clean up well. Go propose to my daughter as you ought. I'll arrange for the special license. We'll make the ball a betrothal announcement."

Will needed a chair to crumple into. The duke hadn't offered him one. Even though this was what he'd known was expected of him, he hadn't anticipated it coming with *approval*. He'd had his arguments prepared against this moment, but they all seemed ungrateful in the face of the duke's graciousness.

"She deserves better," Will muttered, hating his lack of eloquence in stating the obvious.

"That's up to her to decide, isn't it?" the duke said in a desert-dry tone.

There was a glimmer of hope—let the duke think Lela was deciding. And while she did so, Will could finish the task of finding Rose's kidnapper and would-be murderer.

Will wasn't entirely certain that the delay wasn't a bomb about to explode overhead, but he grasped any crumb allowed. He hadn't wanted to insult Lela or the duke or lose his entire future in a grandiose gesture of defiance. But if he could just be allowed to talk to Lela. . .

He feared she would make the wrong choice. Damn.

"Women do not always choose with their heads, sir," Will said, swallowing hard.

"You got yourself into this. You can get yourself out," the duke countered darkly. "I'd thought to marry her off to a man of consequence, but if it's a dog trainer she wants, then one willing to sacrifice his life for her is good enough for me."

That's what he'd be doing, Will knew—sacrificing his life. Without his dogs, he was nothing. The daughter of a duke needed a gentleman on her arm, one who could help her start a school for the deaf, which required London and not the Cotswolds. It required tailored coats and soirees and rubbing elbows with men he didn't like or respect or even understand. He couldn't ask Lela to give up her dreams to follow his.

He hadn't planned on attending her ball. He'd planned on walking Ajax around the perimeter, sniffing out the guests, as hired help. He thought he might muffle her noises just as easily that way. After a while, she'd find someone more suitable who would cause her to focus on him, and she'd forget all about Will.

Defiantly, he found a glass on the sideboard, poured himself a swallow of brandy, and threw it back. "Yes, your grace."

He spun on his heel and walked out without being dismissed. That's how gentlemen did it. He'd watched his arrogant older brothers for years. He knew the routine.

It just wasn't who he was.

STILL FEELING the effects of Will's eye-opening lovemaking, shivering and oddly uncomfortable in her own skin, Lela feared she was coming down with a cold in truth. She didn't have the luxury of mooning over the impossible, however, not with half London pounding at the door. At least Will was still in the house, muffling all the frantic gossip among the servants, which seemed to lead to much clattering of pans and dropping of coal.

She needed someone to talk to and help her understand her confusion.

Fortunately, Lady Aster arrived on schedule to interrogate suitors. Of course, Aster was Will's sister-in-law and not exactly impartial. Aster brought Celeste, who already knew everything since her husband was the one who had been out half the night searching for them. Lela thought she might like having family around her when she needed them, but only if Will was near to make conversation easy.

But having Will around presented an entirely new set of difficulties, which her cousin proved the moment she entered Lela's private sitting room.

"Has Will proposed yet?" were almost the first words out of Aster's mouth. "His astrological signs indicate he's due for happiness and love. I haven't completed the finer aspects of your chart yet, but you look like a perfect fit."

Without giving Lela time to absorb that declaration, Aster swept her up in a hug. "I am so glad you're safe. You have no notion of what ripples you caused in the universe last night."

Celeste leaned over to kiss Lela's cheek. "We were devastated when we heard you'd come to trouble. None of us has slept all night. I am so glad you're both back and unharmed."

Lela wiped away tears and hugged them back. "I'm so sorry we did that to you. It was all my fault. Will had everything in hand, but I had to panic." She wished to tell them more, but the knocker kept rapping below and the servants were still in a frenzy and even Will's presence couldn't muffle all the conflicting sounds.

"We are telling everyone that you were with Celeste and Erran last night," Aster assured her. "The ball shall go on as planned." She waved the list of houseguests they meant to investigate.

"Your sisters were scraping the bottom of the barrel to invite this lot," Celeste said, snatching the list. "Most of the men are in desperate need of wealth, barring one or two who want your father's favor. Most are from good families, I suppose. Will is a much better choice."

Well, she couldn't expect Will's family to say any less. "Will wants to train dogs," Lela pointed out, grateful to air some of her concerns. "He has no interest in London or the deaf school I would like to organize. I don't believe we have anything in common except gossip."

"She's lying," Celeste told Aster with humor. "Shall I cajole her into telling the truth?"

Lela clenched her fists in frustration. "I want you to *help* me, not tell me what to do!"

"We want to help Will too," Aster pointed out. "He needs someone to give him reason to settle down. His chart shows that he's ready to give up traveling. He's a good choice."

Calming her rattled nerves by sipping tea, Lela attempted listening to the conversation in her father's study, but Will's nullification ability was working too well. Neither of them appeared to be raising their voices, at least. She hoped that was a good sign.

So, this was what it was like to be almost normal, carrying on a normal conversation in which she was expected to participate reasonably. She rather missed being senseless. "We cannot make any announcements now, even if Will should be foolish enough to ask. I must use the ball to lure hungry suitors. Until we determine which one has a recently deceased brother and sister-in-law or has come into an unexpected inheritance, Bess and her children are in limbo."

"The infant is doing so well that Christie is likely to adopt him if we don't bring mother and child together soon. We really must act quickly," Celeste agreed. "Our letters aren't producing many answers."

"And I'm sure Rose is anxious to have her mother back," Lela added, relieved to have the discussion turn away from her. "It's hard to know what's going through her head, but she keeps watching the street."

Aster sorted through the abundance of cards and acceptances already collected. "You've had responses from almost everyone. Moira has sketched out the ballroom decorations. I'm glad you set the date early. Parliament will be letting out shortly and everyone will be heading home."

Celeste sipped her tea and looked at Lela with concern. "You plan to reject Will's proposal, don't you?"

Hit with a direct blow, Lela acknowledged the emptiness gaping in her middle. She didn't think she could answer with any coherence. "It's impossible," she murmured.

Even as she said it, the noise of the household crashed in her head with the impact of a battleground.

Damn insufferable Ives. . .

Take your hands off me, you. . .

Put the pot on the table not. . .
Fish, get yer. . .

A shovel scraped. Coal rattled. A carriage rumbled over cobblestone.

Lela held her hands to her ears and bit back a scream. *Will had left,* without a word to her. She couldn't think. She couldn't bear it.

Before her guests could question her behavior, a footman arrived with a note. Concentrating on one of the maids singing in a distant room so she could uncover her ears, not daring to hope, Lela tore open the missive. Astounded at the indecipherable scrawl, relieved that it was from Will, she wished she'd waited until her family had departed before opening it. She needed time to digest the contents, savor his brief words.

She tucked the paper in her pocket, smiled brightly, and lied. "We are about to open the doors to the parade of visitors. I have developed a dreadful catarrh from the storm last night. Will one of you ladies please make my apologies for me?"

Too perceptive, they regarded her with suspicion, but her family was never stupid. They gathered their things, arguing over who should preside over the parlor. Deciding they would both do the honors, they departed.

Lela clung to the paper, sniffing the faint smell of Will's soap, fearful of what the words might tell her. That he was gone, she knew. Where he had gone, she didn't know. With a sigh, she opened the note.

I am gone to Rcihmond. Tlak latre. Will

Not a gentleman's practiced script by any means, but the thickness of the ink strokes said he'd put a great deal of effort into those few words. The right letters were all there, just oddly scrambled.

So, she couldn't read, and he couldn't spell. Well, she could *read,* she just couldn't focus on what she read. And he could spell, he just didn't put the letters in the right order. That didn't make either of them dumb or uneducated, just. . . different.

They might not have a lot in common when it came to worldly interests, but on the inside, they understood each other. How did one make a marriage of that?

Twenty-one

WILL HAD decided it would be faster to leave the dogs and ride to Richmond than to hire a cart to carry the animals. After all the rain and the time since the villain had written the letter, he didn't hold much hope that Ajax could find the scent.

The direction the duke's secretary had provided for Lord Baldwin, one of the impoverished guests Jacques had marked as a possibility, was easy to find in a small town like Richmond. He could ask questions around the neighborhood without Ajax. If Will remembered correctly, Baldwin was one of the three gentlemen they'd met in the tavern the day they'd left Yatesdale with Rose. Young, slightly-built, he hadn't engaged in fisticuffs as Clayton had. The older gentleman with the lavender handkerchief must have been Rush, the presumed man milliner.

Clayton was the more likely villain, given his tendency to drink and violence, but Will wanted to check the one living furthest out first. Besides, he was more comfortable asking questions in the country.

He stopped in the tavern nearest the tidy three-story townhouse Baldwin called home, but none of the men in there were familiar with the gentleman. They did tell him, however, that it was a rooming house.

So wearing gloves to conceal his bandaged hand, Will walked in the garden gate and knocked on the door. A mob-capped housekeeper answered. "I heard there might be rooms to let here, ma'am," he said, holding his tweed cap in his hands. He'd chosen his own rural clothes for this expedition.

"There is only a single room," the housekeeper said, looking at his attire with disapproval. "We're a fine establishment, catering to gentlemen. We seldom have a vacancy, but Lord Baldwin has just moved out, having come into a small inheritance. He had only the room at the top, not a full suite, and we didn't have more space to offer him."

A small inheritance? Was the search this easy? But while he was here, he'd have a look around.

"I know his lordship from school," Will lied. "I hadn't realized he lived here. If you'll give me his new direction, I can ask him to give me a reference."

His approval rating apparently rose. The housekeeper ushered him in and showed him upstairs to a low, timbered attic room that would give him headaches every time he walked into a beam. He pretended to take an interest in the polished floor and window and let his hostess rush off to find Baldwin's new direction.

Had Lela's bookish suitor already taken over Bess's estate, such as it might be? Her home may not have been entailed. Baldwin could have sold it to pay for city housing.

Will looked about for any scent identifiers the man might have left so he could test it on Ajax, but the room had been scrubbed clean, the linens washed, and he couldn't haul furniture back with him.

The housekeeper handed him a scrap of paper with a direction. Will thanked her for her time, and said he would talk to Baldwin and get back to her.

When he stepped outside, he studied the housekeeper's scrawl. Unscrambling the words with his tired brain, he let his eyebrows soar in surprise.

Baldwin now had the same city location as Lord Clayton.

IN THE PRIVATE upstairs sitting room above the public first floor parlor where Aster and Celeste were accepting her callers, Lela sat at a table with the deaf-hand-signal book. Rose bounced from window to window.

Without Will to muffle sound for her, she was having difficulty focusing on the voices below, but at least Rose wasn't making any noise. The child carried a doll from the nursery, showing it the world out the windows, while Tiny explored the carpet.

I hope Lady Aurelia. . .

We are so excited that the duke. . .

Please give our best wishes. . .

Not letting that nasty vermin. . .

Lela yawned. This was why she had difficulty focusing, she decided. No one in the parlor said anything worth listening to, and kitchen quarrels were incessant. She opened one of the picture books she'd brought into the parlor, found a picture of a little girl, wrote G-I-R-L on a piece of paper, and opened the hand signal book to the appropriate illustration.

Rose had climbed up on a sofa to watch out the long windows overlooking the entrance. Lela approached her, hoping to persuade her to look at the books, but Rose pointed at the window and frowned. What had the child seen?

Given the cruelty that had marred Rose's small world, her heart beat accelerated. Would Rose recognize whoever had attacked her mother? She didn't seem agitated, though, just concerned.

Lela caught a glimpse of two gentlemen being let in through their front door. Looking down on top hats told her nothing. She saw no horse or carriage in the street. She placed a finger to her lips in the universal sign language to tell a child to be silent, and then she concentrated, *hard.*

Aster and Celeste were already entertaining several mothers and daughters and one or two gentlemen. Several of the women made their excuses as the newcomers were introduced. That could just mean their visiting time was over—or it could mean the ladies disapproved of the newcomers.

"Good afternoon, Lord Rush, Lord Baldwin," she heard Aster say smoothly, letting Lela know who was in the room as she had this past hour—provided Lela listened.

Rush was the gentleman who lived with his mother, Lela remembered. Lord Baldwin was a slight gentleman, bookish. He'd offered her a rose and tried to propose, but she'd brushed him off.

Neither seemed likely sorts to heave an expectant mother and her child into the cold, then beat them brutally. Or to descend into kidnapping.

But then, she would never have suspected any of their guests to stoop so low.

She listened to the new arrivals offering the usual gallantries while Celeste explained that Lela was suffering from being out in the rain.

It was only the child's reaction that was interesting. Rose had her nose and sticky palms pressed to the window. At least she wasn't saying *bad man.* How could she ask the child if the men were familiar?

She couldn't, plain and simple. It might take months to teach the child to write whole words. Rose knew a few, but even then, she might not know names. Or their connection to Bess. And Lela didn't dare endanger the child by taking her downstairs to introduce her to the company.

Frustrated, she concentrated on the banal conversation below. Aster and Celeste had a list of the house party guests and would know these two were on it. They questioned the men on their enjoyment of the party, what they'd been doing since, anything that occurred to their creative minds.

Rush and Baldwin responded with platitudes, as any gentleman might. Rush had been enjoying the theater. Baldwin said he'd recently taken new accommodations. Rush said he'd acquired a country estate and was thinking of removing there once everyone left the city.

Lord Rush had been living with his mother on the other side of the park. . .

Before she could finish that thought, a maid rapped on the door. Annoyed, Lela nodded at her to enter.

"One of the gentlemen's grooms has took sick, my lady," the maid said, with a curtsy. "He says not to bother his master, but he'd like to come in for a bit of hot tea. Cook says she won't have him, and there's a bit of a pother."

Ah, so that was the quarrel in the kitchen. "Cook is correct. We allow no strangers inside the house. You have my permission to disturb the gentleman in question. Do you know who it is?"

The notion of an outsider nosing around inside the security of her father's house made her itch. Lela glanced at Rose, who hadn't turned at the maid's entrance but remained plastered to the window.

"Jack'll ask, my lady." The maid bobbed and hurried out.

Lela wished Will were here. He could have Ajax check each guest as he left—and take a sniff of their grooms as well.

Uncomfortably, she realized Will would rather sit on the steps waiting for visitors than come inside and talk with the guests. There was part of the enormous divide separating them. She could not save lives by training dogs as he did and must. She could only better the world by using her wealth and position in society. And the twain could never meet. As Will's wife, she'd have to become a recluse again, living in the country while he traveled.

She returned to the conversation below. More new arrivals, women this time. She recognized the voice of the footman asking for a word with Lord Rush—he must be the gentleman with the ill servant.

His lordship sounded peeved, as any wealthy aristocrat might. With interest, Lela stood to look out the window with Rose. She could hear the gentlemen making their farewells. The footman would be providing them with their hats.

A minute later, the two gentlemen reappeared on the front step. Rose patted the window excitedly. The older of the gentlemen—Lord Rush—glanced up, but he shrugged and hurried down the step with the slighter Lord Baldwin on his heels. They waited on the street for their vehicle to be brought around from the mews.

"Da," Rose said worriedly. "Dabro."

Dabro. How did one translate that?

A small cabriolet rolled around the corner, the groom smartly whipping the horses to a halt without splashing the gentlemen on the curb. He leapt down to assist the men into the seat. He didn't appear ill.

And Rose shrieked hysterically.

WILL RETURNED to a house at sixes and sevens. He'd intended to change into city clothes and track Clayton and Baldwin, but Rose shrieked and ran down the staircase to throw herself in his arms. Tiny followed, yipping and leaping against his legs as if this were a new game. Lela was shouting at servants in the upper halls while his sisters-in-law ushered confused guests out the front door. Servants ran about in bewilderment, and he had a good mind to turn and walk out again. Ajax and Tiny made more sense than this domestic confusion.

Rose buried her face against his shoulder and refused to release her grip on his neck, so Will stalked up the broad marble stairs to the family's private floor as if he belonged there, despite his mud-splattered rural clothes. He ignored the stares of his brothers' elegant wives. He saw only Lela rushing down the corridor from her chamber, garbed in the battered cloak and old bonnet she'd worn the other day to disguise herself. In grim determination, he stopped her.

"You will *not* go out without me," he said, surprising even himself. He did not generally go about ordering anyone but his dogs.

"Rose has seen the villain, I'm sure of it!" She circled around him and headed toward the front of the house. "We must find that groom."

So much for ordering Lela to do anything. Was she even *listening* to him? And where in hell was she going now?

Still carrying Rose and trailing the yipping terrier, Will strode after her. The walls of the upper hall were covered in silk and adorned with gilt-framed artwork. The carpet beneath his muddy boots was softer and thicker than some of the beds he'd slept in over the years. His brother's estate at Iveston might be as large as a duke's palace, but it had always been a hovel in comparison to this grandeur. The all-male Iveston household he'd known had few servants and no women to care if the floors were bare and dirty. He had been content living as if the place were a barn. Here, Will feared his every step polluted the space he traversed.

Worse yet, Rainsford strode out of his study to confront him while Lela continued on.

"What the devil is all this caterwauling about?" the marquess demanded in the cool, controlled voice for which he was known.

Will admired Rainsford's lean elegance and the aristocratic graces the marquess used as a shield, but he didn't necessarily *like* Lela's half-brother, not the way he liked the more earthy duke. With malicious intent, Will pried Rose from his neck and thrust her at Rain. "I'm trying to find out. Here, you take her while I try to make Lela focus."

He'd called her *Lela*, as if he had the right to the intimacy. Which, given what they'd done last night and the duke's command, he did, Will realized with a jolt. Rainsford didn't seem to appreciate the familiarity though. He glared at Will and instead of hauling Rose back to the nursery, he followed him after Lela.

They found her in the private sitting room overlooking the street, pacing the carpet and giving instructions to her bewildered maid, who looked up at them in relief when they stormed in.

Lela accepted the child her brother thrust at her, hugging Rose and stroking her hair to calm her down. "Thank goodness, you're here, Will. I think she's seen the villain who cast her out in the cold and beat her mother."

Rainsford drew in a breath with a distinct hiss. "Here? The villain was *here*?"

"Driving Lord Rush's carriage, I believe. The man called Crockett? The description we've had seems apt, but he was in cloak and hat, and I didn't have a good look. I can only wonder that Rose recognized him, except she seemed to be familiar with either Lord Rush or Lord Baldwin before she even saw their driver."

"And just exactly what did you think you could do about it?" Will all but shouted. He bit his tongue when she cast him a look of annoyance.

"The only thing I can do, listen," she said. "I thought I might question Lord Rush's servants, at the very least. He is only across the park."

"And you think he might confess to attempted murder and kidnapping and you'd haul him off to prison?" Rainsford asked in incredulity.

Will started liking the man a little better. There was some soul behind that mask at least.

"We have to start *somewhere*!" Lela cried, looking to Will with a plea in her eyes.

"She's right," Will acknowledged with a shrug, knowing he irritated the marquess even more. "We can't let a murderous villain discover that the witnesses to his evil are still alive. If this groom is the man called Crockett, we need evidence."

"Rose said something that sounded like *dabro* when she saw Rush and Baldwin. I think she knows one of them, and that might be her name for them."

Rose watched them intently, tilting her head close to Lela, perhaps to hear her speak. At the sound of the familiar word, she nodded and began gabbling.

They all stared at her in astonishment. Generally, she did not utter a sound.

"We need a translator," Rainsford said dryly.

"We need a plan," Will countered. "Baldwin has just moved into the City. Do we go after him or Rush?"

"Lela is going nowhere," Rainsford said with the same authority as Will had just used.

The subject in question shoved Rose at her brother and walked out. With a shrug, Will followed her. He was damned no matter what he did. He might as well go with the more pleasant company, even if she did wish to string him from the highest tree.

Twenty-two

FURIOUS AT BEING treated like an infant, Lela raced for the stairs down to the public floor, only to be met with an onslaught of loud chatter inside her head.

Is the lady mad?

Do you think we should leave her like this. . .

Rainsford should handle. . .

Let Will. . .

She halted on the stairway, pressing hands to her temples as the noise in her head escalated. Will was following right behind her. *Why wasn't Will blocking the noise?*

Back in the sitting room, when he'd been present, she'd been fine. Almost.

While she hesitated, Will caught up with her. With the boldness she'd allowed him by her actions last night, he grasped her waist and hauled her back up to the family floor. That got her attention—as it did Rain's. Her brother's shocked expression almost equaled her moment of rare fury.

To her shock, she could think again. Why now and not a moment earlier?

"I've been focusing on *you*!" Lela said angrily when Will set her down in the upper hall. "If I'm thinking about you, I don't hear much else. But if I'm *angry*, I block you too."

He didn't set her down but his expression was one of bemusement and. . . hope?

He hugged her tighter. "We'll work that out later. Right now, I want it understood that you are going nowhere near that villain. I cannot bear another night like the last," Will announced with a firmness he seldom used. Using his bandaged palm at the small of her back, he pushed her past Rainsford, who still held Rose, toward the front sitting room again.

"But I can *listen*," she insisted. "The villain could be talking about his misdeeds right now. Or planning more. I think he tried to worm his way into this house by saying he wasn't feeling well!"

Will stopped to stare at her. She turned to one of the maids hovering in the corridor. "Tilly, take Rose back to the nursery."

Rose refused to go with the maid but wept and reached for Will. Looking more bewildered than any man deserved, he took the child back from Rainsford. He returned to stalking toward the family sitting room, sorting his thoughts aloud. "First, let us determine who the coachman belongs to and which one of the dolts Rose recognizes. Neither Rush nor Baldwin seem likely to order the killing of women and children."

"Your brother hinted that Lord Rush is a molly, but why would he court me, if so?" Lela asked, throwing off the nasty bonnet and plopping down in a seat at the window overlooking the street, still agitated but more focused now that she could watch Will. "It must be Lord Baldwin, but I've never seen him with anything more dangerous than a book in his hand."

Rainsford looked as if he might explode. "Who taught you such cant?"

Will, thankfully, ignored him. Not many people ignored a marquess, and certainly not to listen to *her*. Lela thought she might preen, until she realized Will's half-brother was a marquess and Will had experience in ignoring brothers.

"I am not a green goose," she insisted. "I do not perfectly understand except that sometimes men who never marry, like Lord Rush, prefer men to women. It's of no concern to me, but it does make it seem unlikely that he would marry for wealth or otherwise."

"He might to hide the illegality of his predilections," Will suggested.

"But if Lord Rush is wealthy, he doesn't need any meager inheritance Bess might have."

Will set Rose on the floor, caught Tiny, and dropped the terrier in the child's lap. Rose settled down to hold her pet and warily watch the adults.

Rainsford stalked up and down the carpet. "Rush's *mother* is in funds, but I wouldn't call *him* wealthy. He wasted his father's inheritance in his youth. He seems to have an allowance from his mother now but not enough to haunt the clubs."

"Where did his mother come into wealth that her son does not possess?" Will asked, reasonably enough. He filled a chair near Lela's seat and sprawled his long legs across the flowered carpet.

Even in his country tweed, Will overpowered the room with masculinity and an innate nobility, Lela decided. If she must make a fool of herself over any man, she'd found a good one. And blessedly, all the gabble in her head faded without her having to do more than watch him. With practice, she might learn to focus better.

For now, she had to settle her pounding heart by looking away from Will so she could listen to what Celeste and Aster below were doing—apparently instructing servants that visiting hours were over. She returned her attention to the men.

Rain shrugged at Will's question. "Rush's mother is from York, so I'm familiar with the family. Her father is a wealthy merchant who provided her with a large dowry when she married a baron. My supposition would be that when the last Baron Rush died, his wife kept her dowry and possibly more. Her son, the lavender-loving Lord Rush, would have inherited his father's title and entailment but not necessarily funds. After a brief mourning, his mother married Viscount Simmons. Her merchant father was exceedingly pleased, and she was again well provided for in the settlements. Those monies would most likely come to her at his death also."

"Lord Rush's mother remarried?" Lela asked. She'd never paid attention to London or Yorkshire gossip, but she knew human nature. "Does she have more children? Or is Lord Rush her only child?"

"I don't know the particulars," Rain said with a scowl. "It's not as if they travel in our circles, and Rush is a decade or more older than I am. Far too old for you." He frowned formidably at her, and she stuck her tongue out at him.

"I never met the late Viscount Simmons," Rain continued. "His estate was more in Northumberland and North Yorkshire, and I heard he wasn't a social sort. I have a vague memory that he left a son, but he'd be more Rush's age than mine."

"Might the elder Simmons be a heavy snuff taker?" Will said, looking up from Rose and the puppy.

Lela and Rain both turned to him expectantly.

He shrugged his big shoulders uncomfortably. "An old Lord Simmons used to come through the village on his way to York and stay at our inn. The maids hated cleaning his room because of the stench of snuff. I could only have been nine or ten at the time, but I remember him grumbling about his wife and her son's expensive sojourns to London. He may have been a viscount, but he never struck me as more than a country squire with muddy boots, threadbare attire, and a filthy habit."

"Simmons may have preferred living in the country, and his wife had grown tired of it," Lela said with a shrug. "With wealth of her own, she could do as she pleased. Not all aristocracy lives in each other's pockets."

Could she do that? Live in London and start a school while Will returned to traveling? But Aster had said he was ready to settle down. What was she to make of that?

"Why do you ask?" Rain demanded in irritation, missing the obvious.

"If Lady Simmons gave the viscount a son, he would be Lord Rush's half-brother," Lela explained. "Lord Rush may have grown up in a surly viscount's rural household, with a younger brother who inherited a title and possibly an estate greater than his own."

Will rubbed at his eyes—an indication that his sleepless night was taking its toll. "So lavender-loving Rush might have had a snuff-sniffing stepfather, one who did not travel in aristocratic circles, and whose son may have followed in his grubby path."

At least he was following the path of her thoughts. "So Rush's half-brother might have been a country-loving viscount who married Bess just to get a son to inherit so his citified older brother wouldn't?" Lela suggested.

"Simmons' *half*-brother could not inherit his title or any entailment," Rain said with scorn. "There is no blood connection between their fathers. There would be no benefit in murdering Simmons' wife and child, if that is who they are."

He stopped pacing, apparently remembering the tale Lela had told him. He studied Rose playing on the carpet. "But there may have been dower funds that would revert to Simmons' *mother* if there were no wife, child, or surviving siblings. The estate itself would be in the hands of an executor, presumably one searching for the next in line to the title. The process can be long and drawn out and the estate funds might vanish during the search."

"Unless Viscount Simmons' heir is Bess's son," Lela said, also studying the silent child on the carpet. "Rose could be a minor heiress, and the nearly-orphaned infant in the marchioness's nursery could be a viscount. Bess may be a viscountess. If she was no more than a serving wench prior to marriage, she may have a right to fear her husband's wealthy, aristocratic family."

"And if the executor handling the estate happens to be the infant's half-uncle, Lord Rush?" Will stood up. "We need confirmation, but I'm not waiting. It's time to take Ajax out."

WILL COULDN'T easily disguise himself amid the throngs of Mayfair. He had the Viking proportions and distinctive bone structure of an Ives. The small, aristocratic world his brothers moved in knew of Will's existence and habits. The dog confirmed his identity if any had doubts.

It was the woman at his side that confused him as well as everyone else they passed. She was dainty, with the graceful bearing of a lady as she glided along, holding his arm. She wore abominable black bombazine and the heavy widow's veil of a much older rural matriarch. Most of Mayfair might not recognize Lela's form, since she did not come to town often. But her face. . . once they met her, they would know her. And the men would be stumbling over their feet to acknowledge her—hence, the ugly veil.

And she was walking on his damned arm on his way to a potential villain's house as if she were a nobody. They both had bats in their belfries.

True, they were surrounded not only by the duke's grooms and footmen but those of his brothers. The servants lurked on street corners, in the alleys, held horses and carriages all up and down the thoroughfare. Theo probably had one of his telescopes aimed at them. Jacques would be in a coffee shop nearby, all for the sake of Lela.

Unaccustomed to having his actions so closely observed, Will was deuced uncomfortable. He prayed to all that was holy that the two marquesses had better things to do than watch him at work. It wasn't as if his brother or hers discussed their plans with him. Rain had stormed off, leaving Will the responsibility of looking after Lela. That made him sweat enough.

"Really, Will," she murmured as they approached the rear of Lady Simmons' townhouse, "I doubt the lady keeps weapons under her parlor cushions. This is much safer than all the plans you and Rain suggested."

"Waiting for confirmation of our surmises would be *safer*," he complained. "I could have led Ajax down this alley without your company."

He'd given Ajax the ransom note to sniff again, but the dog hadn't picked up much, as Will had feared. Still, searching for Rush's driver would be easier without Lela on his arm. Only the lady who had barely left her room before, now couldn't be persuaded to stay in it.

He was terrified that she'd come to harm again. The world needed this compassionate lady. *He* needed her. But the duke had sheltered her for too long. Will couldn't smother her as well, much as he would like to.

"You can't hear what's happening inside that house," Lela insisted, as she'd been doing since Will had said he was taking Ajax out. "Why did the carriage driver try to come into our house? He was obviously not ill as he claimed. He may have been up to no good. They could be talking about it even now. Hush, and let me listen."

Will swallowed his pride and acknowledged her gift was far more useful than his when it came to cities and people.

The alley had no personal stables the way the duke's grandiose home did. These were narrow townhomes. Walking down the delivery alley led them past kitchen gardens on either side. Will kept his mind open to dog scents as Ajax obediently sniffed the mud and fences, while Lela *listened*.

Will noted one of Ashford's grooms loitering ahead. He knew another of the duke's men whistled on the corner behind them. Lela should be perfectly safe. He just wasn't accustomed to sharing his searches with anyone, much less a woman.

And there was the crux of it—the duke wanted him to marry his beautiful, intelligent, talented daughter, who might possibly help him in his searches for lost children and other victims. If she'd been anyone other than a duke's daughter, Will would have been thrilled to have her talent at his side.

He was an inverse snob. He thought the nobility couldn't do what he did.

Lela gripped his arm tighter and tugged him to a halt. He couldn't hear anything. He linked with Ajax, who had found an interesting scent. Will couldn't tell if it was the *right* scent.

"Lord Rush is arguing with his manservant," she whispered. A moment later, she added in a puzzled voice, "He doesn't speak like a servant."

Which was when Will began to suspect the truth. How the devil did he handle this? Delicate ladies shouldn't be faced with indelicate matters. Real gentlemen did not allow their ladies in situations like this in the first place. He was no gentleman. . .

"Cornett," she murmured again. "His man's name is *Cornett*. They are arguing over money and. . . privacy? Really, he sounds almost as educated as Rush. He speaks in military terms of cutting losses, taking the offensive, not retreating, gaining ground. . ."

Cornett. Crockett? It could be coincidence. Or sheer lack of imagination. *Cutting losses*. . . Rose and Bess?

The mastiff woofed and Will turned his attention to what the dog was telling him.

Lela stiffened and tugged him toward the alley exit. Will needed to linger. . .

A door opened and a man shouted, "You've the spine of a guppy!"

Forgetting what Ajax was sniffing, Will hurried Lela out of the line of fire.

"You've the soul of a guttersnipe," a deeper voice retaliated. "And the imagination of a cretin! My way is safer, and you know it. You're just jealous."

Will put Lela in front of him so the man storming into the alley could only see his broad back. He shoved her at the tall footman whistling on the corner, who nodded and signaled a nearby carriage.

Lela resisted. Of course, she resisted. But she didn't head back to the alley. Instead, she turned the corner toward the main street in front of the house.

Will swore under his breath and glanced helplessly at the footman. Neither of them was likely to manhandle the duke's daughter in public, even if she looked little better than a dowdy domestic. Will strode after her.

"The Cornett person is objecting to Lord Rush courting me. He's insisting that they retire to their rural estate. Lord Rush wants my dowry and to stay in town. It's all very tawdry," Lela said angrily as she marched down the walk. "There are reasons I never listen to people."

Will's gut lurched as he imagined what else she'd overheard. Rush's manservant must also be his lover—a lover who wouldn't want Rush marrying and bringing an inquisitive female into their lives. The pieces began to fall together in a ghastly picture. "So why are we not in a carriage heading back for your home?"

"Because I want to know what Lady Simmons thinks about her daughter-in-law's disappearance," she stated with a deadly resolve that brooked no argument.

"They mentioned a disappearing daughter-in-law?" Will asked, looking around for the carriage. Public manhandling or not, if these people knew anything of Bess's torture and near-death, he wasn't letting Lela near them.

"Lord Rush seems concerned about the whereabouts of his brother's missing widow and child and isn't convinced that they won't return and claim the estate Cornett wants them to occupy. If they're talking about Bess, he doesn't seem to know she's supposedly dead. I believe Rush is mostly innocent, but I'm surmising from Rose's reaction that his manservant most decidedly is *not*."

Will stepped into the street, halting the duke's carriage that had been following them. Before Lela could protest, he flung her inside as soon as the footman opened the door. If there were murderers running about the street, he wouldn't allow Lela in their path.

Ajax howled as a long-legged gentleman in a black coat ran out of the alley in their direction.

Will swung to block the runner. The dastard looked up, saw him, and reversed his direction. Will unleashed Ajax. "Find," he ordered.

The bitch knew the command and knew to connect it to the ransom note. Without hesitation, she raced after the fleeing servant. That meant Ajax had scented the writer of the ransom note. Will was torn between racing after the blackguard and protecting Lela.

"Damn you, man, come back here!" A man's shout echoed from the alley. *Rush.*

That decided that. Will mentally ordered Ajax to bring down the fleeing servant. Cornett screamed as the mastiff pinned him to the walk. Will braced himself for the encounter with Lela's lavender-loving suitor.

He hadn't prepared himself for Lela leaping out of a moving carriage. She shouldn't even be able to unlatch the damned door!

Ahead, Cornett shouted and a knife flashed in his hand. *Ajax!*

Without hesitation, Will removed his brother Erran's inventive, three-shot pistol from his pocket. Rush and Ajax were in between him and his target, blast it. He ran, deliberately smashing into Rush to remove him from his path so he could find a better angle to stop Cornett from gutting the mastiff, who was merely holding him down.

"Don't shoot, don't shoot," Rush cried in horror. "Corny, stop, don't hurt the dog!"

Even with one hand bandaged, Will preferred fists to guns, but he wouldn't allow Ajax to be hurt any more than he would allow Lela to be. He took aim.

Lela screamed. Torn between the dog and the woman he loved, Will had no choice. He swung around to aim at anyone causing her harm.

Not a soul touched her. She'd removed her veil and men ran from every corner to surround her. She'd summoned her own reinforcements.

Will swung back to the villain, but Ajax had intelligently sunk her teeth into the wrist brandishing the knife. Cornett wouldn't be stabbing anyone soon.

He had half a mind to put the gun back in his pocket and walk away. He was a peaceful man, a man who went about his own business and left others to theirs. He worked alone, with responsibility for no one but himself.

And now, because of a duke's daughter and his own stupidity, he was wielding pistols, ready to take off heads, and he had half London on his heels. And a self-satisfied lady waiting for him to catch a villain.

Twenty-three

"I AM FEELING exceedingly vaporish," Lela announced, taking the arm of a footman. She watched in satisfaction as a murderous-looking Will planted his big boot on Cornett's arm. Spitefully, Lela hoped Will broke it. The man deserved it for attempting to knife a dog. Ajax obeyed a silent command and sat back, tongue lolling innocently.

"Please, Lord Rush, if you would. . ." She turned to the older man with graying sideburns, who appeared torn between rushing to his friend's aid and the approval of the members of society gathering around the scene.

He barely gave Lela a second look. He knotted his hands in anguish as Will hauled Cornett to his feet. "Please," he said, "Corny was only protecting himself from a vicious animal. I will pay for any harm."

Lela rolled her eyes. Since Will and her not-besotted suitor paid her no heed, she had to assert herself more forcefully. She was fully focused on Will, so summoning her wits was easy enough.

"Lord Rush, you will take me to your mother this instant," she commanded in a no-nonsense tone that mimicked her father at his worst. "Mr. Ives will not harm that vile creature unless I give the word."

Will glared at her for her presumption, but he pinned Cornett's arms behind his back and marched him down the street. The manservant was tall but almost cadaverous. He could not match Will's strength, no matter how much he struggled.

"You will go nowhere without a battalion of trained soldiers," Will contradicted her. Before she could object, he jerked his head peremptorily at someone behind her. "If Lady Simmons is at home, we'll *all* pay her a visit."

Lord Rush suddenly looked petrified. Lela swung around to see Jacques Ives-Bellamy leading a policeman through the throng. Will's younger brother looked as delighted as if he were in the audience of a good production of *Midsummer Night's Dream*.

"The rest of you may depart. The lady is in good hands," Will ordered, wearing a ferocious scowl.

And every wretched man on the street did as Will commanded, bowing to his authority even though he dressed like a rural squire. Within minutes, the crowd had melted away. The policeman took Cornett, who fought his hold until smacked with a nightstick. Jacques took Ajax. Lord Rush, looking petrified, led the way. And Will held Lela's gloved hand pinned to his arm as if he'd never let go.

"What do you think you are doing?" she asked under her breath.

He gave her one of those dark masculine looks from his long-lashed eyes, the kind of a look that made her insides flutter but focused her mind exceedingly well.

"Clearing the air," he said succinctly.

"Of the stench of villainy?" she suggested.

He nodded approval and returned to ordering people about—as he most likely always did when commanding rescue missions. Her insides fluttered even more, although she had a strong urge to beat him about the ears with the policeman's stick.

Will was not a man who would melt at her feet, but she understood him—as he understood her. Rather daunting, if she thought about it.

Jacques winked at her and lifted his tall gray hat. "I'll take the animal home, shall I? She's served her purpose, I believe."

Will grunted. Lela nodded. She was attempting to follow a multitude of conversations, but Will's presence kept her head spinning. Perhaps she would be better off without him.

The thought sent her into a panic, and she clutched his arm tighter in realization. Once this was settled, he'd be gone.

Lord Rush's door opened before anyone knocked. A stout lady of formidable years and exuding disapproval filled the entry. "Hammond, what is the meaning of this hullabaloo? The entire household is abuzz. Come in and leave those common fellows—"

Her tirade halted when Lela stepped forward. She doubted she'd ever met Lady Simmons in more than a reception line, but if the viscountess was from Yorkshire, she knew the duke's family. "Lady Simmons, I believe?" she said sweetly. "There's been a bit of a bother, if we might impose on your hospitality for just a few moments. . ."

"My. . . my lady, of course," the widow stammered, before

bestowing a frosty glare on Lela's companions. "I cannot imagine you wish these ruffians to accompany you. Really, Hammond, I told you Cornett would end up in gaol. I cannot understand why you have suffered him all these years."

Before any of the men could answer that, Lela stepped aside to gesture for the anxious bobby to lead his prisoner inside. "On the contrary, my lady, we need the aid of these gentlemen to solve a mystery."

When the lady stood there, stunned and blocking the entrance, and Lord Rush did nothing but stammer helplessly, Will emitted a soul-deep sigh. With a curt apology, he took Lady Simmons' silk-clad arm and all but pushed her inside, out of the way.

"Bit of a brute, eh what?" Rush muttered, extending his arm for Lela to take now that Will was inside.

Lela considered that. Once upon a time, she might have agreed, if "brute" meant large, intimidating, lacking patience, and inclined to do as he wished and not as told. But it was only Will's clothes that allowed him to be considered more animal than gentleman, which was what Rush implied.

"Entirely a man, and a gentle one at that," she replied. "A brute would have shot your manservant on sight."

He dropped her arm the instant they crossed the portal. Will was there to take it. She sent him a blinding smile that made him blink and freeze. And then, with that assurance she loved so much, he smiled back and led her after Lady Simmons into the parlor.

Will had smiled. At her. She walked on clouds.

"BESS?" LADY Simmons asked in confusion. "Why would you want to know about Bess? She's probably consorting with. . ."

Standing behind Lela's chair, Will coughed to cover up what she was undoubtedly about to say and nodded at the duke's daughter.

The lady cast Lela a mortified look and moderated her tone. "My daughter-in-law is no better than she should be, I fear. I cannot imagine where she could have got to. Is she wanted by the law?" she asked, almost hopefully. "Is Rose safe?"

"You do not communicate with her, even though she's carrying your grandchild?" Lela asked.

Will noted with approval that she kept her voice neutral. He knew families didn't always talk to each other or even like each other, and in this case, there might even be good reason for it. Bess wasn't the most tractable, pleasant person he'd ever encountered. However, it wasn't their place to judge.

"Grandchild?" Lady Simmons looked to her son, who had collapsed in a faded wing chair and stared only at his feet. "Bess is with child? Why wasn't I told this?"

And then her eyes widened, and she stiffened. The old lady hadn't lost any of her sharp wits. "She could be carrying the next viscount! *I should have been told.*"

Before anyone could question further, there was a commotion at the front door. Will winced, recognizing the deep voices of authority ordering the servants about. He squeezed Lela's shoulder and returned to the foyer.

Sure enough, both marquesses had bullied their way in. Without giving it a second thought, Will grabbed their elbows and shoved Rainsford and Ashford back out the entrance. "You do not want to have to testify in court later. This is what I do. You go do whatever it is you do."

Rainsford tried to swing around again. "Lela. . ."

"Is mine," Will stated firmly and emphatically. "I will see to her."

And he felt fine saying it. He filled with joy saying it. He was blatantly insane and Rainsford's look confirmed it, but Will didn't care. The lady was his, just as soon as he asked her.

Remembering how she'd rejected every other proposal she'd received, he had a sinking feeling about that. Which made him shove harder.

There were two of them. They could have overpowered him. But Ash merely tipped his hat in acknowledgment. "Find a better tailor," he admonished, before striding off.

Lela's brother looked mutinous. Will shut the door in his face and threw the bolt. "Don't let anyone in," he told the duke's terrified footman.

Lady Simmons was still upbraiding her son about being kept in the dark about her younger son's wife and child. Lela smiled at Will as he returned, and he thought his blood heated to boiling. Before he could decide how to steer the subject back on topic, Lela spoke for him.

"Lady Simmons, are you saying that. . ." She hesitated over Bess's real name. "Lady Bradford Simmons has a life interest in your younger son's estate, and that if her child is a boy, he will inherit the title and lands? There is no doubt about the marriage documents?"

"I shouldn't think so," the older woman said huffily, turning her attention back to her guests. "Our family solicitor would have made certain all was in proper order before settling Rose's portion on her. Poor Rose will never be right, so I provided for her future. Hamm is her executor."

Will kept his eye on Cornett slumped against the wall with the bobby standing watch over him. Will knew from experience that once the servant's lies were revealed, the rogue would attempt to flee. Cornett was a tall man with a military bearing. He would be dangerous.

Before he asked any further questions, Will placed himself in the room's one doorway and nodded to the footman, who discreetly stood behind Lela and blocked the window.

"Your son's wife is under the impression that her marriage isn't legal," Will explained, wishing he had Erran's silver tongue. "She has been removed from her husband's home. Are you aware of this?"

"What?" Lady Simmons turned immediately to her son. "Did you know of this? Why would. . ." And then she turned an ashen gray and slumped over, holding an arm across her chest.

Lela was on her feet at once, rushing to the lady's aid. A mouse of a woman appeared from the shadows with smelling salts in hand.

And Cornett shoved from the wall, as Will feared. Caught by surprise, the policeman didn't grab him fast enough as the rogue dashed straight for—not the door where Will stood, but Lela.

Will roared. Lela dodged. The scoundrel didn't have time to do more than grab at her hat before Will was upon him, wrapping his fingers in the cad's over-long hair, yanking his head back, and plowing his fist into a bony jaw. Cornett flew backward, off the floor, into the arms of the duke's footman.

"Don't hurt him," Rush shouted. "Whatever he's done, it's all been for me. I shouldn't have denied him. I shouldn't have insisted on staying in town. It's all my fault."

"We've seen enough. Take them both to the magistrate," Will ordered. "Bind Cornett's arms and hobble his feet. I'll be down to testify shortly."

"Hamm's a good boy," Lady Simmons whispered as more maids arrived to help her up and a footman ran for her physician. "I told him to find a nice wife, that he'd need someone when I was gone." She glanced at Lela. "I never dreamed he'd seek so high as you, my lady. It's a pleasure to meet you."

Will wrapped Lela in his arms and let her weep as the lady was led away. "Because of you, Bess and Rose will have their home back. Think happy thoughts."

She sniffed and nodded against his shoulder, letting him lead her back to the waiting carriage.

In a few days, Lady Aurelia would hold her grand ball, with every eligible bachelor in town at her feet. Will had to give her the opportunity to see if she could tolerate the society events she'd been raised to attend. There might never be another woman for him, but he had to let her discover if there might be someone more suitable for her.

The duke's orders be damned. Lela needed to spread her wings on her own terms. Will refused to cage her as the duke had.

Twenty-four

RIDING BESIDE the carriage taking Rose, her infant brother, and the wet nurse back to Bess—Lady Simmons—Will wished for the company of his dogs. But he'd left Ajax guarding Lela and given Hero to his brothers to take to Iveston.

Not knowing what the future held, he could make no other plans. His entire life rested upon the answer to one impossible question. How had he ended up in this predicament?

Will's gut ground as he imagined Lela happily preparing for her ball. The house had been full of women nattering about decorations and gowns. Now that she was learning how to cope with the noises in her head, she wouldn't miss him.

But Will missed her, far more than he'd ever imagined. Every time he thought of something he wished to say to her, he jotted it in a little notebook he'd picked up in the city. He wanted to offer her poetry as her other suitors did. All he had was a misspelled scrawl with foolish lines like: *I almost heard you laugh when Tiny stuck his nose in Rose's porridge bowl.*

He missed Lela's laugh and her feminine understanding and the way she made his day lighter. He missed her scent of vanilla—he'd finally learned the name for her sweet bakery aroma. And he spent way too much time recalling that night in the freezing warehouse—except it wasn't the cold he recalled. He'd always thought he'd wanted a large woman, but delicate Lela. . . Lela felt like a part of him that had been missing.

But instead of courting her, he was escorting Bess's brood to their home. They'd agreed to meet at the late viscount's estate. It was a long ride from London in the upper reaches of nowhere, but the weather held and they arrived on time.

Rose's home was a vine-covered block stone house. Will could hear the child's excited cries as she recognized the familiar sight, so he knew they'd done the right thing. She'd been upset to leave Lela, weeping and refusing to go with the nurse. Will hadn't seen any other choice but to take the child himself. It was probably safer this way. If he'd been left alone with Lela for any length of time—

If he had any chance to make a future in civilized society with Lela, he had to eliminate the animal part of him that he'd followed for so long.

For her sake, he was trying very hard to be a gentleman, but he was still a man with all the faults of his kind. And Lela wasn't helping him be strong. She'd pouted and flirted and pressed her breasts into his arm until he'd almost been ready to fling caution to the wind and Lela into bed. Almost. Only his desire that she have what was best for her had kept him on the straight and narrow.

Shortly, he'd be on his way back to face temptation and possible rejection of his tentative new hopes and dreams. He'd never spent much time dreaming before. He was wary of it.

Bess rushed out to greet the carriage as soon as it stopped. She looked better now, stronger and healthier. The respite from worry and fear had wiped the lines and shadows from her eyes. She was a tall, strong woman who joyously swung Rose up in the air much as a man might. But she wept like any weak female when the nurse climbed out carrying the infant.

She was the type of sturdy woman Will had once thought he wanted. But now he understood it wasn't a woman's body that mattered most, just as a woman's aristocratic parentage shouldn't put him off. It was hard to adjust his thinking, but he meant to stop and tell Miranda good-bye before returning to London. He'd never raised her expectations. He didn't think she would be heart-broken or even miss him. He would be the one to suffer if Lela rejected him.

Holding the babe while Rose chased after Tiny, Bess turned her tear-stained face to him. "I cannot thank you enough. What will happen to Hammond and Cornett? Will we be safe now?"

Lord Rush had turned on his lover after learning what the valet had done. They were both broken men. Will didn't see the need to expand.

"After half England learns what they did to you? They have no chance of stealing your home again. Whatever the courts decide, your son's title and inheritance are safe. The rest is up to you, I suppose." Will was still uncomfortable explaining since he seldom fully understood all the layers of human reactions—but Lela did. He needed her here with him.

"You saved our lives, then you saved our futures," Lady

Simmons said gratefully. "How can I ever repay you?"

Will shrugged uncomfortably. "By helping others when you can, I suppose. It's what people do. Lady Aurelia said she will be sending you a book of hand signs to help talk with Rose, but she wanted to make copies first."

Bess looked both shy and elated. "Lady Aurelia has been a saint. I must find a good way to thank her as well. Won't you come in? The house has been empty, but there's still water and tea. It's been such a long journey!"

Will dug in his pocket for the letters Lela and his brothers had written to explain all that had happened. "Forgive me for not accepting your invitation, but there are still daylight hours left, and I'm in something of a hurry. You're to write if you have questions, and I believe the magistrate will be corresponding with your solicitor, so he will be speaking with you as well."

Bess shifted the infant so she could reach for the packet. She wore an expression of awe as she studied the seal and the elegant script Will could never produce. *"The Right Honorable, The Viscountess Simmons,"* she said in wonder, reading the direction. "They address me as if I'm truly one of them."

Uncomfortably, Will recognized the feeling. Bess was no more than the bastard of some poor unfortunate vicar's daughter, but she was a viscountess by way of marriage. He was a bastard son of a much higher sort, with the breeding and education Bess could never attain. And yet, he still felt astonished at being recognized as a gentleman.

He'd have to go beyond that flaw in his thinking if he meant to propose to the daughter of a duke. He had no idea where they'd go from there if she actually said yes. He needed to hear that *yes* before he could make a single plan.

He was far more prepared for a *no*. Or to be ignored while Lela listened to the strains of a waltz instead of his impassioned plea, he acknowledged with grim humor.

He left the little family laughing and hugging and promising to write. He left the carriage in his dust. He had to see Miranda, then make London in four days' time, and the weather was threatening to turn.

***

STANDING UNHAPPILY in the middle of her suite as family and servants swirled around her, Lela cried, "Will isn't back. Can't we wait until he is?"

Her maid tightened the strings of Lela's exquisitely embroidered corset, designed just for the gown another maid held ready. "You have shrunk to nothing," Addy scolded. "You must eat."

"I don't want to eat. I should be with Rose and Will, not standing here like a useless fashion doll." Lela took a nibble of the meat-filled roll Christie shoved between her lips.

Aster and Celeste had brought in reinforcements in the form of the marchioness for the evening. Christie, Lady Ashford, had a way of bringing order out of chaos while seeing that everyone had what they needed, when they needed it.

She frowned at Lela now and held up the rest of the roll. "Eat. William will be here when he gets here. He's not likely to vanish or melt in this rain. We'll not have you fainting from lack of nourishment tonight. The rumors would be dreadful."

Lela rolled her eyes. "The gossip is already hilarious. It's obvious no one knows Will. As if he'd do anything improper!"

Well, he had touched her in ways no other man had, and she fully intended that he do so again—if only he would return! The wretched man insisted on doing what was right and proper at all times, when all she wanted to do was fling aside proprieties and tell the world to go away. She supposed that reflected her privileged upbringing.

"He has enough against him without allowing rumors to circulate," Aster admonished, unintentionally contrasting Lela's freedom to Will's more restricted background.

But Lela hadn't really been free until Will had come into her life. If only they had time to talk and plan, they might make their differences work—if only he would see that!

Aster used the looking glass to adjust the bodice of her multi-colored evening gown and continued speaking over Lela's thoughts. "It's not as if it's easy to explain that Will has rescued a viscountess and her family when society knows nothing of them. They only know that Lady Simmons had an apoplexy in his presence, and that a baron is under arrest because of Will's charges. We must use this occasion to make the *ton* see him as the hero he is."

"As if I'll be able to think two words without Will in the room,"

Lela said in frustration. "I'm learning, but there will be hundreds of people present. I had so counted on him—"

"In which case, you definitely should go without him," Christie scolded. "You must learn to stand on your own. It's only by being able to act independently that you can be a true help to the husband you choose."

The marchioness was older and wiser and had a gift for knowing how people felt. She sailed through the halls of society with head held high, confident of her position—unlike Lela.

"Don't," Celeste warned, coming to help the maid lower Lela's wide skirt over her head. "I know that expression. Do not give us excuses about your inability to think and need to be somewhere quiet. You have been hiding all your life behind that excuse. You owe it to Will to go out there and enjoy yourself. I cannot imagine how that poor man is suffering out on the cold road while he knows you're in a glittering ballroom, surrounded by suitors."

"Do you think he even cares?" Lela whispered her fear. "He rode off as if eager to see the last of us. He's probably on his way to Scotland, relieved to be free."

Aster, Celeste, and Christie all broke into gales of laughter.

Lela wasn't reassured. They didn't know Will as she did. They were thinking in terms of their own Ives males, the legitimate heirs who walked through society with cynicism and confidence, doing as they pleased. Will wasn't like that. Underneath that muscle, he was a gentle, honorable man. He respected his brothers and society, as they hadn't always respected him. He was accustomed to rejection and going his own way.

He didn't need her.

He was trying to show her that she didn't need him.

"Sometimes, men need to be hit about the ears with a big stick," she muttered, which sent her family into more gales of laughter.

With the grim preparation of a soldier going off to war, Lela allowed them to powder and paint her face, drip her with diamonds and pearls, puff the ice-blue silk of her gown to perfection, and put her into heels that raised her to eye level with half the gentlemen who would be attending. Glaring into the looking glass, she saw a crystalline ice princess. If that didn't scare off suitors, they were more stupid than she expected.

***

WILL RUBBED his hand over his still damp jaw, feeling plucked, shaved, and basted for roasting. Ash's valet had done his job so well that he now felt more like the marquess than himself. Even the coat and trousers tailored just for him felt as if they belonged on one of his brothers. And the shoes... he glared at the offending pieces of useless leather as he stomped up the stairs, past the gleaming lamps illuminating the duke's palace for this grand affair. The shoes were worthless for anything except dancing.

It had been a dozen years since he'd been forced to prance around a ballroom.

At his expression, liveried servants inched out of his way. With a scowl, Will strolled past guests glittering in jewels and stinking of expensive perfumes. He probably knew some of the gentlemen. He'd made his reputation by training dogs for the highest ranking nobles in the kingdom, after all. Most of them didn't know his work in training rescue dogs, but their tenants had occasionally benefited from his talent. The tenants weren't at a duke's ball, and the men he'd worked for probably thought he was one of his brothers in these exalted corridors.

So he felt safe acting as if he owned the place, brushing past the throngs on the broad marble staircase, behaving as if he had no one to account to or for—unless he ran into the duke or Rain. He'd like to avoid them for as long as possible.

He could hear strains of a waltz drifting from the ballroom on the top floor. Would Lela be there? Or would she be in one of these crowded public rooms with the champagne and cards and food?

Or in a private niche being wooed by some upstart Will would have to heave over a banister?

It was nearly midnight. He'd been riding all day. Saying farewell to Miranda had felt right, but now that he was here... He was having doubts again. But he hadn't worn out himself and the horse to give up now.

He reached the top floor. It was well past the time for receiving lines and announcing guests. He strode in without interference, searching for his only purpose in being here. He should have brought Ajax. He almost smiled at the image that conjured. But he was here to prove he could be a gentleman when necessary, so he had left the dog in her kennel.

The center of the ballroom swirled with dancers. The edges

were crowded with clumps of black-and-white intermixed with exotic colors, all laughing and talking above the music.

Lela wasn't tall. She would disappear in this mob.

Will walked the perimeter, searching. He saw his brothers and their wives among the swirling dancers. Except for Aster, they were all tall and easy to discern. He'd hoped to see Lela dancing and enjoying herself. He wished he knew what she was wearing. Aster's peacock gown stood out among the crowd, but he'd never seen Lela wear wild colors.

He investigated every clump of males he passed, fearing she would be at their center. She wasn't.

There was no garden path for her to be led down here. But there was a balcony—and the kind of quiet she'd prefer. Gritting his molars, Will shoved open the glass doors and stepped into the cool night. Lanterns had been lit up and down the length of the building, but there were plenty of shadows in between. Couples strolled about, cooling off after dancing, having intimate conversations.

Could he ever have that with Lela? He longed for it in ways he didn't understand but wanted to experience.

"Your eyes are like a sunlit sky, your skin rivals the pearls in the sea. . ."

Will cast his eyes heavenward and followed the babble of drivel.

"Oh, look, there is Cassie! I really should ask about her modiste."

Will grinned at the familiar voice and the addled reply.

"Lady Aurelia, please, I'm trying to—" A strapping black-and-white form stepped out of the shadows, following a fleeing vision in icy blue.

Will debated flipping the magpie over the balcony wall, but he couldn't take his eyes off the vision racing toward him. He braced himself, prepared for her to run straight into him. She wore her pale hair in a marvelous construction of curls and diamonds, and his first urge was to divest her of all that fol-de-rol. Her neck was so slender, how did she hold her head up under the weight?

But then Lela's eyes lit and she threw herself straight at him. Will held out his arms, caught her, and held her tight against his chest lest they both topple into the garden below.

"Will! I *knew* you were here. I've been doing so well, but the instant you entered, I knew it. So it isn't just because I'm focused on you, although I am. But you're *special.*" She flung her arms around his neck.

He had no idea what she meant but he nearly died and went to heaven having her heart beating against his. This moment made every minute of the last grueling week worth the exhaustion. Closing his eyes, Will clung to her, drinking in her scent, enjoying the softness against his hardness, letting her pleasure heal all the tiny wounds in his heart.

It didn't matter if she was a duke's daughter. This was Lela, his heart and soul.

A well-dressed gentleman stalked by, muttering. Another waltz struck up inside.

"I've come to do this properly," Will warned, half-carrying her through the open doorway and back into the ballroom. "If you mean to tell me you wish to ask Cassie about her modiste, do so now."

She laughed and let him take her hand and waist in a proper dance hold. "Oh, I heard him this time. I am very focused. I've been listening for you all evening. But I saw no reason to change what worked so well before. Being an addle-pate is convenient."

"You are a malicious woman." Will did his best to hold her correctly and not bury his nose in her hair and hug her so she pressed against his cock, where he wanted her. But his blood raced and he completely forgot his fatigue now that he had her in his arms again, swirling her about the floor. "Shall I tell you about Bess and Rose until I can dance you through this mob to an exit?"

"Yes, please, servants door to the right. Oh, this is sheer bliss! I was terrified you would stay away because you couldn't dance or some such flummery. I'm so glad you're here."

He glanced down to see why she was tall enough for him to think improper thoughts about covering her in kisses and admired her heeled shoes. "How do you dance backward in those things?"

"You carry me," she said with a laugh. "Is Bess well?"

Trying not to step on her feet or those of any around him, Will circled with the crowd. They passed the duke and the marquess, who looked startled as Lela laughed out loud over one of his stories. She wasn't theirs anymore. She was *his.* Holding his not-so-icy princess, Will told her tales of Bess and Rose. His blood heated with every brush of her glove, trill of her laughter, and hint of her perfume. She swayed like a dandelion wisp in his arms, until he located the nearly hidden exit by the punch table.

With relief, he slipped her from the crowd of dancers into the silk hangings disguising the servants dark hall. Lela found the latch to the door leading to the third-floor private rooms. After the duke's injunction, Will had explored this unused upper story thoroughly, searching for just the right spot. He led the way down the shadowed corridor now. If he was to do this, he would do it his way—with her full attention.

Lela gasped in amazement when he flung open a door to a small bedchamber lit by oil lamps. A fire crackled in the grate, and a bouquet of blue and white flowers waited on the dressing table.

"Is this your room?" she asked in amazement. "Is this where you've been these last hours while I was terrified you would not appear?"

"I will always be there when you want me to be," he asserted, rummaging in his pockets for the little notebook, nearly panicking when he couldn't find it. "I paid one of your footmen a great deal of blunt to prepare this room." He found the book in a different pocket and exhaled in relief. "I've spent these last hours riding hell-bent for London through a rainstorm and then at Ashford's being buffed and basted and shoved into these clothes like so much sausage."

She laughed, and he could swear her eyes sparkled as she watched him with eagerness. Her happiness was in his hands now. The responsibility no longer overwhelmed him. He knew Lela in ways he didn't even know himself. He had much to learn about being a gentleman and not a dog, but her acceptance gave him confidence that she would teach him, because that was who she was.

He handed her the notebook. "You need not look at this right now. You already know I cannot give you pretty phrases and poetry, but I give you my thoughts so you might read them when you are not too distracted. They tend to be all about you these days."

She emitted a cry of delight that was even better than the music carrying perfectly through the walls.

She held the book to her breasts—which weren't covered by the usual flimsy bits of lace and muslin but exposed to his lascivious stare in all their pearlescent glory. Will could almost imagine the pink tips budding beneath the silk. He dutifully kept his gaze on the smile flickering about her lips, and had to pinch himself to prevent bending over and stealing a kiss. *He* was the one too distracted to speak.

"Pretty words don't always come from the heart," she murmured, easing closer, so his head spun from her scent. Rose tonight, not vanilla. "Will, if you don't say it, I will, but I am terrified I'll send you fleeing into the night."

"Does this look as if I'm going anywhere?" he asked gruffly. "How can I go anywhere when my heart is here? If it takes magpie clothes and city houses to woo you, I'll comply, because I cannot go on living without you. And I know I'm a presumptuous fool to even think a woman like you could be happy with a man like me, but I have to ask. Lady Aurelia, would you consider marrying me?"

Her smile lit the room better than a thousand lanterns. Still holding the foolish notebook, she circled his neck with her slender arms and stood on her toes to kiss his newly-shaved jaw. "I love you, Mr. Ives-Madden. I think I have loved you ever since you carried a weeping little girl and her filthy puppy out of a ravine for me. I have loved you more for every minute I've been in your company. I would be proud and delighted to be your wife, without magpie clothes. . . *magpie*? Honestly, Will, where did that come from?"

He laughed. He roared with laughter and joy, lifted her from the floor, and spun her around in time to the bouncy tune coming through the wall. "I love that I don't have to explain myself to you and love when you demand explanations," he said senselessly. He was too giddy with disbelief to do otherwise. "I love that you look like an ice princess but hide a heart so fiery with love and compassion that you hear what others do not. And I want to make love to you here, right now, before you can change your mind. Or maybe so you can change your mind. I'm terrified I'll terrify you."

"I thought you'd never ask," she said demurely, tugging at his starched neckcloth. "You look very uncomfortable in this. Shouldn't it come off?"

Will gulped and stayed her hands by pressing them against his linen. "Is that a yes?" He studied Lela's beloved face, the expressive eyes and laughing lips.

"That is an unqualified yes, sir," she said, covering his cheek with kisses.

Wanting to say what he didn't have the words to say, Will pressed his mouth to hers.

She responded gratifyingly, sinking into the kiss with all the desire and need he felt. He still couldn't believe it. He'd dreamed of this for nights on end, telling himself he was a fool, but here she was, returning his fervor with a passion all her own.

He moved his kisses to her throat, and she moaned in a manner that hit a visceral chord and had him instantly hard. He heard the notebook hit the floor. He kissed the sweet flesh of the round orbs rising above her bodice. She nibbled his ear.

"Tell me to stop now," he said, hiding his anguish that she might do so. "I will wait for the vows to be said if I must, but right now, I am the animal I'm trying very hard not to be."

"You are no animal! No more than I am an addle-pate." She yanked off his neckcloth and ran her fingers from his throat down to the bare chest she'd revealed. "I have wanted to do this since the beginnings of time. The sausage suit has to go."

Will unfastened his coat buttons and eagerly wriggled out of the confinement. "You don't know what you're doing," he remonstrated, because she was innocent and *didn't* know.

"I am a Malcolm. I know exactly what I'm doing," she reminded him, helping him tug the coat sleeve off. "We don't keep all those journals for naught." She stopped a moment to gaze up at him with delight. "Your notebook is like a journal! You may be the first Ives male to actually write down his thoughts."

"They are very badly written thoughts." But Will's mind wasn't on the damned notebook. It was on the rise of her breasts above that shimmering ball gown. He flung his coat at a chair and reached around her, hunting for the hidden fastenings of her bodice. He fumbled, nearly ripping the gossamer gown from her back.

"But you wrote them for me," she murmured, turning to work at his waistcoat buttons. "That means more than all the poetry in the world."

Will had no reply to that. He'd wanted to give her a special gift, and he'd had naught else. He simply loved her a little more for understanding. "There was one morning when the sky was blue and gold and fair and I saw you in it, but I could not paint the words the way I saw it."

She stood on her toes and scattered kisses over his jaw. "You make me see myself through your eyes. Blue and gold and dawn mean far more to me than poetry about pearls."

Will sighed in relief as her bodice finally came off, giving him access to the corset. He wanted to take his knife to all the delicate strings, but she was a Christmas package wrapped up in silver ribbons, and he refused to be hasty. "I wish I could paint," he murmured, untying and loosening the whalebone structure. "I want to immortalize this moment."

Lela gasped as he finally pried her loose from her garments and lifted her breasts free.

She remembered this moment of freedom from the warehouse. Their mutual pleasure wasn't half so clear then as it was now, with light to illuminate Will's reverential expression, and his words of love to warm her heart.

She could see his delight as he worshipped her with his hands, and then, with his mouth. "This is what I listened for," she murmured, sliding her hands over his hard, linen-covered chest while he kissed her breasts. "Not the words, but the need."

Blessedly, Will didn't argue with her irrationality. He merely raised his mouth to hers and kissed her deeper, entangling his tongue with hers and telling her of how their bodies were meant to blend. Her sensitized breasts ached brushing against his stiff linen.

"I vow to love, honor, and take thee in equality into eternity and beyond," he murmured against her ear, before dropping her gown to the floor.

The words of the Malcolm marriage ceremony, Lela knew, although altered to promise her more. He offered her the heritage they shared, admitted that they were more than just a dog trainer and a duke's daughter, but the future of their family. He *understood*. That he could so humble himself for a woman's need for words solidified her love until her heart nearly burst with it.

"I do not need to wait for vows said before a priest," she said, kissing his chest through the linen. "I take thee now, as husband, to love and honor into eternity and beyond." Malcolm vows were more lasting than those said in a church. They sealed their fates.

The music in the ballroom rose in a crescendo. The fire bloomed higher. Light and laughter filled the air as Will carried her to the bed. They had so many thoughts and fears that hadn't been said, but the spirits and their eternal vows spoke for them. Whatever the future held, this moment promised that they would share it together.

It wasn't a grand bed. It barely fit Will's large frame. But the linens were fresh and the mattress was soft, and Lela sank into it as he covered her with his heavy weight.

Will ran his strong workman's hand from her garter, up her bare flesh, to her buttocks. Lela thought she might expire of desire. She parted her legs and rubbed herself against his straining trousers. She had yet to see his full masculinity. She was curious, but curiosity could wait. She needed his knowledge of how to release this spiraling need.

But instead of easing her tension, he increased it. His beautiful dark eyes studied her with intensity, watching her reaction with pleasure as he covered her face in kisses. He caressed her with excruciating gentleness, then breathed his hot desire over her breasts until she feared her blood would boil through her skin. He tore off her flimsy chemise, leaving her bare except for her stockings, and his expression of joy awoke her to a whole new pleasure. She shivered with it as he shoved her garters down, admiring what he uncovered. Flames danced everywhere he looked. She wanted to tug his hand down to touch her as he had before. She ached. She melted.

But she wanted to see him too, so she reluctantly waited.

Kneeling over her, he cast off his shirt, diverting her from her needs to admiring the raw masculine flesh and muscle revealed. She wanted to speak her appreciation but she was speechless. She caressed the light river of hair flowing between his taut male nipples, across the rippling muscle of his abdomen, and disappearing inside his trousers. She tried to sit and kiss him as he had her, but he straddled her, preventing her from rising.

"It will hurt," he warned her. "I cannot promise otherwise this first time."

"I hurt now," she whispered. "Show me more."

Concern crossed his broad face, but he opened his placket with practiced skill. Instead of removing the tight trousers, however, he caressed her between her thighs, distracting her from what he hid. Lela cried out, needing to open for him but confined by his weight.

He rubbed and caressed as he had that other night, bringing her to the brink of enlightenment, pushing her that one last step until she flew apart, heaving and crying like a mare in heat while the musicians played a jaunty folk tune on the other side of the wall.

And then he was shoving inside her, bracing her thighs apart with his big hands, piercing her with a stallion's pizzle until she bit her lip to prevent screaming from shock.

He stopped and began kissing her again. In relief, she complied eagerly, holding his square jaw and covering him with licks and bites and joy. He caressed her breasts until a river of desire flowed from his touch to the place they joined.

"I love you," he murmured. "I love and worship you and I would be proud if you were to bear my child. And as much as I would like to say that I will not share your bed if you ask it of me, I cannot. I want you far too much. So tell me to stop and send me away now, or bear with me until I can show you the pleasure of a marriage bed."

"Don't stop," she whispered, drunk on kisses and the need to feel that thickness all the way inside her. "Please don't stop. I will die if you stop."

"To hell with consequences, your father, and all the whispering maggots back there," he murmured.

"My family will merely tell them I was overcome as usual," she whispered back. "They will not miss us."

With that last obstacle removed, he touched her between her legs again. His caress made her rear off the mattress—and impale herself on his maleness. The shock of tearing tissue tore a sob from her throat, but then he was inside, filling her, teaching her the power of joining.

And it was pain and bliss and struggling to find one without the other until he cupped her buttocks, lifted them, and drove deep.

She cried out as he shuddered and spilled within her. Then the passion he'd taught her exploded deeper and more satisfying than before, leaving her limp and weeping with the immensity of what they had done.

"Mine," he whispered, caressing the tangles of hair that had fallen from her pins.

"Mine," she whispered back, sliding her hands over his muscled derriere and squeezing until he buried a roar in the pillow.

Twenty-five

LELA WATCHED anxiously as Will walked around the sturdy three-story stone cottage. The grounds were extensive and neatly tended. She could hear the gentle lapping of the river not too far away. Richmond was close, but not nearly as loud as the city. Now that she'd learned to focus, it was easier for her to visit London, but she relaxed more in the country.

She held her breath as her new husband examined the stable, kennel, and dovecote hidden behind the trees and hedges. "It is not the Cotswolds, I know," she said nervously. "But Father's steward said this was the best of his unattached properties. I can ask for another, I suppose."

"But they would not be near London," he said, understanding. "I chose the Cotswolds not just because they were more central, but because I could afford no better. I do not need to be central so much if I'm not traveling. And if your dower brings this property, I will have all my funds to spend on us."

She thought he said that with satisfaction, and she thrilled that she could tell so much of what he felt from his voice. With Will, that was a valuable gift. "Copying and distributing the hand sign book won't cost too much, will it? I have too much to learn to start a school like Bridey, but if I can help others. . ."

"A school may happen in time, but the book is a good start," he agreed, taking her in his arms and holding her, just as she needed. She was still far too uncertain of her place in the wider world he had made his own, but he never let her fret. He encouraged her tentative steps toward a freedom she'd never hoped to attain.

"I would love to think I can help children like Rose to communicate," she said with a sigh of contentment as his hands rode up and down her spine. "I don't like being a useless ornament."

He laughed, that deep bass laugh that shivered her bones in delight. Will laughed and smiled more now, she'd noted. She thought she might be partly responsible for his new outlook.

"You are as ornamental as those trees lining the yard. They

make a pretty picture, yes, but they also provide shade and a windbreak. Some of them flower and provide nectar for honey. In the fall, the fruit-bearing ones feed us." He bent his head to study her up-turned one. "You are more beautiful than any tree or flower, and far more useful." He grinned. "Especially in bed."

He still had the power to make her blush when he looked at her like that.

He caught her knees and lifted her from the ground. Lela cried out in surprise, then expectation as he carried her up the stairs to the house. The doors opened as if the servants had been watching out the windows.

Blessedly, he did not molest her in front of the staff but set her down with triumph so they could both admire the towering, gas-lit entry.

The staff bowed and curtsied and Will impatiently held his hand to her back as she responded as she ought. Her new husband would never woo and charm, but she had no doubt that he would treat the servants with more respect than most.

His notebook had been a revelation. Will couldn't spell worth a farthing, but his thoughts. . . probably deserved publication. He wouldn't, of course. He was too private. But even if he wasn't a leader of men, he possessed the kind of power that directed the leaders, out of the public eye. And with so many men of authority within his sphere of influence, he could help her accomplish everything she'd been raised to believe she should.

She would simply have to learn to be the person in the public eye, because Will preferred dogs to people, and she understood that too.

But in their home, they could be anything they liked. Lela examined the floor-length draperies in the front parlor as if she had any idea whether they were old or needed replacing. "We will have to establish a household budget," she said, because that was how she'd been taught.

"Or we can give the housekeeper a purse and tell her it must last the year," he countered, uninterested in coins but striding for the next room.

She ran after him, considering his singularly unorthodox method of keeping house. Of course, he'd never had a house to keep!

She almost plowed her nose into his back when he halted in the doorway.

"Is the house too noisy for you?" he asked with an odd inflection.

"I hadn't thought about it," she admitted, stopping to consider now. "You are admirably muffling creaks and squeaks, and there doesn't seem to be a close neighbor who talks loudly. And the river creates a nice background burble when I think about it."

"I am almost disappointed." He stepped aside to allow her into what appeared to be a music room. "I've always wanted to learn to make music, and I'm looking for an excuse to learn."

"Oh, my, look at the harp! And the piano. And is that a lute on the wall?" Lela dashed around the room, discovering its treasures—benches full of music sheets and cabinets made for instruments. "You would need an excuse *not* to learn!"

"Do you think so?" He hit a piano key. "I have no idea if it's even in tune."

"Surely a music teacher could not be so costly. And we'll meet other people who love to play, and we can have evening musicales where I might learn to converse even if I'm not watching you."

He looked down at her with that warm chocolate gaze that could melt her knee bones.

"We could have children who learned to play so you need not even notice if I'm not in the house." His voice was a low, seductive rumble.

And the thought did not fill her with fear as it might once have. Instead, she felt a thrill of expectation deep inside her. She caught his hand and led him back to the hall. "Should we explore the upstairs before we decide?" she asked in her best attempt to sound enticing.

"We most certainly should," he agreed, placing his big hand at her back and guiding her up the stairs. "Do you think you will be happy here at those times when I must travel?"

"That depends. How likely are your hounds to howl the whole time you are gone?" she asked pertly as they hit the upper corridor and began opening doors to examine bed chambers and private parlors.

"That depends on whether their howls are reassuring or annoying. I can command them to be quiet if that's your preference. A dog trainer has a few uses." He opened the door at the front of the house, overlooking the trees and river.

Floor to ceiling windows created the effect of entering a bird's nest overlooking the countryside. Lela cried out in delight and ran to examine the balcony beyond. Will closed the door.

The bed was large and neatly made.

They both ran to throw themselves across it at the same time.

Their laughter christened the old rafters for the years ahead.

Acknowledgements

As I SAID EARLIER, these books would never be written without the generous enthusiasm of my many readers. But it takes an entire community to build a book, and I want to bow gratefully to the team who produces the finished product. In no particular order, I thank my patient husband who provides the elegant formatting and attempts to keep up with my many changes. Mindy Klasky tempers my wilder plot deviations and helps provide structure. Phyllis Radford, my wonderful editor, finds all those niggling details I tend to ignore and then has the patience to proof my typos. And the wonderful crew of Book View Café provides the logistics and promotion that I'm much too disorganized to do on my own.

I'm sure I've left out a few names, but they understand the limits of my off-the-wall mind. Bless all of my silent partners!

GET A FREE PATRICIA RICE BOOK

Thank you for reading *No Perfect Magic*.

Would you like to know when my next book is available? I occasionally send newsletters with details on new releases, special offers and other bits of news. If you sign up for the mailing list I'll send you a free Patricia Rice novel. Just sign up at **http://patriciarice.com/**

I am an independent author, so getting the word out about my book is vital to its success. If you liked this book, please consider telling your friends, and writing a review at the store where you purchased it. Reviews help other readers find books. I appreciate all reviews, whether positive or negative.

***

Find more of Pat's books on her website: **http://patriciarice.com**
Sign up for Pat's newsletter to be the first to know about her next release! *http://patriciarice.com/sign-up*

If you enjoyed this story, try these PATRICIA RICE books!

The World of Magic:
The Unexpected Magic Series
MAGIC IN THE STARS
WHISPER OF MAGIC
THEORY OF MAGIC
AURA OF MAGIC
CHEMISTRY OF MAGIC
The Magical Malcolms Series
MERELY MAGIC
MUST BE MAGIC

THE TROUBLE WITH MAGIC
THIS MAGIC MOMENT
MUCH ADO ABOUT MAGIC
MAGIC MAN

The California Malcolms Series
THE LURE OF SONG AND MAGIC
TROUBLE WITH AIR AND MAGIC
THE RISK OF LOVE AND MAGIC

Historical Romance:
The Rebellious Sons
WICKED WYCKERLY
DEVILISH MONTAGUE
NOTORIOUS ATHERTON
FORMIDABLE LORD QUENTIN

The Regency Nobles Series
THE GENUINE ARTICLE
THE MARQUESS
ENGLISH HEIRESS
IRISH DUCHESS

Mysteries:
Family Genius series
EVIL GENIUS
UNDERCOVER GENIUS
CYBER GENIUS
TWIN GENIUS

Praise for Patricia Rice's novels

MAGIC IN THE STARS

"Rice packs her tale with whimsy humor and mayhem. . . and takes her readers on an amorous adventure in this magical tale."—Joan Hammond, *RT Book Reviews* 4 1/2 top pick

FORMIDABLE LORD QUENTIN

"Rice has crafted her novel with plenty of witty, engaging characters and a healthy dose of romance. Clever Bell is a splendid protagonist, and readers will cheer her efforts to get men to take her seriously and treat her as an equal."–*Publishers Weekly*

MERELY MAGIC

"Like Julie Garwood, Patricia Rice employs wicked wit and sizzling sensuality to turn the battle of the sexes into a magical romp" –Mary Jo Putney, NYT Bestselling author

MUST BE MAGIC

"Rice has created a mystical masterpiece full of enchanting characters, a spellbinding plot, and the sweetest of romances." *Booklist* (starred review)

THE TROUBLE WITH MAGIC

"Rice is a marvelously talented author who skillfully combines pathos with humor in a stirring, sensual romance that shows the power of love is the most wondrous gift of all. Think of this memorable story as a gift you can open again and again." – *Romantic Times*

About the Author

WITH SEVERAL MILLION books in print and *New York Times* and *USA Today's* bestseller lists under her belt, former CPA Patricia Rice is one of romance's hottest authors. Her emotionally-charged contemporary and historical romances have won numerous awards, including the *RT Book Reviews* Reviewers Choice and Career Achievement Awards. Her books have been honored as Romance Writers of America RITA® finalists in the historical, regency and contemporary categories.

A firm believer in happily-ever-after, Patricia Rice is married to her high school sweetheart and has two children. A native of Kentucky and New York, a past resident of North Carolina and Missouri, she currently resides in Southern California, and now does accounting only for herself. She is a member of Romance Writers of America, the Authors Guild, and Novelists, Inc.

For further information, visit Patricia's network:

http://www.patriciarice.com
http://www.facebook.com/OfficialPatriciaRice
https://twitter.com/Patricia_Rice
http://wordwenches.typepad.com/word_wenches/
http://patricia-rice.tumblr.com/

About Book View Café

Book View Café Publishing Cooperative (BVC) is an author-owned cooperative of over fifty professional writers, publishing in a variety of genres including fantasy, romance, mystery, and science fiction. Since its debut in 2008, BVC has gained a reputation for producing high-quality ebooks. BVC's ebooks are DRM-free and are distributed around the world. The cooperative is now bringing that same quality to its print editions.

BVC authors include New York Times and USA Today bestsellers as well as winners and nominees of many prestigious awards, including:

Agatha Award

Campbell Award

Hugo Award

Lambda Award

Locus Award

Nebula Award

Nicholl Fellowship

PEN/Malamud Award

Philip K. Dick Award

RITA Award

World Fantasy Award

Writers of the Future Award

Made in the USA
Lexington, KY
02 July 2017